The Unquiet Mind
Sara Alexi is the author of the Greek Village
Collection.
She divides her time between England and a small
village in Greece.

http://facebook.com/authorsaraalexi

Sara Alexi
THE UNQUIET MIND

.

oneiro

10/15

Published by Oneiro Press 2014

ISBN-13: 978-1502882721

ISBN-10: 1502882728

For Sophia

Part I

Chapter 1

'Yanni, we cannot survive with just one donkey.' His mama sits with his baba at the wooden table outside. She is picking out tiny stones and pieces of grit from a plate of split peas in front of her. An onion and a handful of dill wait inside next to a pan of water by the two-ring gas stove

'We'll manage, Mama.' Yanni keeps his hands in the front pockets of his jeans and arches his back to stretch. 'We have Suzi and the goats.' He scans the small plain they call home. The ground is flat and bare, and even in the summer heat there is no rasping sound of the cicadas, as there is not a leaf or a twig for them to perch on. It is still, silent, peaceful. His gaze drifts along the east ridge, stark against the endless blue sky. His eyes are drawn, to the left and down, as usual, to the sea, flat like oil reflecting the early morning sun. A thin line of white ruffles the blue, the day's first commercial hydrofoil on its way to the mainland. From this height, the vessel, packed no doubt with commuters and tourists, is as insignificant as an ant.

The uninhabited southern side of the island cannot be seen from here. In that direction, the landscape dips and raises again to the pine trees at the top. A brief stretch of the legs beyond that point and he could stare out, on a clear day, to see a hint of Crete, hazy in the far distance.

'And the cheese,' Yanni's baba adds quietly, concentrating on twisting the ends of the rabbit snare he is fashioning out of a piece of thin wire, wiping his sweating hands on his dust-coloured trousers.

'Yes, the cheese, that helps,' Yanni agrees.

'Suzi is old. You have said yourself that she tires quickly,' Yanni's mama continues, looking over to where the remaining donkey is loosely hitched to a post by the well. The animal's head hangs down, eyes closed, ears twitching at flies. 'And the goats and the cheese are not enough and you both know it. We would not have survived last year without Dolly.'

Yanni closes his eyes. A line puckers between his brows. He twists his moustache with his left hand. It's a donkey man's moustache which he has encouraged since the first sign of downy hair in his teens. It has now matured into a fine display. Maybe it would look more appropriate on a man twice his age, but he preens it as though it lends gravitas to his thirty-three years. His right hand reaches into the breast pocket of his loose shirt for his tobacco pouch.

'Yes, she was a good beast.' Yanni's baba glances sideways at his son, his voice as quiet as a prayer.

Yanni lights his cigarette and sighs deeply as he exhales, re-pocketing the pouch next to the small book that nestles there. His mama is waiting for him to say something. He turns to take the wooden trough from where it sits by the front door and steps to the well.

'Baba, tell him.' The speed at which Yanni's mama picks grit from the split peas increases, her movements sharper as she speaks.

Yanni's baba says nothing. He catches his hand in the snare, pulling the wire tight.

'No one listens to anything I say round here,' Yanni's mama states, standing, wiping her hands on her apron and then taking up the plate of split peas. She rolls a little from side to side as she walks, rubbing her hip where it aches. Lately she has complained the aching is stopping her sleeping. She ducks into the house. The two men remain silent, exchange a glance. She returns presently with a pale, sand-coloured shirt and needle and thread. 'Yanni you need a donkey and a wife. There, I have said it.'

'For the thousandth time,' Yanni says quietly to Suzi, setting the trough of water in front of her. He pats her neck and the donkey responds with short snorts which dislodge some flies from her nose. After a moment, she lets her head drop to drink, curling her lips to suck in the water.

'It may be for the thousandth time, Yanni, but until the day you bring her home, I will continue to say it. She could help me with the milking and the cheese. She could even go down with you maybe, help with the tourist trade.'

Yanni rolls his eyes. 'You have no idea what you are talking about.'

'I know a little female charm can work wonders in any trade.' She winces as she stabs the needle into the shirt and withdraws her finger to suck on the wound.

Yanni's baba lays his snare on the table and goes into the two-roomed stone house. His wife watches him go, shaking her head.

Behind the house, the ground is dusty and barren. From a low-walled enclosure come occasional soft bleating sounds. The little stone house and the walls of the enclosure are thick with flaking whitewash. The shutters of the single window in the cottage are painted a bright blue and stand open, allowing room for a large geranium on the sill, suggesting they are never closed. The scarlet flowers shriek against the pale surrounds, draining the colour from the aging terracotta roof tiles.

'And grandchildren.' She looks back at Yanni, who has his back to her, watching Suzi drink as he smokes. 'Yanni?' Her tone becomes softer. 'We are getting old. We need some new life around here. Who will be your company when Baba and I are gone, eh?'

Yanni pats Suzi's neck again and grinds the end of his cigarette into the dust. He looks straight at his mama as he passes her, but he doesn't speak. Rounding the end of the house, he passes the sheep pen and heads up the incline in the direction of what is left of a crumbling, circular windmill. A tower of human sweat and struggle, a beacon to head home by after a day spent watching the goats at the far grazing ground. His ancestors built it, dragging stone after stone from the now-dry river bed. Stones worn round and smooth by water, demanding bucket after bucket of mud cement to bind them together, to hold them erect. Back in those days, there were several families living up here on the ridge at the top of the island, a community of farmers tending huge herds of sheep and goats. They grew their own food and even planted wheat on the high plateaux, and Yanni's ancestors were the ones to take the step from grinding by hand to building the windmill. The mill that became the central point of the community. They were the family everyone would look to back then— his baba has so often told him. But then the river stopped gushing and tumbling over those rounded stones, the water seemed to just soak away until it became a stream, became a trickle, became a way for snow to melt into the ground until now, eleven months of the year it is nothing more than just another dry ravine. As the water dried up, the wheat failed, there was no water for the animals and one by one, the families left too. Yanni's family have been lucky: even now, their well still holds water. Not as it was once—so plentiful they could share—but enough. If they are careful, they have water until the very last weeks of October. Then they pray. Today, the windmill, with its sails gone and the thatched roof slipped off into the dust, provides a makeshift shelter for the goats, and the insects tunnel holes in the mud mortar, making their own tiny communities and reducing the once-proud building back to the earth.

Around the outside of the mill, a fence has been erected to contain the goats, patched and repaired more times than either Yanni or his baba care to recall. Yanni cannot remember a time when it was not there. The wooden stakes, one by one, have been replaced with metal rods, hammered into the ground with the boulders hauled from the river bed by their ancestors. The chicken wire between these stakes billows and sags where tiny hooves have tried to climb in expectation and excitement of freedom as Yanni or his baba come to release them morning and night. If you were to ask Yanni's baba how many goats he has, he would reply, 'Many', and if you pressed him, he might wave his hands and shrug, 'Many, many', but ask Yanni and he would tell you, every year, 'Never enough'.

They used to take turns to take the goats and sheep to graze. Now it depends on the old man's energy. When he is not feeling too strong, it is hard on Yanni because twice a day, he must also walk down to the port. Once in the morning and again after *mesimeri*—siesta—when everyone wakes. It is a fast half an hour journey on the way down, but more than an hour back up, but there is no choice. Unless he makes the journey, Yanni cannot hire the labour of his donkeys to the people using the daily cargo boat that comes to the island. Everything comes by boat: roof tiles and toilet rolls, bottled water and scaffold planks, and it all needs to be distributed around the steep amphitheatre of houses they call Orino Town. A pair of donkeys can earn a modest living; three and you can be the breadwinner of your family. One, and there is not time in the day, nor energy in old Suzi, to do the number of trips necessary. Besides, the cargo boat unloads to whoever is there and you get paid by how much you haul. It is just basic maths that the more donkeys you have, the more you make.

But if he is lucky, in the mornings, he can convince tourists off the boats to let him carry their bags to their hotels, or even give the more adventurous ones from the daily cruise ships a ride. That is light work for his beast, it pays well, and more often than not, they tip well. The sort of work that can make you greedy, as he knows only too well. He has paid the price, and now Dolly is dead.

His baba comes out of the house in time to see Yanni kicking the stone that secures the gate in the fence around the windmill, and the goats tumbling from their enclosure, bleating their excitement as they jump and run towards the hills. The crude bells around their necks clonking and donging, a noise so familiar that it soaks into the hillside. Yanni settles into a steady pace as he strolls after them.

'Leave him alone, Mama.' Yanni's baba picks his snare from the table and examines it. 'The more you pressure him, the more he will resist.' Taking up an axe leaning against the house wall, he looks around for a good-sized stone. As he moves with the axe in his hand, its metal head rocks loosely on its wooden handle. 'You need to be a bit psychological. The more you tell him, the less he will want it. You need to be clever and find ways to make him think for himself that he needs a wife, make it his idea. Same with the donkey.' Putting the butt of the handle on the dusty ground, he raises the stone and hammers the wooden wedge that has worked loose.

'Psychological! If we left it to you men to think for yourselves, we would still have holes in the roof, half the goats we have now, and no donkeys at all. We would never have moved on from when we first got married.'

Yanni's baba tests the axe head, which now resists. 'Ah but it was so romantic lying in our bed looking up at the stars, just you and me.' He nudges her shoulder as he passes. 'You forget all that?'

She giggles and stops sewing, eyeing her husband from head to toe, seeing not the bent and aged man he has become but the Adonis she remembers. He takes the half-empty trough from in front of Suzi, whose eyes have closed again, and puts it back by the door, setting the axe in to soak, for the wooden handle to expand, tighten his repair. With the splash, Yanni's mama breaks her stare.

'Stop it. This is serious.' She is telling herself as much as him. 'We are going to struggle with the wage from one donkey and as far as a wife is concerned, he is not getting any younger and we most definitely are getting older.'

'Yes, but Yanni is Yanni. He is content.' Yanni's baba stands for an idle moment. His son has taken the usual route to the hills at the back of the island. One or two of the white goats can just be seen dotted among the pine trees. The cicadas will be deafening up there. In a minute, he will see the tiny silhouette of Yanni as he leaves the trees, climbs the bald top of the hill, and sinks over the other side.

'Is he content? He spent so much time with Dolly for company, I wonder what is going to happen now she is gone.' She cuts a thread with her teeth and searches the garment for any other areas needing repair. Her needle digs in, begins again.

'Sure, you build up an understanding when you work with an animal for years, and her death was so unexpected.' Yanni's baba dips his head into the house and reappears with a paper bag and a small tube of glue.

'About time,' Yanni's mama says, looking at the broken pottery pieces that he pours from the bag onto the table. 'You are just like Yanni. Everything takes a year and five minutes. Five minutes to do and a year to think about it.'

Yanni's baba moves his wooden chair a little closer to his wife's. She looks at him shyly and the corners of her mouth twitch into a small smile.

'Didn't take me a year and five minutes to marry you, did it?'

She wriggles a little in her chair as he leans into her, before she stiffens. 'What will it take to make you think about this seriously?'

He stops sorting the pieces and turns to her, his arm over the back of his own chair. She in turn puts down her sewing and turns to face him. They look into each other's eyes and he leans towards her and kisses her briefly on the lips. 'There is hope, you know,' he says as he pulls away. Her shoulders drop, the arch in her eyebrows flattens, she waits for his next words. 'That boy spent hours talking to Dolly, up and down to the port. With the wind in the right direction, you could hear him mumbling away to her.' His hand slides across to her chair back. His thumb finds her shoulder, her neck, her earring, which he plays with to make it glint in the sun. She nods her head. 'She was his companion and now she is gone, there will be a hole in his life.' He strokes her wrinkled cheek when he sees the look of fear for her son in her eyes. 'He will want to fill that hole. It may drive him to another donkey. It may even drive him to a wife.' His own wife's eyes are locked in his gaze. 'And he is an honest man.' She nods again at his words. 'He will only spend the money on another donkey. He would not take advantage.'

The old woman's face brightens. 'Take him, Baba, take him to the mainland, show him a little of the world, let him see the beautiful women on the mainland and show him how to buy a donkey.'

His hand drops from her face into his lap. He looks back at the broken pot awaiting his attention. 'Ach, I am too old for that and I have been up here for too long to go amongst men.' He cannot look at her as he speaks. 'He is a man now. He does not need his baba to hold his hand.'

Yanni's mama stands, the shirt in a ball in her hands, the needle lost amongst the folds. She throws it with force on the table; it lands softly. She stomps inside.

Chapter 2

Yanni kicks the stone that secures the gate in the fence around the windmill, unaware that his baba's eyes are on him. One of the kids bleats at him, its front hooves rasping on the chicken-wire fence as it tries to climb out, its back legs trying to follow. The whole fence threatens to collapse, oscillating on the stakes that, over time, have rattled loose in the ground. 'Take it easy. Slow yourselves down. Nothing is going to happen fast in this heat.' Yanni rubs its stubby horns, the animal's neck arching to reach his hand. This heatwave so early will make the animals more thirsty. They will put an even greater strain on the well this year.

Before the gate swings free of the stone, he ruffles his own sandy hair smooth. From this vantage point, the house looks cosy on the small flat plain. Beyond and down the hillside, the sea stretches undisturbed to the horizon. The sunshine that glints on the waves is almost too bright. He looks away and rubs his eyes, his dreams still lingering. He had that dream again, dreamt of her, not as she was then, but as she would be now, a grown woman, with chestnut hair shining in the sun, a smile that makes the hairs on the back of his neck stand on end. Sophia. The muscles around his eyes wish to return to sleep. He wipes his whole face on his shirt in the crook of his elbow and then twists the ends of his moustache between finger and thumb. The action gives a sense of control.

With his back to the goats, he turns to his left, facing downhill. The town and the port itself are hidden from view by the pine trees below him but the water tanker is visible on its way into the port. Soon it will dock with much shouting and line throwing. Spanners wielded, pipes attached, stopcocks turned, and the daily water supply will be pumped up the hillside to a reservoir from where it can be delivered to the houses in town. The two thousand or so inhabitants, and the same number of tourists—do they know how much they depend on that water tanker coming every day to the island? It is low in the water as it arrives, weighed down by its dense cargo, and bobs lightly on the surface as it leaves. The water is brackish and not fit to drink but is used for bathing and watering gardens. Many houses have cisterns under the ground to store the rainwater that runs from their roofs in the winter, but there is rarely enough to last all summer. For drinking, there is only bottled water, litres and litres of it, carted to every house. Too heavy to be taken by hand, and so every person on the island depends on the donkey men.

The tanker disappears behind the pine tree tops into the harbour, entering the bustle of a different world. Yanni exhales, grateful not to be a part of it, glad of his solitude, his hilltop situation allowing him to stay on the outside looking in. Here there are no social expectations on him, no rules to govern him. His shyness around people can remain hidden. The goats settle around the gate, awaiting their imminent release. His feeling of gratitude for his solitude is cut short. He may yet have to be part of that world even if only briefly, face a trip off the island, go to the mainland. He shudders at the thought.

Tucking his denim shirt into his jeans, he tightens his belt and turns his attention back to the goats. Another kick moves the stone securing the gate to one side and the herd pours out as one mass. Feeling eyes upon him, he looks down to the house. His baba is standing there staring back, perhaps wishing he was taking the goats out himself. One or two remain within the walls of the windmill and in a stride, Yanni chases them out to follow the others. Originally, the mill was roughly plastered and at one time painted. Here and there, patches of plaster cling to the stones, but mostly, it has flaked off over the years. The floor is earth and goat droppings. The smell is faintly acrid.

'Come on, come on then,' he calls and then whistles through his teeth. The goats bleat, run, bounce, and frisk about, spreading out, the brown and black and white wiry coats melting into the hillside. Their dull bells clonk and clank, indicating their whereabouts, arpeggios with no resonance, an orchestra of one-note soloists, the sound enchanting, filling the hill, a gently dramatic moment. Yanni's heart expands.

'Why do people rush?' he asks the air as he stands watching the bobbing white tails fan out.

As he walks, he overtakes the animals that follow in a loose pack along the track up through the top cluster of pine trees, over the bald crown of the island, and down onto the steep still back side of the island. Here the cicadas are deafening, their rasping love call sung loudly and desperately, their brief lives above ground lived to the full; a few days to find a mate before their energy is gone and they fall to the ground. Both goats and shepherd leave the trees and noise behind them and take a path that heads down the hill to the water's edge. The bugs' cacophony mellows, then fades and becomes intermittent. Not far down the path is a smooth rock in the shade of a lone almond tree where Yanni sits, the tree's trunk black against the blue sky, the branches dark, twisted and knotted in shocking contrast to the soft white blossom.

The animals spread out, settle, and begin to eat, each bite bringing them closer to Yanni, slowly gathering around him until he picks up a small pebble and throws it at the billy goat with the large curling horns. The animal sidesteps away with a clang of his bell, and the other goats follow him, resuming their feast some distance away.

'What to do?' he asks the silence. Dolly's soft muzzle invades his thoughts, a wisp of an image amongst many. She may have been a tool for work

17

but she was a wise and gentle beast, a good companion. He will probably never find another donkey like her for intelligence and willingness to work. And what will happen when the summer delivery work is over and the island grows quiet? Will he be able to keep his promise to the foreigner?

The American said he wanted to start building his house in September. The ruin he has bought is high up in the town, not as far as the pine trees, but nevertheless many steps from the port. Some stone remains from the building that once stood there, but more will be needed, brought by donkey from somewhere else on the island. Also every timber, every tile, every bag of sand and cement, every pipe, every light switch, every chair, every plate, knife, and fork will be brought in on the rusting old cargo boat. It has been agreed, he has shaken on it. He and his donkeys will do the job, haul everything up to the 'plot with a view', as the American referred to it. Even before the building work commences, there will be the rubble to clear from the site. Bags and bags of it. The charge is by the bag, two bags to a mule.

This work would see him and his parents through to the spring with ease. But with only one donkey, the American might not tolerate the time it will take. Will the builders wait? It is more likely that the American will just hire someone else as well. No one has fewer than two animals. With three donkeys working side by side, his work will be less, his pay will be less.

'I have no choice,' Yanni tells himself. The nearest goat looks up from its grazing, mouth chewing, dull yellow eyes staring blankly. 'I must go to the mainland.' The goat wiggles its tail and bends its head again. The idea does not sit easily; he never imagined he would ever leave his island, not for any reason. He has never really managed with people. It seems to him that everyone agrees to an unspoken big pretence of 'civilisation', but the truth is people are no different from his herd of goats. They all want the best branches for grazing, the deepest shade to stand in, and really there is no thought for the other goats beside them, just an unspoken pecking order. But he does not see life like that. He knows the herd will fare better if they work as a whole. His mama is always saying that his way of thinking ends up with him being taken advantage of, but is any other way better? Only last week, he advised a German couple to use the taxi boats once a week to take their bottled water along the coast to their newly bought summer house. If he had not done so, he would have delivered water to them every day for weeks until they wised up. His suggestion saved them a lot of money. It left him with less work. His mama was cross.

'What business is it of yours to advise this man, Yanni?' she scolded after he relayed the day's events to his baba.

'But how could I look this man in the eye after taking his money day after day, knowing I was taking such advantage?'

'Any other donkey man would have,' his mama sulked.

It is a lot easier if he just keeps himself to himself.

His hand fumbles as he takes the book from behind his tobacco pouch in his pocket. The book Sophia gave him all those years ago.

It falls open at a familiar page. When she gave it to him, the words seemed like nothing but squiggles. Now he can read, now he knows it off by heart. Under his moustache, his lips tighten. He briefly snorts, his head nodding. The irony is not lost on him. It was her brightness that lit his soul and his ignorance that lost him his chance. With diligence and help, he put his ignorance behind him. But it was in losing his ignorance that he came to know that she could have once been his.

If he had stayed ignorant, maybe the pain would be less now.

He strokes the page and reads the verse, in English, that she ringed with her own pencil all those years ago. Who says adolescent love is not as deep and real as any other?

Thus much and more; and yet thou lov'st me not,
   And never wilt! Love dwells not in our will.
Nor can I blame thee, though it be my lot
   To strongly, wrongly, vainly love thee still.

Looking out to sea, Yanni scans the horizon. He focuses there, his vision holding nothing but sea and sky. He stares hard, willing his mind to settle on nothing until his thoughts pass like dreams, forming of their own accord, all relating to the island, his island, where he was born and his family have lived for centuries. If he can have his wish, he will die here having never seen another land, living nowhere but in the stone hut. He has no wish to see more or do more. He is almost content. Sophia has faded as the years have passed, she will fade more still until one day, he will have perfect peace. He rolls up his sleeves. The sun has found its strength, the promise of the usual scorching summer.

His mama has no idea what she is saying when she suggests he get a wife. It would be like tearing out his heart and throwing it under stampeding hooves, a demand to dismiss his loyalty to Sophia. For what—an easier life? The very harshness of his life keeps the memory of her alive, the stark contrast highlighting her tenderness. Sometimes his mama does not know him at all. But then, Mama never did know about Sophia.

So long ago, he needs to learn to let her go. She was no more than a girl then, and he was just a boy. He can picture himself back then in colourless, shapeless shorts, his skin as brown as chestnuts, his hair always growing too fast for his mama's scissors to keep up with. Sophia wore dresses that had no wrinkles, her hair always neatly combed, but she was always quick to take off her shoes once they were away from school. She climbed the scrubland above the town like a goat. He would run, fall, run again, lose her, find her, call for her. She would call back; he

21

seemed always to be trying to keep up. Away from school, they played as if they only had one mind. He lost all sense of self and felt a contentment he has never known since. But at school, his awkwardness would return, the giggles would begin behind his back, and he and Sophia would become two people again. He her silent follower, she his defender.

'You laugh and pick fun, but you are children who play with toys and sleep on your mothers' laps when Yanni is out doing a man's job, herding goats and milking sheep.' She would stand, in the playground, with her hands on her hips, her back straight.

'We can smell the work he does all too well.' Hectoras would usually be the one to reply, trying to gain Sophia's attention for himself.

'And without it, you would have no milk to suckle on. Until you have a job of your own, I would not be too quick to judge others.' She was outspoken, brave, afraid of no one.

How much of a different person will she be now? Across the water, all grown up. Off the island, in a land of sophistication, complex rules, and modern ways.

With each green bite, the herd moves nearer to him, now almost on top of him as he lies back in the sunshine, looking up at the cloudless blue sky. A hoof clips his foot as the animal's blind march for food moves it forward. Yanni throws another stone; the goats scatter away, startled. He will wait for them to eat their way towards him again, one more stone's throw, and he will take them back.

The time comes too soon. He pockets the book which has been lying on his chest. He uncurls slowly and calls his animals with a whistle. The goats eat on but as he walks, they munch towards him until they finally lift their heads and follow him, now hurrying, now taking a bite, back to the windmill's corral. He listens for any distant bells that may have wandered, but the hillside is silent. He looks over the scrubland. Here and there are houses which are now nothing but ruins, piles of stones. Where walls remain standing, gaping holes are left where the roofs once were, and blind eyes show lifeless interiors. It won't be many years before Mama and Baba follow Dolly, and then what? Will he remain alone up here with all these ghosts or will his life change so much that only the cottage will remain and that too will lose its roof and eventually the walls begin to crumble?

Chapter 3

The animals leap and push back through the gate toward the windmill, hurrying to be first inside the corral. Yanni secures the gate with the stone and strides down to the house. The chairs around the wooden table at the front of the house are empty. His mama and baba, even at this early hour, forced inside by the growing strength of the sun. A tempting aroma of rosemary and tomatoes drifts from the open door. Mama will be standing by the stove fed by a gas bottle, spoon in one hand, pan handle in the other, chattering away to Baba, who will not hear a word. Cooking is a practical excuse to be inside, in the relative cool when the temperature reaches its heights outside. The food she prepares will not be eaten until the evening brings a wisp of a breeze and the sun loses its strength, and only then will the outside table be laid. If work keeps Yanni in town, or fatigue lengthens his return journey up the endless hill, his food will be set to one side, kept warm, and when he arrives, both Mama and Baba will sit at the table to keep him company even though their bellies will be full.

The bucket is already at the bottom of the well. Yanni hauls it up, fills two waiting pails and, slowed by their weight, takes even steps back to the goats to pour the water into their troughs. How would life have been if the well had dried up along with the others? Maybe it would have just hastened the inevitable. They wouldn't be living up here, and his life would have been different right from the start. He would probably have spent more days at school. In fact, that would have been guaranteed without goats to look after. He pours the water into the troughs and the animals drink greedily. He returns to the well.

He pulls the bucket up again, brimming with ice cold water. He trudges steadily back up to the goats and after decanting the last bucket, Yanni kicks the gate closed again.

Swinging the empty pails, he heads back down home. He should set off soon for town, but first he checks on the pregnant ewes that seem content in their low-walled enclosure behind the house. The enclosure always makes him smile. It is a standing summary of who, or rather what, has always determined his life. He thought, at the time of building the low walls, he was making a choice, having a say in his world. The naïvety of youth.

'I will build a new room,' he can remember saying, so proud, so young, around the time he knew Sophia, and he began to gather stones. Boulders for the base and smaller stones as the walls rose. 'You will have your bedroom back,' he announced to his mama, who just smiled. The house is made up of two rooms, the second of which is the only bedroom. It

25

has no windows, just a space filled with a thin mattress on a wood-and-rope base and a curtain for a door. A room that became his the day he was born. It was not the greatest prize in the world to offer back to his mama. Besides, she and Baba seemed quite happy to sleep on a similar bed in the main room. But he was at an age when a room separate from her and Baba would give them all space and at that age, he felt the need for some privacy, too.

So he had begun. A few stones here and a boulder or two there, the walls began to grow, until, on returning from grazing the goats one day, he found his baba had topped the wall with wire fencing and herded all the pregnant sheep into the half-built room, its walls now tall enough that they could not jump out.

After the ewes gave birth, the lambs took over, and after that the kids, by which time the sight of livestock in the half-built room had become familiar and Yanni had the feeling that his separate dwelling would never be finished.

The following year, the 'house-pen,' as it was by then referred to, was whitewashed, even along the top where the next row of stone would have been laid, and Yanni let go of the idea that it might one day be a room of his own. Sophia had left the island by then and he lost, well, what was it, a spark, energy, hope? Besides, the animals must come first. Their welfare determined his life, just as they had determined the days he could attend school in the brief years it was available to him. It had to be that way. It was their livelihood.

He walks round the end of the house-pen, one eye checking the distended bellies of the ewes. The scoop for the barrel sits on its lid. The wide-bellied sheep bleat with anticipation. Inside the pen, dividing walls have been erected. Some of the animals are bullies who leave the others hungry. Yanni gives some grain to these large animals first, adding a calcium mix, before repeating the process for the others, the wide bellies gently pushing each other out of the way.

His mama rounds the corner of the house, bottle in hand, and she lifts one of the newborn lambs out of a separate corral and tucks it under her arm. This starts a frenzy of bleating from it and from the two that remain in the pen. These are the rejects, unwanted by their mamas. They were pushed away when they tried to suckle and had to be rescued before they starved.

He and his mama walk together, with no need for talk, to the house front. She smells of onions. Sitting with the lamb on her knee, its little hooves dig holes in her woolly skirt as it nuzzles and pushes the bottle she holds. In no time, the bottle is nearly empty and its actions grow stronger until it is sucking air. She pulls the empty container away and the lamb's bleats fill with panic until she lifts it and gently takes it back and puts it into the pen with the others. They head butt each other and jump on the spot for a moment before she takes out the next and repeats the process.

Yanni knows that in a day or two, more will be born and soon after that, it will be time to make yoghurt. The thought is pleasing. Bread and yoghurt for breakfast. It reminds him that he must bring up more flour to make bread. The sack they have will soon be empty and he must fix the crack where his mother says heat is leaking from the domed bread oven that leans against the house wall nearest the well. Unless his baba has fixed it already. He goes to look at it.

His mother finishes with the lambs and returns, wiping her hands on her apron, which is already dirty from this morning's chores. It will be washed and hung on the line by the time he comes back for lunch and a sleep at *mesimeri*.

Yanni smiles at her and heads towards his donkey.

'You okay, son?' she asks. He nods. 'Going down?' He nods again. 'Can you get your father a coil of fence wire whilst you are in town? And we need more coffee. We only have Nescafé left.'

Yanni feels no need to answer. He would bring the town to her if she asked, but is glad that she would never ask. The mass of people is as unnerving to her as it is to him, and he cannot remember the last time she went down there, not her or his baba.

The wood and leather saddle creaks as he lifts it and places it on the donkey's back. Suzi is sleeping in the warmth and she starts awake and then immediately drifts off again as Yanni fastens buckles, loops, and ropes.

'What do you dream, my beauty? Of flat fields full of flowers and trees for shade, Dolly by your side?' He stops to consider her. Her muzzle is greying.

'Yanni, here, give her some more water before you go,' his mama says.

The water splashes from the bucket into the bowl she has given him, from which Suzi drinks her fill.

Yanni deftly rolls a cigarette while her nose is in the water. When he is sure Suzi is satiated, he takes the bitless bridle and scans the ridge. There are two ways down. The way they came up last night, along the ridge a way, past the monastery where only eight monks now live. The old ways are fast dying out, even on the island. That way follows a paved track down through the pine trees. Or he can go the other way, down the compressed earth track which is quicker but steeper.

'Don't forget the wire and the coffee,' his mama reminds him. His baba appears in the doorway, makes eye contact and nods.

The compressed track heads directly for the port and then straight down past the older monastery that has long since been re-designated for nuns. He will take it slowly, with Suzi finding her feet.

'Did you hear me?' his mama calls after him. He continues walking, raises his hand to acknowledge her without turning, and then bows his head as he lights the cigarette dangling from his lips as if it is windy, which it is not. There is not a breath of air. Just sun, heat, and lower down, the sound of cicadas.

The scrub and the weeds have not all turned brown with the sun's heat even on this, the exposed side of the island, but it is only a matter of weeks before the moisture will dry out in this heatwave, the air will become even stiller, the insects' calls will grow ever louder, and summer will suck everything to a crisp.

The donkey kicks up dust along the ridge. Yanni's cowboy boots, softened with age, disturb little as he glides foot to foot with no hurry. The smallest threads of cloud hang very high up in the flat blue sky and Yanni walks for a while with his head tipped back, watching them shift and change, drawing on his cigarette without removing it.

When he reaches where the land starts to drop more steeply, he watches his step. Small boulders buried in the hillside make good footholds. Suzi, alert now, takes it even more slowly, her haunches dropping and rising as they make their way. As the path flattens a little, they become less vigilant again and then the convent appears in the dip; an ancient stone building the colour of honey built around a courtyard. A tiny domed church squats as the centrepiece, flanked by spears of cypress trees that spike the sky.

When Yanni was a boy, there were three nuns. Now there is only one, Sister Katerina.

He watches the building as they descend. The shutters are closed, with only the Greek flag, barely moving, indicating the possibility of life. The only change over the years has been the height of the palm and cypress trees within the walls, each year pushing a little higher. The position is spectacular, its foundations tucked in a dip, but the windows of the cells must boast a panoramic view of town and sea and the mainland beyond. Yanni has only ever been in the courtyard, the church, and the dining hall from where you can see nothing of the outside world.

As he draws closer to the large main door, there is the familiar smell of jasmine. Under a stubby tree, he loops Suzi's reins on a hook that was hammered into the wall for that very purpose, Sister Katerina told him as a child, when he would swing from it himself. Yanni faces the door and turns the big cast iron ring, lifting the latch inside. He pushes it open with his shoulder. The scrubland is transformed within the walls to blossoms and roses, bougainvillea and dwarf trees. He has seen it many times before but still, it catches him unawares and he hesitates before crossing the threshold. The neatness and order attracts him but at the same time repels him. He feels he should wipe his boots every time he enters even though he is still outside.

Chapter 4

'Ah, there you are.' Sister Katerina's familiar, gentle voice puts him at his ease. He does not reply but smiles instead. He uses one hand to twist his moustache at either end and looks down at the ground to avoid her gaze, shuffling his feet. The first few seconds in her company always have this effect. Her calmness, her grace take a moment or two for him to feel, well, if he is honest, to feel he can just be himself. Truth be told, he feels like this in everyone's company but he knows that with Sister Katerina, his discomfort will be short lived.

Puffing, she straightens herself from bending over the flower beds and brushes her hands on her white apron, which she takes off as she walks across the courtyard, away from Yanni, who follows. They enter the cool stone building, with its low ceiling and dark wooden beams that support age-stained sticks packed with earth above, in the traditional manner. A long refectory table occupies the centre of the room with carved and uncomfortable-looking chairs standing stiffly down either side like soldiers, polished and waiting for nuns who will never come. Along the walls, at roughly equal intervals, are old, time-darkened icons but otherwise the room is bare, white, still. There is little the sister can do to make the room more homely. Up against a window, she long ago placed two wooden chairs on either side of a small, now well-used, table. On its polished surface is a vase of flowers.

With a gentle gesture, she invites Yanni to sit, which he does, slouching in the chair until he is comfortable, his initial unsettled feeling forgotten. They have sat many hours across from each other like this, Yanni deep in concentration, his cheeks burning as he tried to learn, at his request, the letters of the Greek alphabet. But after mastering more Greek than the average school boy, his passion to learn, instead of being satisfied, seemed to grow. His determination did not illicit any question from the sister, of which he was glad, for although he had a reason to learn, he still could not understand the pleasure it gave him. After a couple of years of short systematic bouts of study, her surprise registered when he asked if she spoke English. He can remember the look on her face; he had thought nothing could disquiet her until then.

'I will have to reassess who you are, Yanni. I have made the common mistake of presuming to know you and yet here you are surprising me again with your desire to learn,' was all she said. She didn't ask why he wanted to learn English.

Over the days that turned to months and then years, Sister Katerina seemed to always be available whenever he wanted to learn. He'd pick up her list of shopping every few days and take it to be filled out by the supermarket when he went into town to hire out his animals. He brought her goods up to her on the way home. This would be the time when he would linger and conversations became lessons until, after years of patient repetitive work and much frustration for Yanni, who felt Sister Katerina must consider him slow, she sat back and said, in English, 'Yanni, I have no more to teach you.'

Excitement played in his stomach as he drove Dolly and Suzi homewards that day. He could not wait to find a suitable place to pull the donkeys to a standstill. He called the beasts to halt halfway up and balancing, leaning against Dolly, he drew out the book that Sophia had given him and let it fall open. This long-anticipated reward, he had reserved until this moment. This was his big prize.

This was the day that he would read what Sophia had circled. Today he would understand the message she had left him.

He heard his heart in his ears. He swallowed and prepared himself, for good or bad, whatever the words on the page were going to tell him. But maybe, just maybe, the words would give him peace, help him to let go, return to the contentment of solitude he had before he met her.

He read, the words swimming in the excitement he could not contain. Then came the confusion and the heavy understanding that it made no sense as his heart sank and disappointment snuffed out his hope.

It began 'thus', a word that looked simple, but which he had never come across. And then 'lov'st'. He had never seen such grammar. What was 'wilt' in such a context? Flowers 'wilt', but in this sentence, there was nothing to 'wilt'. The words began to smudge behind unspilled tears and he closed the book and hid it away. He stopped carrying it for a while and Sister Katerina remarked on his lowness of mood some weeks later. He had tried not to let it show but in her graceful company, he could lie in neither mood nor deed.

She did not push, only supported in her compassion, and he surprised himself one day by confessing all: Sophia being in his class at school, her intelligence and uncreased clothes, her eager smile and her confidence. The teasing from the other boys that he received at first because of the smell of livestock, but later, when he had missed too many days of learning through lambing time, for being stupid. Sophia had stepped in, branded them all bullies in a way that no one could argue with, and bid him sit next to her in class. He had fallen in love. The boys teased all the more and he lost the confidence to speak up in class and then, eventually to speak in school at all. He avoided his peers and only spent time with Sophia. He confessed that he and Sophia had skived off school to play in the pine forest and he confessed the day she gave him the book and said she was going away as she stared at him in a way that he could only interpret as longing. She put the book in his hand, opened to the page she had marked, and he had looked down and not understood a word and when he looked up again, she had gone, running down the hill towards her home. The next day, she had left the island leaving nothing behind but the indecipherable book, which was the reason for all the learning and now a source of great frustration.

Sister Katerina listened as she always did, silently, attentively, and then she sat quietly.

'May I see the book?' she asked. Yanni held back the sacred tome from Sister Katerina's outstretched hand. No human hand had touched it but his since Sophia had given it to him. She sensed his hesitation and withdrew her hand to her lap. Ashamed of his reluctance, Yanni laid the book on the table. It fell open at the page with the circled words. She leaned forward and studied the page before sitting upright.

'Oh my!' she exclaimed. 'It is another language again … Shall we learn it?'

'It is not English?' Yanni asked.

'Oh yes, but as different to the English that we have been learning as ancient Greek is to Modern Greek.

'You know this language?' he asked hopefully.

'No.' She smiled so sweetly, her eyes shining. 'But we can learn together.'

Yanni feels heat rising to his cheek even now as he remembers, at that time, standing and leaving the sister without a thank you or a good-bye. For a while, he felt he had nothing to say to her. This new hurdle in his path seemed almost too great to climb. He stopped by for the shopping lists and dropped the things she needed back as usual until one day she asked him to go to the post office to check her mail. She had never asked such a thing before, but one shop or another, or the post office, it made no difference to him. A thick parcel was waiting. He glanced at it briefly to make sure it was for the nun and heard his own intake of breath. Both his name and Sister Katerina's were typed on a label adhered to the brown paper. It was the second post he had ever received.

He remembered the first all too well. It was a letter around his eighteenth birthday and he can remember feeling intimidated by how official it seemed. His name written by hand and the postmark over the stamp, those printed black lines had intimidated him. Reasoning with himself did not help. Even though he knew his birth had not been registered and he would not be listed in any official office, he felt sure it was draft papers for his military service. He looked again and again at the flowery handwriting on the envelope on the way home, but always his eye was drawn to the stamp, the official-ness of the black printed squiggles over it. He stopped to open it several times but he never quite managed it, his fingers freezing, rigid.

He arrived home late that day to a concerned Mama.

'Oh there you are, *agapi mou*.' She looked years older when she worried. How much more worried would she be if he had to go away to the army for two years? He could never bring that amount of anxiety to her. He walked to her open-armed greeting and, with a sly movement, he let the letter slip from his fingers and down the well as he passed. He hoped and prayed nothing would come of it, and nothing ever did. In time, he forgot all about it until the parcel came for the sister and all those feelings of fear returned.

He hoped a mistake had been made and that his name should not be there at all. It filled him with fear. He stuffed it into the sack on Dolly's side and tried not to think about it. A letter was easily lost but a parcel, and one also addressed to someone else?

The big, solid wooden door was open that day and she waited for him on the bench inside, amidst the pink roses, the orange bougainvillea, the purple wisteria, clusters of cultivated red poppies, and a many-petalled yellow flower he could never remember the name of no matter how many times she told him.

He handed her the parcel.

'Thank you, Yanni,' she said and he turned to leave, the colours of her garden too big a contrast to his mood to remain. 'Stay a moment,' she said, so softly he thought he might have imagined it. He hesitated. She remained unmoved on the bench by the tiny church in the courtyard and patted the seat next to her. He felt like a child as he sat.

She pulled at the package, but it wouldn't be opened until Yanni offered his help. From his pocket, he took a small penknife that he used to clean the donkey's hooves, wiped it on his shirt sleeve, and slit the string and tape that was binding the brown paper.

'Look, Yanni, it has come, and we may begin our studies again.' Her voice tinkled like water, a grin from ear to ear.

Yanni was surprised at that moment to realise that Sister Katerina derived as much satisfaction from teaching as he did being her student. Her smile was generous, encompassing, and her eyes were alive, the skin around them crinkling in her pleasure.

He looked at the contents of the parcel. Two books in her lap.

'Look, a more comprehensive English dictionary and "Understanding and Explicating English Poetry".' She laughed, a laugh that fitted with the gentle, bright flowers of her garden. 'We will need the one even to understand the title of the other,' she said and laughed again. They began to study again and as they learnt, piece by piece, he told her more about Sophia and, over time, the situation became clear, allowing Sister Katerina to understand Yanni, the reason for the distant look in his eyes and her own place in his life.

Chapter 5

Sitting opposite him now, upright, poised, she picks up the pen. She continues to smile as she puts pen to paper. 'Do you want a coffee?'

Yanni shakes his head. Once in a while he drinks coffee, but generally he doesn't. It makes him dizzy. And he hardly ever drinks anything stronger. Ouzo goes straight to his limbs, making him so relaxed, he almost falls over himself—or at least fall asleep.

'Water? I will get you water.' She stands and walks gracefully across the room in her long black habit, her black headdress wrapped around her face, cupping her chin so only her features show, her back a little bent. She disappears through an arch and returns with a metal jug and two matching beakers. Putting them on the table, she leaves Yanni to pour and takes up her pen again. He drinks and watches her as she concentrates on her writing. 'Sister, have you ever been off the island?' Yanni opens the conversation. Sister Katerina pauses before gently exhaling.

'Well, I was born in Athens, so the short answer is yes. But I have been here since I was about thirteen so not really, not as an adult, and certainly not since I was ordained.'

Yanni looks past her at a small icon hung on the wall at the end of the room. His eyes flick at his own internal snapshots of Sister Katerina in her habit hovering over imaginary city pavements. It is impossible to imagine.

'People talk about the mainland as if the people there are so slick, they would have the shirt off your back and you would thank them for it before you have even said hello.' It is a long sentence for him and he takes a moment before asking, 'Do you think there is any truth in that—really?' His features are unmoving. There is a slight tremor in his voice but he wonders if it is more something he can feel than something that can be heard.

Sister Katerina's calm is in her eyes, in the way she sits, the way she talks. 'I think people are people the world over. They will treat you as you allow them to treat you.' She takes a sip of water. A brightly coloured butterfly settles on the windowsill. 'Most people describe their own lives in the way they treat others. Those who feel the world is harming them harm others in word or deed, and those who feel the world is a gift, who are grateful, treat others as if they are part of the gift.' The words are soft as silk, spun from a compassionate heart.

'Don't those two sentences contradict each other?' Yanni follows her gaze to the butterfly. 'Either they treat you as you allow them to treat you or they treat you as a reflection of their own world. Can it be both?'

The butterfly dances in through the open window, circumnavigates their heads, and flies out again. They follow its swooping progress into the garden. It lands on a rose and stays there for a full minute before flying to the next flower, where it spreads its wings in the sun. 'Maybe they can,' the sister ponders. 'The way people begin to treat you reflects them but when you respond, with kindness and love or otherwise, you draw your boundaries. People rarely want to hurt kindness or love, no matter how scared of it they are.' She closes her mouth. Yanni looks over to her. Her eyes are flitting back and forth but she does not see the outside world, she is sieving through her thoughts. 'Unless we are talking about people who are extreme, who block out everything. People who hurt so much and are so scared they presume there is no love in the world and attack as a form of defence.' She pours more water.

The butterfly closes its wings.

'That is what I am asking—is that true of the people on the mainland?' Yanni says.

Sister Katerina waits before she answers.

'No more so than anywhere else. But, you know, maybe their expectation of how their lives should be is different. There is a limitation to our comfort here on the island. Even for the rich, if their air conditioning breaks down, they know they must wait for the repair man to come from the next island. They know they will be uncomfortable for a day or two. It is a part of life; we accept it here on the island. But on the mainland with all the modern conveniences and the abundance of material wealth everywhere, maybe they expect that in their lives, there should no discomfort. Which appears to make any hardship worse, perhaps? But I am just guessing. Maybe we should study some psychology?' The sister, not expecting an answer, nods over her reflections as they continue their observance of the flowers. A lizard scuttles into the open and remains motionless on the warm flags in the scorching sun.

'I was not even two when I fed my first lamb,' Yanni remarks.

The lizard jerks its head to look at them.

'It was so soft and gentle, I named it *Moro Mou*, My Baby.' He chuckles. He can feel his cheeks warm so he repeats the phrase in English to take the focus off him.

Sister Katerina smiles.

'She died the week I named her.' Yanni twists his moustache and the lizard darts away. 'The first of many. I learnt not to love them so much and I never named another.'

'I remember you doing the same with school,' Sister Katerina says quietly. Yanni frowns slightly, struggling to make the connection. 'You couldn't wait to get home to your mama to tell her all about your first day, do you remember? You didn't have the patience to get all the way up the hill, so you came running in here to tell me all about it, that day and every day for the first two weeks. You loved it so much.' Her smile fades. 'But then lambing took precedence and as your time was needed up on the ridge, you dismissed school. You told me, maybe you have forgotten this, that it was an "inconvenience that got in the way of real life".' She smiles, but it does not reach her eyes. 'Pushing it away because you loved it so much, perhaps.' They lapse into silence. The lizard reappears. Another butterfly, or perhaps the same one, comes and sits on the windowsill. Yanni wonders at how much life there is if you sit still long enough to see it. He finally shifts in his seat, breaking the meditation and Sister Katerina speaks. 'I wonder if we protect ourselves from our fears by choosing to love people we cannot get near so they cannot hurt us.' She turns to look at him.

Yanni meets her gaze.

'Like choosing to love God?' Yanni asks. His moustache twitches at the corners of his mouth as he struggles not to grin. Sister Katerina gives him a mock stern look and then glances at an icon to let him know that her God is watching them, hearing every word.

'Or in loving Sophia,' Sister Katerina challenges.

The butterfly leaves the sill and flies up and over the wall and is gone. Yanni is not in the mood to discuss his love for Sophia. He gazes out over the convent wall, up to the hill tops, a nice safe distance.

'Right.' Sister Katerina breaks the stalemate and picks up the piece of paper before her. 'The list is not long. The vegetable garden has come into its own this week.' She checks what she has written and replaces it on the table to add an extra item at the bottom, folds it, puts it in an envelope, and seals it before handing it to Yanni.

The sunlight is blinding as they leave the cooler interior. Sister Katerina walks with him through the garden, 'Sto kalo,' she calls and then she leans on the heavy door to shut it after him. Just before it fully closes, she stops.

'Yanni, where is Dolly?' she asks, holding the door open a crack.

Yanni's shoulders sink and his brow knots. His hand comes up to smooth his hair from front to back. The sister opens the door wider.

'She is dead,' he says, blinking.

'Oh Yanni, I am so sorry. What happened?' Sister Katerina comes out of the gates and goes to rub Suzi's nose.

'On the way towards the boatyard. The path has narrowed.' He looks at the floor and twists one toe in the dust. 'She was carrying a foreign woman.'

'Oh my goodness, the woman as well?'

'No. She is fine, and she has given me money to buy another donkey.' His tone is flat.

'Really?'

'From the mainland.'

'Ah … I see,' she says. The 'ah' is elongated, expressing her new understanding of the topic of conversation they pursued earlier.

Yanni waits, hoping she will say something helpful. She is looking into Suzi's eyes and her hands explore the softness of her muzzle.

'You and Suzi will be sad for a while. She was a good donkey.' Sister Katerina pats Suzi's neck and now looks Yanni in the eye. 'Do you have time to come back in and talk a while longer?' Her invitation is tender, but Yanni cannot hold her gaze. Dolly feels too far away right now and the mainland too close. He shakes his head. He takes up Suzi's rein and nods a farewell.

He walks a few steps, Sister Katerina returns inside her fort, the door thudding closed behind her.

Yanni stops, rolls a cigarette, and flicks open his lighter. He pulls on Suzi's reins and they begin to walk away.

The edge of town, at the top of the amphitheatre of houses, is quiet but as they descend, the noise begins; doors open and close, windows are shut, people call to one another.

A group of women pass, chattering, their black-encased shoulders drooping with the weight of their shopping bags. Children run, chasing one another, careful to avoid Suzi's rear end. Stories of children being kicked to death have been drilled into them since birth. Shops appear among the houses and their open doors offer cool interiors. A wide array of their goods trickle onto the pathways. Taverna tables and chairs line the way here and there as they get nearer to the port.

The lace makers have draped their wares over shop doors, on chairs and tables which all but fill the pathway onto the harbour front itself. Little old ladies in black sitting outside their tiny emporiums twist their fingers and crochet tools to weave items for which neither Yanni, or his mama, could ever find a use.

They look up from their work to smile at him because he is a familiar sight, but none of them know him well, although they all know him by name, know his nature—and leave him to his solitude.

Around the port's three sides, the shops are open and each has claimed as much of the walkway space in front of them as they think they can get away with to display their wares without passers-by being forced into the water. Jewellers compete with designer clothes shops next to art galleries, reflecting the wealth of the visitors who, on holidays and at weekends, descend on this island.

The cafés are full, extra chairs have been put out, not even a space left to walk between one café to get to another, the chairs and tables trickling all the way to the water's edge and here, hopeful cats sit and watch and wait for the fishermen who will come home at some point.

A cruise ship has just come in and deposited its catch of tourists. By this, Yanni judges that he is late, might have missed his chance for easy money. The stragglers are still disembarking, the eager ones already engaged in haggling with the lace makers and drawn into jewellery shops.

All the donkey men are there. Mimis is helping an Asian girl onto his lead mule while her friend stands giggling, waiting to be lifted onto the rear animal.

Both girls wear long-sleeved shirts, white gloves, sunglasses, and very broad-brimmed hats.

'Hey Yanni,' Hectoras' gruff voice calls. Yanni pulls Suzi toward him. Hectoras turns to a passing woman. 'Lady—donkey. Take bags to hotel?' He uses his limited English to tout for business. The woman ignores him.

'Hey Yanni,' he repeats. 'When are you going across to get a new donkey?' Next to the mass which is Hectoras, almost hidden by his bulk, stands Tollis, pulling his jeans up on his slim hips, his animals not needing to be held. Tollis' method of approaching the tourists is to make eye contact and then vigorously point at his animals—a little brown donkey and a fine ass with a glossy black coat. His English is for money only; he can count, and this is enough. It is a bit of a mystery, once Tollis has got a foreign client, how he communicates to agree where he will take them, but he seems to manage. He points again and the woman shakes her head.

'It is good that she is paying.' Hectoras refers to the tourist lady who was on Dolly when she slipped over the cliff. Nothing remains private for long on the island.

'Sure, why not, she is a foreigner, she will have plenty of money,' Tollis agrees whilst raising and lowering his eyebrows at a passing Japanese girl and pointing at his ass.

Yanni says nothing.

'So when do you go?' Hectoras asks.

'Not sure if …' Yanni begins his sentence but lets it peter out unsaid.

'Big cut in your salary if you don't,' Hectoras encourages.

'It's not like there are any for sale on the island,' Tollis offers.

'Oh no, you don't want to get one from here, they are all too interbred. Go across to the mainland.' Hectoras and Tollis turn to look beyond the port across the water to the blue hills in the distance, under the clear deep blue sky.

'Over there.' Tollis points. 'Behind that hill above a small village near Saros, over the other side of the peninsula. You know Saros, right?'

Yanni does not answer. Although he has no desire to leave his island, he feels there is some shame in admitting that he never has.

'Yes, yes, jump on one of the water taxis to get across, then just take the bus up to Saros. You'll get a lift from someone if you start walking to the village and then it is just a stretch of the legs to the breeder. It's a good stretch, mind, but do-able if it is not too hot,' Hectoras confirms. 'Got Bibby from there.' He pats his lead mule's neck.

'Donkeys too, or just mules?' Yanni's mouth hardly opening to form the words, his reticence betraying his will.

'Donkeys, mules, asses, hinnys, whatever you want.' Tollis points to his animals in quick succession as another group of foreign girls walks past. They giggle and hide their mouths behind their hands, chattering shyly to one another. Two of them pause and then step forward and nod their heads at Tollis, who grins, showing a missing tooth to one side, adding to his cheeky character. The girls giggle all the more.

A blonde lady with fine, floating clothes and a large monogrammed suitcase pauses to hitch up a handbag on her shoulder, bangles glinting in the sun as they slide down her arm, six months' donkey pay on her feet in the form of a flimsy pair of sandals. The sort of woman who thinks nothing of tipping a day's pay, not aware of how generous she is being.

'Lady, would you like me to take your bag to your hotel for you? It looks heavy and it is hot.' Yanni approaches her.

'Oh, English.' She sets down the suitcase gratefully and her shoulders relax. 'You speak English. Wonderful.' Yanni steps forward to take her bag.

'You sharp-talker, Yanni. You didn't learn to gabble in English like that at the school I went to,' Hectoras teases, confident the lady does not understand Greek.

'Same school,' Yanni mutters. Hectoras' bullying days have not been forgotten.

'Yeah, but you were never there, always with your goats, that or you skived off with, er, what was her name?'

Hectoras' left hand goes up to his throat, the fingertips feeling a scar under his chin. His voice is goading, challenging Yanni.

Yanni ties the suitcase onto the side of Suzi's saddle: once round with the thick rope, underneath, and a simple hitch to stop it slipping. The woman catches her breath and searches in her handbag, from which she retrieves a pair of overly large sunglasses that swamp her delicate face.

'What was her name, Yanni? Smart … Smartest girl I've ever met. What was it? Oh yes, Sophia. Do you remember? Left the island when she was only a teenager, didn't she? To become a nun in that place over near Saros.'

Yanni clicks Suzi on.

'I bet you haven't thought of her for a long time, have you?' Hectoras asks, but he has lost interest; Yanni does not rise to the bait and another tourist is approaching.

Chapter 6

Before they are halfway up to the hotel, the foreign woman begins to complain about the heat and the number of steps that climb ever upwards through narrow alleys between the whitewashed houses. She looks longingly at Suzi, who is laden with her suitcase. At this point, Yanni would normally suggest that she take a ride on Dolly, and his fee would double as a result. But now he can make no such offer. At the hotel, the woman dabs her forehead and neck with a tiny lace-edged bit of material and catches her breath. She is in no mood to tip. The cool air-conditioned interior of the hotel beckons and the journey up is forgotten. Yanni returns to the port and watches as work is offered to his colleagues who have more than one animal.

Up a narrow alley just yards from the port is a little shop that sells groceries. Despite its size, it does a healthy trade, and, although they have their own mule, there is sometimes work to be had delivering goods to demanding customers. Not today, however, although they are very sorry to hear about Dolly.

When the evening cargo ship groans into the harbour, metal creaking, crew shouting, Yanni gets a couple of runs with water bottles up to another shop, higher up in the town, where four paths cross. A shop that is crammed to the rafters with cold drinks, fresh vegetables, bread, fire-lighters, home-pickled olives to be scooped out of big jars, face cream, string, hair clips and all manner of day-to-day items. It's a sweaty walk up to the houses in this part of town, but the owners are compensated for their efforts by the most fantastic views across to the mainland, out over the sea, which is dotted with floating islands. The grocery shop saves them a walk down to the shops in town. The shop owner, hemmed in behind the tiny counter with two caged singing birds and an ever-friendly dog, charges higher prices because all the goods have to be brought up by pack animal. But those who frequent her Aladdin's cave understand and accept this as they push past fly swats and oil lamps that hang from the ceiling to get to the worn wooden counter where they will be greeted with a smile. Besides, so many of the ancient stone houses in the town are holiday homes to rich Americans, English, and French. Their time on the island for the summer months is spent without a thought for money, or so it appears.

The donkey men generally share the four-paths-shop work between them, one of their daily staples. Yanni is more than usually glad of the work today. As Suzi clops her way up steps and eases her way around the tight corners of the narrow path, there are several times when Yanni encourages her along but calls her Dolly. Each time the inadvertent mistake falls from his lips, his throat tightens and he reaches for his tobacco pouch.

As the day's light fades and the whitewashed houses turn pink and the sea begins to darken, the mainland across flattens to an even indigo blue. Yanni looks across to the mainland that stretches away to the west and east. It seems to stretch on forever.

Down in the harbour, lights in the cafés are coming on. The donkey trade has all but stopped for the evening; it is time for him to head home. Hectoras is standing by his mules.

'How about an ouzo and a game of *tavli*?' Hectoras hitches up his trousers around his ample waist as he speaks; the white lining curling over his twisted belt. Yanni opens his mouth and closes it again. It is an unusual offer.

For Hectoras, it is obvious which café to choose. The name over the door tells anyone who wants to know that Costas Voulgaris is the proud owner. Costas never sided with Hectoras at school, nor did he defend Yanni, unless things went too far and Sophia was not there. He trod the middle ground with wit and goodwill. He is, above all, a diplomat. A skill which no doubt held him in good stead when he went to America to study. But the island lured him back and now he makes coffees and talks to the foreigners in their own tongues.

'So you are going to the mainland, Yanni?' It is the man himself. 'You know, I have lost all interest in leaving the island since my adventures.' Costas

Voulgaris pulls out a director's chair for Yanni to sit, nearest the harbour edge and next to Hectoras.

'You want something, a lemonade perhaps?' Costas asks.

'I'll have an ouzo,' Hectoras demands. 'No ice.'

'No,' Yanni answers, but it comes out louder than he intended.

'It's not that I would mind going anywhere, rather that I cannot see the point, do you know what I mean?' Costas says as he walks away to get their order.

'I er …' Yanni stumbles.

'He's right,' Hectoras mumbles, 'and you know why?' Without looking at it, he kicks out the chair Costas offered to Yanni even further. Yanni looks at Suzi, who is snoozing, and lets go of her rein so it just dangles, and then he slides into the proffered chair. He will sit just for a moment. Suzi will find the journey home easier the more rested she is and the cooler it gets as the day passes into evening.

They stare across the water, side by side, to the mainland.

'It's too big,' Hectoras states. 'The mainland, it's just too big, don't you think?'

Yanni has no reply.

'This town, Orino town, is just a tiny dot. A lot of people huddled together.' He slaps his belly and his hand rests there, one finger finding its way between buttons to scratch his hairy navel. 'We collude in the idea that this place is important, but we are ants.'

Yanni wonders if he will lose the light if he sits too long. He still has to deliver Sister Katerina's goods. A cloudy lemonade is set before him, the ice tinkling against the glass. He looks up to tell Costas he does not want it, but the owner-cum-waiter has already turned on his heel and is inviting some German tourists to sit, have a cold beer, enjoy the sunset.

'At school, they try to make you think the island is important,' Hectoras continues. 'And then, just as they begin to succeed, the teacher tells you how big the rest of the world is.' He takes a long drink from the glass of iced water that came with his ouzo. Costas, having seated the Germans, is now clearing used glasses from the table behind them. He stops to watch people disembark from the converted fishing boat that offers day trips to the more obscure beaches around the island. Many of the tourists are sunburnt, they all move languidly, animated but tired, bags bursting with flippers and masks, sunhats and sun-creams, towels over their shoulders. Their own particular tribe.

Hectoras continues. 'The lies they told us at school, eh Yanni?' He guffaws quietly to himself.

'Ha, and who did the most lie telling, eh Hectoras my friend?' Costas gently taunts him as he passes by. Hectoras plucks a serviette from the holder on the table and wipes his face. He takes a second and lifts his chin to wipe his neck, the sweat running down a line of discoloured puckering and briefly collecting in the thin skin of a deep indentation before continuing down to the sharp distinction where his shaved beard meets the unshaved hairs of his chest.

Yanni pushes himself up a little from his slouched position. Hectoras drops what's left of the tissues in the ashtray.

'Do you see what I mean though?' Hectoras ignores Costas and takes a sip of ouzo. 'We think we can handle the world because we can handle this tiny little island.' Putting his drink down, he turns slightly to face Yanni. 'Now, here is the interesting bit. You hardly went to school at all. You are a man who walks to the beat of his own drum.' He stops to chuckle. Yanni's eyebrows raise but he continues to stare out across the water. Hectoras' chuckle becomes a laugh. 'You sure you won't have an ouzo?' He looks around to catch Costas' attention, but Costas is talking to two boys who have a puppy with them. When Hectoras hisses through his teeth to gain Costas' attention. He looks up and acknowledges the two raised fingers, an ouzo each.

'So here's the thing. Seeing as you never did much schooling, do you have any idea how big and how different the mainland is?' He waits. Yanni feels he is expected to say something, but nothing comes to mind. He pictures the goats running over the hills in the early morning light; he must get back to sleep to start a new day.

Hectoras looks around to see if his ouzo is coming. Yanni looks at the sky, tries to judge how long the light will remain. Suzi is still sleeping. She should be rested enough by now.

Two ouzos arrive and one is put down in front of Yanni. He tries to object, but it is simpler to let it sit there next to his lemonade, which is also untouched. Hectoras is silent again, still waiting for him to say something.

'Everywhere, people are the same,' Yanni finally says. 'We are born, we scrabble about living, and we die. The rules do not change because you live on a small island or a large one. The only differences one man has from another are his own rules in his head. His honour.'

'There, you see.' Hectoras sounds triumphant. 'You have not changed at all.'

'Hectoras, is there something you are getting at?' Yanni takes out his tobacco pouch. He will have one cigarette and then he will go.

'You are going across to the mainland,' Hectoras states, as if the decision has already been made.

Yanni's fingers begin to fumble with his tobacco pouch. 'Maybe,' he mutters.

'The day before I went up to Athens to go into the army, I was terrified. You never did do the army, did you?' It's a question he neither expects an answer to, nor does Yanni intend to give him one. Being born halfway up the mountain has made conformities, such as registering his birth, more effort than it was worth. In the world of lists and paper, he does not exist. But he does not want to discuss his business with Hectoras.

Yanni lights his cigarette and takes a long draw, his lighter still burning.

'Until I was called for the army, I had never been off the island. The day I was due to leave was the most frightening day of my life. I can still remember the cold sweat that was running down my back. The ferry pulled in. It was the big old steel ship back then, you remember them.' He coughs out a laugh. 'My mama and baba standing so proud and I ran, ran to the nearest café and locked myself in the toilet. I was just in time.' He chuckles at the memory. 'But then I could not get out. My hands were shaking so much, I could not open the door. In the end, I had to call out and the waiter came. The most terrifying day of my life became the most embarrassing. But I was glad for the humiliation of being locked in the toilet. It took everyone's focus away from my trembling bottom lip and my cold sweats. And for why? All because I thought the rules would be different, that the big world would be beyond my understanding.' He finishes his ouzo.

'So my question is, if I had not been to school so much and learnt the differences between this tiny island and the big world out there, would I have felt so much fear?' With narrowed eyes and a smirk on his lips, he glances across to Yanni.

Yanni leans forward, picks up the glass of ouzo that is reflecting pinks and pale blues in the setting sun and, putting it to his mouth, throws his head back and swallows it in one.

'Ah!' Hectoras replies. 'I see.' With this, he takes a cigarette from the soft pack in front of him and, lighting it with a match that transforms his features grotesquely in the half-dark, he watches Yanni's face.

Yanni grips the chair for moment and then without a word stands and strides stiffly to Suzi, who wakes with a start. It is difficult to see who leads who from the harbour.

Chapter 7

The cobbles under Suzi's hooves click in time with the heels of Yanni's boots. They lapse into a familiar rhythm and Yanni's thoughts give way to a mercifully pleasant blankness.

The wide path narrows and grows steeper and finally peters to nothing but a dusty track, used by few. It zigzags steeply out of town.

If he were to leave the island, what if something should happen and he were to never come back? His mama and baba are growing ever older, and things that would have once not affected them now present insurmountable obstacles.

Thoughts of them ageing brings also the inevitability of their deaths. One day, he will be alone up there, and what woman would ever choose such isolation? They cluster like chickens, needing the social whirl of each other's company. If he is ever to even consider marriage, he must be ready to live in town. Something he can neither afford in money nor in peace of mind. There is not a woman alive who would choose to be his wife, if only because of his circumstances. After his parents are gone, he will not be choosing to be alone up there. He will be forced to be alone.

Isolation is different from solitude, and what if something happens to him? When his baba slipped and broke his ankle over at the far grazing area, he crawled the distance home on his knees. It took him four hours and his knees were shredded. If Yanni had not been at home with his phone and his donkeys, it would have been another four hours to crawl into town. Baba would never have made it, and he was a younger man then.

The monastery door is ajar, a slash of light taming the rough ground outside.

'Well hello.' Sister Katerina's voice breaks through his gloomy thoughts as he pushes the door open. 'Late tonight. Did you get everything?' she asks with energy in her voice. She scans his face. 'Yanni?' she asks more gently.

'I was thinking,' he answers with no elaboration.

She takes her favourite seat by the little church from where there is the best view of the garden. There is a jug of water and two cups.

Yanni uses the moment to take the things he has brought for her from town inside. He puts them on the end of the long table before returning to sit with her.

'Ah ...' A sigh that is almost a yawn is her greeting on his return. The sunlight is now nothing but a soft glow, somewhere between day and night.

'I was thinking of whether I have to go over to the mainland, Sister,' Yanni says.

'Oh I see, and your dilemma is in wondering if you can put off the inevitable, perhaps?'

'Inevitable?' Yanni asks.

'Maybe it is time?' she says with a glance.

'Are we talking in riddles today, Sister?' Yanni laughs quietly, respectful of the mood in the garden.

'It would not only be a donkey you were buying.'

Yanni frowns and waits for her to explain.

'Let me ask you a question.' She straightens her robes over her knees. 'If there were a good donkey on the island for sale, would you buy it?'

There is a pause.

'Yes, I would.'

'So it is not from not wanting a donkey that you are not leaving the island, then?' A quick roll of her eyes acknowledges her tangle of words. When the smile drops from Yanni's lips, she adds, 'Fear's a funny thing.'

Yanni turns from her to look over the garden. He reaches for his tobacco but, with a sideways glance at the nun, replaces it in his pocket. Instead, he grinds a pebble into the dusty earth with the toe of his cowboy boot.

'We all feel fear when we face something new. There is nothing over there that you need fear. There is not a big demon out there eating islanders for breakfast or anything.' She laughs at the thought and her mirth judders through her body. 'Perhaps this is a lesson being offered to you so you can learn to trust yourself. Trust yourself with people perhaps, realise you have as much right to be here as the sun or the …' She looks around herself to name something else, at which moment Suzi calls out her loneliness: big heaving bellows as if she knows her cries will never reach the ears of her lost long-eared companion. 'Or the donkeys.' Sister Katerina acknowledges the sound. 'Sometimes we name a feeling we do not recognise as fear, but it may in fact be excitement, or anticipation, or expectancy, but we just have not understood it, or ever connected it with that particular event that we are experiencing. It is only as we step over that threshold, into the fear so to speak, that we can truly name it.'

'Yes but meanwhile, we are feeling fearful,' Yanni offers.

'That's what I am saying. It is not really a feeling. It is a thought, a pre-emptory thought. That's the demon, and he is not on the mainland.'

'You never mention God when you lecture me,' Yanni says.

'Do I need to?' she asks. 'I have always found logic works better with you.' Her eyes dance a little, waiting for his response.

'I think you are the demon that eats islanders for breakfast,' Yanni rejoins, his attention being drawn by the sound of Suzi scraping her hoof on the ground outside. She will be hungry. He is also hungry.

'There is another thing, too.' Her hand raises to the cross around her neck. 'Sophia.' She waits. Yanni stops breathing for a second. 'I cannot tell you how she is in the nunnery near Saros; maybe she has moved to another nunnery. But even if I did know anything about her life, I think it would make very little difference to you. The Sophia you hold in your heart, who keeps you from being at peace, is not the Sophia who has spent the last nineteen years in God's service. Maybe it is time to face that, too; realise you are holding onto a dream, an imaginary person. Go Yanni, visit her, realise she is not the same person. Give yourself peace.' The last sentence she says with energy.

His throat is too constricted to speak. He smooths out his moustache and then wraps his arms across his chest. 'No.' He says it quietly.

'Yanni, we have spent many hours together learning, and it was not revealed to me until recently what all the learning was for. Do not use the dream, a dream that, if treated right could turn into a lovely memory, to hamper your life.'

'But …' His voice is almost a whisper.

'Again, we have fear, but is what you feel fear or is it another emotion that you will not truly know until you meet her face to face? Maybe it will be relief, relief that you can let her go. Or excitement, excitement that you no longer have your loyalty to her holding you back.'

'But it may be heartbreak at my loss.' Yanni is not sure if he says the words out loud.

'And the fear is you would not cope with that loss. That is our ultimate fear, I think, the fear that we cannot cope.' Sister Katerina makes it all sound so easy.

'What if I cannot cope?'

65

'What does that even mean, Yanni? How would it manifest itself if you "could not cope"? What would it look like?'

'I don't know.'

'Ah, so now you fear the unknown again. Maybe "Not being able to cope" feels like sadness, or emptiness, or even hopelessness.' Katerina waits for some acknowledgement of what she has said. Yanni lets his arms drop to his lap. 'Feeling sad or empty or hopeless doesn't feel nice, but how long do those feelings last? We cope with them, Yanni. It is part of human nature.'

He leans forward, his elbows across his knees, his head hanging.

'The truth is, Yanni, unless you go and you face these things, nothing will change. You will continue on the hill there with your parents, a piece of you yearning for a love that will never be, until God takes your family and then you will be truly alone, and maybe you will have missed your chance to find love and your dreams will be of little comfort then.'

The garden is quiet. The day of buzzing and searching for nectar is over for the insects. The roses in the twilight look black, the moonlight gives a glow to the edges of the paths where Sister Katerina has whitewashed. Yanni wipes his hands down his jeans, sits back, and takes a deep breath.

'So you will go?' Sister Katerina asks lightly.

'So I just walk up to the convent door, knock, and ask to speak to her? What if she doesn't want to speak to me?'

'For that, you must trust in God,' she says. 'Besides, I have something that I really need to have delivered to that convent. I would not trust it to go by post, so this is the only way. Will you deliver it for me, Yanni?' The request is so gentle, but even in the moonlight, he can just see her eyes are sparkling, mischievous, alive. He nods; what else can he do? After all she has given him, the hours of her time, the patience, all he has learnt, how could he say no to anything she would ask of him? Especially something so simple as a delivery? It is so little to ask, and while he is there, he can buy a donkey.

'Good.' Sister Katerina draws out the word and rolls to her feet to glide indoors, returning after some time with a paper parcel bound up tightly with string. She hands it to Yanni.

Yanni turns it in his palm before finding a pocket in which to store it.

'Now, you should go tomorrow, I think.' Nothing she says sounds rushed or pushing, but her delivery is emphatic nonetheless. 'Don't you have some family in the village over there? A second cousin was it? He came here once, I seem to remember. What was his name? Your mama will know.'

Yanni feels he is falling into a hole. It seems not only that he must go but somehow, it has been decided that he must go tomorrow. The ground is opening beneath his feet and he dangles.

Sister Katerina must see his hesitation as she takes a gliding step towards the boundary door. Yanni

67

reacts by standing and walking mechanically by her side.

'Tell your mama that if she needs to telephone your second cousin so he can prepare for you, she can come to use the convent phone. Also, as long as you are on God's business, tell your mama you will be safe and I will be praying for you—personally.' She indicates his pocket with the missive. 'It makes sense for you to buy your donkey whilst you are there, does it not?' They are at the big wooden door. Yanni nods his head compliantly. As an afterthought she adds, 'If your mama has any worries tell her to come down to me anyway.'

With this, she gently bustles Yanni out of the door, handing him a delicate rose that she nips off from the nearest of her bushes for him to give to his mother.

Outside alone with Suzi, it is quiet. It is dark.

A day to get there, a day at the convent and the donkey breeder's place, and a day to travel home, he reasons, but he doesn't really believe he is going anywhere yet.

He puts the Nun's parcel in the saddle bag and his hand automatically reaches for his tobacco pouch.

Chapter 8

It is dark. There is a door, no, a window, a light beyond. So bright. Better to keep his eyes closed, just for a moment. The bed he is on, sagging, soft, swirling. Still swirling with his eyes closed. Water would be good. It's possible to make out the shadows of the ceiling. An oblong room. It is not home. But where, what time? It's dark. Do the animals need feeding? He knows where he is, he knows everything, it's lurking just beyond his grasp, teasing, taunting. What can he remember? A boat and a bright sea, his island receding. And then? Then voices, women with bags. Jostling and swaying. A sickness in the stomach. Voices arguing. A goat amongst people, bleating, terrified. More arguing, the goat leaving, more swaying, so hot. A change of people, laughing and rocking and then, and then …

Perhaps if he sits up. Slowly. No, bad idea, lie down. His hand creeps across his stomach, up his chest, over his jaw, sweeping his eyes. Pressing and rubbing his temples does not alleviate the pain or the steady beat of the drum. Twitching his legs, his feet heavy; he still has his boots on. Why would he still have his boots on if he has laid down? Where did he walk? Images of orange orchards, rich and lush, leaves so green, like nothing he has ever seen on the island. And olive groves, with bushy trees thick with fruit and, yes, he remembers that - water coming from pipes beneath them, the ground soggy with the excess. Then? What then? A turn in the road, a school with a brightly coloured fence. Houses with bright blue shutters. And then?

'Hey Yanni, you're awake. Come on my man, let's go.' The light from the opened door blinds him. 'We must eat and celebrate.' A hand grabs his arm and pulls. He shakes it off with a flex of his bicep. The hand has a weak grip.

'Oh, you're not one of these people that are all grumpy when they wake, are you? Come on.'

Like the bucket falling from the well's edge and spilling the water over the parched ground, in an instant, everything returns and soaks in. Being met in the village square by Babis, being hauled into the kafeneio, the open floor-to-ceiling glass doors, clusters of tables surrounded by work-worn faces. So many faces. Babis introducing to everyone his second cousin from the island. Unfamiliar face after unfamiliar face offering to shake his hand, an ouzo thrust into his open palm and a hearty slap on the back from Babis as he takes a sip which makes him gulp and the shot goes down in one swallow. A joke being made of islanders drinking, another glass in his hand, Babis telling expectant faces exaggerated tales of their brief meetings when they were boys, Yanni so much taller and older and wiser. On and on, Babis talked. What could have been said in five words took him twenty minutes. Yanni was tired from the jiggling and pounding and shouting of the journey, so many people, so much that was new and then with Babis droning on, his eyes closed in reaction to everything, shutting down, blocking it out, another slap on the back, another mouthful and then nothing seemed so bad; in fact, he felt quite pleasant for a while. Another glass in his hand feeling smooth and round, the burn in his throat. No idea what was going on, someone said … No, that was Hectoras on the island—on a different day, maybe he … No, it will not come.

'Come on now, Yanni, whilst you've been snoring all afternoon, I've been working, another sale going through, but now I am hungry. Come, the food is on me, my friend. Let's go!'

'Water,' is all Yanni can say.

Babis leaves the room and returns presently. 'Here.' He hands him a glass of water. 'I did think you were chucking it back my friend, but who was I to say? First you seemed all strung out, tense, tongue tied and then after a couple of ouzos, you found your stride. I couldn't keep up. Anyway, it's great you are here. Come, it's late enough; let's go eat.'

'Could we not stay here?' Yanni says, not quite sure where 'here' is, but the quiet seems preferable to anything he can recall of the mainland so far. How many times has he put his hands to his ears, so many people he could no longer tell them apart, and that bus, that jolting about, the speed with which the land passed, who could think that was a good idea? So many people pressed in so close together, and why

71

was that man given such a hard time when he wanted his goat to ride with him, when there was a woman on the seat next to him with a dog on her lap? And that other woman who talked and talked and when she had worn one person to the point of getting off the bus, she began on another and nothing she said had any practical use to anyone listening. Yanni shakes his head gently to try to clear the fog.

'Well it's a bit of a mess here at the moment ... What with Mama going up to her sister's in Athens. Thought she would only be a weekend, but she's been gone two months already.' He picks up a shirt and a tea towel and puts them on the back of a chair by the door. The chair already has an upturned bowl on it, which is none too clean. 'But Auntie is getting better, thanks be to God, so we must not complain.' He crosses himself and gathers together various parts of a newspaper that has spread over the floor. He folds it haphazardly and puts it on the upturned bowl, which it promptly falls off. 'The thing is, what with trying to get myself established in Saros and everything that entails, I haven't really had much time to clean up around here. Which you might find your way to helping me with, Yanni? Seeing as your time will not be as pressed as mine is … But come, let's go. Stella and Mitsos make a good chicken and chips and we'll go to Theo's kafeneio again and watch the match tonight. You like football, right? Even if you don't, it's a good atmosphere and besides, I need to be seen in as many local places as I can, get myself noticed, be the name on everyone's lips, if you know what I mean.' He leaves the room, taking the empty water glass. Yanni manages to sit up, his feet over the edge of the bed. Bright light floods through the doorway and he can see past a table and into a sitting room. There are plates, shoes, shirts, plastic bags, boxes from the *zaharoplasteio*—sweet shop—on their sides, empty of the *baklava* and *kataifi* they once held, the honey and gooey remains puddling onto the tiles. Babis did not exaggerate when he described it as a bit of a mess. Yanni puts his hand to his temple again.

'You want some Depon or aspirin?' Babis brings another glass of water and two packets. Yanni shrugs. Babis opens one of the boxes and pops out two pills from the blisters. 'Here you go.' Yanni inspects the shiny pink pills in the palm of his hand. Very occasionally, his mama took these things when he was young, but very rarely, once a month if that. He wasn't aware men could take them too, but if they will relieve this pain, then why not? He hardly notices them going down.

'Right, let's go then.' Babis waits at the door with his arm outstretched as if to show the way into the sitting room. Picking his way through the things on the floor and using any surface that is not too covered in grime to steady himself, Yanni makes it to the back door. He is not taking anything much in, but that is probably just as well.

'I don't use the front door much.' Babis trips down the steps. 'It's got a nice veranda that looks down onto the back of the roof of the kiosk and the rest of the square, which is great for watching people come and go, but it's easier to come out of this side door then, look, here is the *souvlaki* shop. You hungry, by the way? You must be hungry. What time did you start out? The bus journey's not fun is it? It used to be worse but they have straightened some of the roads.'

Yanni shakes his head. The last thing he needs is the noise of a taverna; Babis' continuous monologue on its own is proving too much. But he must show his appreciation for his second cousin so kindly putting him up. It would not do to reject his hospitality, and he is being very hospitable. Yanni blinks a few times and opens his eyes wide. At least it is dark. Maybe he can manage a taverna and a bite to eat. He will offer to pay. After that, he can make his excuses. He has no desire to watch any football match. He is here to deliver Sister Katerina's parcel, buy a donkey, and go home—and that's it. Three days maximum. He has already wasted the entire afternoon sleeping as soon as he got here, so he had better plan out his time carefully. At least his head is starting to feel a little better.

'Hello Babis.' A petite woman in a sleeveless floral dress greets him as they leave the house. Shafts of light from inside the taverna spread an inviting glow across into the darkness. Someone has wound a thousand tiny lights around the trunk of a tree that stands sentinel between the tables on the pavement, their wooden tops smooth with plastic cloths reflecting the glow. No one is sitting outside but there are sounds of voices from inside the tiny but brightly lit place.

'Out or in?' the woman asks, offering them a choice of any of the four outside tables, each only big enough for two people, with a sweep of her arm.

'Stella, this is Yanni, my second cousin from Orino Island,' Babis gushes.

'Hello Yanni.' Her voice is quiet and warm and her movements those of a girl but her face betrays wisdom only years can bring, and there is a just a fleck or two of grey in her hair. 'Will this do?' she asks, pulling out a chair from the table nearest the tree trunk. 'The usual, Babis? Yanni, we don't serve much, but what we serve is good.'

'You need no more than you offer, Stella. The chicken is always perfect, the sausages are just spicy enough, and everything comes with chips, oh and Stella's lemon sauce, which is to die for,' Babis informs Yanni.

'I can do you a salad if you prefer?' Stella asks Yanni, a small frown on her forehead, a hand on his arm as he eases himself into the proffered chair.

'Are we not going inside then?' Babis looks from Yanni to the glow of the interior and back again.

'Here's good, Babis,' Stella states, patting Yanni's shoulder gently as she does so. 'So what'll it be?'

'Right then, chicken and chips twice I say, with a couple of sausages and beer, right, Yanni?'

'Water.' Yanni's head jerks up, he blinks to clear the swirling feeling. 'Please,' he adds, looking up at Stella.

Babis scrapes his chair out and sits down. Yannis takes his time to try to orient himself. The house they have just come from is on the right side of the square, alongside the taverna where they now sit. A kiosk occupies the middle of the paved area, next to a majestic palm tree with a low circular wall around which a number of Eastern-looking men in shabby clothes sit slumped. Tables and chairs have been set up facing the kafeneio beyond, and a huge television sits on a spindly legged table in its open doorway. Farmers, slightly better dressed than the men under the palm tree, relax here with their ouzo glasses, taking little interest in the Western film that is splashing light onto the road. Mopeds putter by and greetings are shouted.

In the top left-hand corner of the square is a shop which looks more packed with wares for sale than even the kiosk. Next to this is a pharmacy and a bakery.

Next to the bakery, level with him on the other side of the road, is an open door, with a stool outside beside an open window. Balanced on the windowsill, a tray of sandwiches wrapped in cling film hovers half inside and half out. There is a movement at the back of the shop and a tinkling sound, suggesting someone inside is arranging bottles.

A man with one sleeve tucked into his trouser tops brings bread in a cane basket, which he places on the table.

'Hello, Mitsos. How are you? I would like to introduce you to my second cousin, Yanni from Orino Island. Yanni, this is Mitsos, Stella's husband.' Babis grabs at the bread, tearing a piece off and putting the oversized hunk into his mouth.

Yanni moves his chair back, not sure if he should stand to shake the man's hand or not. Mitsos puts down the bread, freeing his hand, which swings to clasp Yanni's shoulder. 'Well, hello Yanni. Stella says I am to ask if you want lemon sauce on your chicken.' His smile is easy and reaches his eyes. Yanni feels Mitsos and Stella could be people who would be happy living on the ridge like him: no hurry, easy-going, and if this is the only eatery in the village, then presumably hard working. There is something of a farmer about Mitsos.

'Yanni's got the biggest goat herd on the island,' Babis boasts.

'Have a herd myself, although these days I don't get to go out with them much, but still, I get involved when they are pregnant and so on. I spend more time here these days …' He makes eye contact with Yanni, a wistful look as though he is searching for high, silent pastures to be reflected back at him. Yanni unlocks his hands from in front of him and reaches for his tobacco pouch.

The chicken is delicious, not at all tough like the ones his mama cooks, but then they only eat their hens when they are old and they have stopped laying. The lemon sauce is amazing, and he wonders if his mama could learn to make it. The sausages prove too salty but Babis is hungry and takes them from him. While he eats, Babis does not talk, and Yanni encourages him to eat more. Eventually, Babis sits back, slaps his hand on his engorged stomach, and concedes defeat. The buttons of his silk shirt are straining and he undoes a notch of his belt. The tail end, which is capped in silver, clicks against the ornate clasp as he does so.

'I would like to make a toast,' Babis says, filling two glasses from the one beer bottle. 'To cousins.' He encourages Yanni to pick up the glass and drink. 'Come on, to cousins! Are you not happy to be here with your cousin?' Yanni picks up the glass and drinks, just a mouthful. 'Oh, and to mothers. Single-handed she raised me, Yanni, and look at me now, making deals to sell houses worth hundreds of thousands, so to mamas.' This time, Yanni only takes a sip. 'Yanni, is that all your mama is worth? To mothers.' Babis raises his glass and they drink again. 'Oh yes and to work! Without which we would all starve.' Babis clicks his glass against Yanni's and the glasses are drained.

'My first sale is going through. I told you, right? Within months, mark my words, I will be arranging the contracts for the sale of many of the houses around here. But Yanni, when I heard you were coming from Orino, I saw it all.' He stops, takes a breath. 'Yanni,' he pauses, this time for effect, 'within a year, I am going to make you a rich man, make us both rich men.' Babis waits for a response. Yanni can think of nothing to say. The drumming in his temples has returned and he is thinking of the brief moment he felt quite pleasant after the second, or was it the third, shot of ouzo he had earlier in the day, when everything, suddenly, seemed more manageable.

Babis raises his hand and clicks his fingers at Stella, who is leaning against the door post.

'Two ouzos,' he demands.

Chapter 9

He had heard about it. Poems, both Greek and English, alluded to it, like being struck by lightning some had said, finding the other half of your soul, he had read. A feeling of completeness, his mama had confessed. Utter nonsense, his baba had countered. Yet there she is. No one ever said it would be terrifying. No one ever said he would feel consumed with horror. But he does. He feels horror at the disloyalty of his emotions to his Sophia. But also horror for ever having loved Sophia in the first place when everything in his being now urges him to take care and protect this missing piece to his life at which he is staring, just a few footsteps away.

Stella puts the ouzo glasses down, one on either side of the table, giving Yanni a sideways glance. He can feel her eyes on him but he cannot look away from the woman across the road who is now shifting her weight onto the stool by the sandwich shop doorway. Her navy calf-length skirt wraps around her knees, her white top twists against her chest. Her face is blank, bored. Her limbs loose, tired. Her hair pulled back into a ponytail, strands broken free and creating untidy halos around her ears. Yet she is perfect in every sense of the expression.

'Yanni, are you listening to me?' Babis pulls him back to consciousness. Yanni catches Babis looking over to see what has taken his attention, but his gaze does not linger, he cannot see what Yanni can see. It surprises Yanni, but at the same time, it doesn't. She looks his way. Yanni grabs the shot glass and downs his ouzo in one.

'*Yia mas*!' Babis cries and he downs his, slamming his glass back onto the table top and attracting Stella's attention. With a wink from Babis, she steps into her emporium and returns with the bottle, which she leaves on their table.

'So what do you think?' Babis is almost jumping about in his seat. Sweat marks are spreading in the armpits of his silk shirt and his brow is shiny in the evening's residual heat.

The woman has met Yanni's gaze and Yanni is stunned. He cannot move.

'Yanni, Yanni.' Babis pulls on his shirt sleeve. 'I don't think you have listened to a word.' He pours them both another measure. 'Drink up and we will go up to the kafeneio and I will explain it again. Stella, the bill.'

At these words, Yanni drags himself to the moment, looks quickly at Babis and then at Stella, who is adding sums on her notepad.

'How many ouzos did you have?' she asks. Yanni has no idea.

'Two each,' Babis is quick to reply.

Yanni half stands and fumbles in his back pocket for money.

'No, no. You are in my village now, Yanni, my guest. Stella, take nothing from him.' Babis pays and Yanni looks back across the road, but the woman has gone inside. 'Here you go, Stella. Keep the change.'

'Thanks, Babis. Nice to meet you, Yanni.' She gathers the empty plates, glasses and forks on top, bread basket on top of that.

'Oh, yes, nice to meet you too.' Yanni manages to break through his own reverie and smile at Stella. Her face relaxes as if she has been worrying about something but now is not.

'Hey Babis, take care of our island friend, won't you.' She smiles now and grabs the ouzo bottle with her free hand to take it inside.

'Of course. Why wouldn't I?' Babis retorts as he stands. 'Come on, Yanni.'

Yanni looks from Stella to the empty doorway across the road and then to the side road that leads to Babi's back door.

'Who … Sorry where …' Yanni's words and feet stumble in unison. The village is moving slightly as if they are at sea.

'Up to Theo's, yes? I'll tell you my plan again and the football is on later.' Babis is almost level with the first chilled drinks cabinet outside the kiosk.

'Look, er, it's been a long day.' Yanni looks up the side road. His feet seem to have grown a size and one is catching on the other as he walks.

'You have all day tomorrow to sleep, my friend. Come, how many times do we have such a great reunion?' Babis says.

'It is very kind and I do appreciate …' Yanni has turned his hips in the direction of the back door of Babis' house, but he is looking over his shoulder at the sandwich shop. He is experiencing the calm feeling he felt earlier in the day after the second ouzo, as if he is floating. He wants to see her again, just a glimpse, to know she is real.

'You don't seem to be appreciating anything much. Why the rush for your bed? Come, I will tell you the plan again and once you understand, you will not want to sleep for a week.'

'I must get up and go to the convent tomorrow.' He hadn't intended to say that.

'The convent, whatever for? I thought you were here for a donkey?' Babis has stopped outside the kiosk. Yanni lowers his voice to reply; he does not want the woman in the kiosk knowing his business.

'I have to drop a letter off for Sister Katerina …' As the sister's name forms on his lips, he no longer floats. The woman in the sandwich shop becomes … becomes what? He stops to think, a mirage perhaps. He looks back to where she was sitting. She is still not there, so how can he be sure she is real? Maybe she is an imagined temptation thrown to steer him off his course. No, to call her a temptress implies notions beyond her ability. A temptress she was not. She was angelic, serene, calm. What was he saying? Oh yes, 'Drop a package off and maybe arrange to see one of the sisters there.' It feels important to state this out loud, make it solid.

The possibility of seeing Sophia is suddenly critical, a return to sanity, his real life. He rubs a hand across his chest, sucking in big lungfuls of air, images of the woman in the sandwich shop crowding his thoughts. One chaotic reaction has folded over another ever since leaving Orino Island; he has experienced such a wreckage of emotions since stepping off the boat that it is entirely possible he is losing all sense of reason. He is certainly struggling with his grip on reality. Falling asleep on the bus with all the noise and clamour around him, how was that even possible? And then he doesn't even remember falling asleep again on setting foot in Babis' house, only waking up and it being evening. He twists the ends of his moustache with one hand, his other seeking his tobacco pouch. It's possible that his feet are not touching the ground. He looks down to make sure they are and, unbidden and, to his mind, wholly inappropriately, he finds he is chuckling.

'Here, have one of these.' Babis pulls out his soft pack and shakes two cigarettes free. They are the last ones and he screws up the empty packet and throws it in the kiosk's swing-top bin, which advertises instant coffee.

'If you want to see one of the nuns, you'd best go tomorrow during the day. In the evening, they will be in prayer and the day after, they won't open their doors to anyone, as they will be preparing for their *panigyri*—celebration. Then there'll be the open day itself, then the clear up day afterwards, so you won't get another chance till after that at the very earliest,' the lady with perfectly set hair inside the kiosk calls out to them. Something in her voice suggests it is her role to pass on as much information as she can.

'Vasso, this is Yanni, my second cousin from Orinio island. Yanni ...' Babis searches for his lighter but Yanni has his own, which he reaches out to offer, holding it lit whilst Babis says, 'Vasso is the heart of the village.' Yanni notices some of her lipstick is on her teeth. He nods to acknowledge their introduction. Babis has hold of his hand, which is swaying, to light his cigarette from his lighter, which Yanni has forgotten he was holding.

'I have had a comment a bit like that before, but I still think I am more like the lungs, with the amount the men in this village smoke. You want your usual, Babis?' She giggles to herself as she turns to the stack of packets next to her inside her wooden hutch. She puts the pack on top of the boxes of chewing gum displayed in front of her little window. The chewing gums compete with boxes of biros, packets of tissues, plastic cups wrapped in more plastic, the gaily coloured writing on the outside telling of the coffee and sugar and dried milk within - just add water and shake for a frappe - packets of biscuits and opened packs of batteries so it is possible to buy just one. Yanni looks away. There is too much to take in.

'Thanks.' Babis picks up the pack and searches his pockets. 'So there you go, Yanni. Tomorrow's your best bet. On their open day, they make food for anyone who goes up there. Most of the village will go. The sisters will all be so busy, you will find no one.' Babis pays for his cigarettes. 'But I suppose it depends on how long you are here for.'

'Then tomorrow it must be,' Yanni says, more to himself than Babis.

'You here long? Yanni, was it?' Vasso asks. Babis nods to the second question.

'No.' Yanni wants to leave his answer at that. To say how long will commit him, even if it turns out to be longer than is necessary. To say, 'As short as possible' might offend, but they are both looking at him. He has to say something. One day to deliver the package to the nuns and see Sophia, one day to buy a donkey and go home? 'Two days.'

'Two days! Is that it after all this time! We will have to make the most of it. See you, Vasso.' Babis swings an arm across Yanni's shoulder and leads him towards Theo's kafeneio. 'So listen, this time. I will tell you the plan. *Yeia sou* Theo.' They trip up the three steps into the high-ceilinged room. Along the back wall runs a counter. Cups and plates are stacked as if used and awaiting washing, clustered here and there along its length. Behind the counter, on the back wall, shelves reach from end to end and as high as a man can reach. Clean cups and glasses cause the shelves to bow slightly in the middle. In the room itself, there is little by way of adornment, no pictures, nothing unnecessary. White walls brown with age and tobacco smoke, metal tables painted pale grey, chipped in places and rusty at the joints, wooden chairs painted the same grey. Stark, basic, serviceable, practical, and a little tired-looking.

A man with a mop of greying frizzy hair nods at them as they enter. His crown of hair bobs with the movement. He is serving coffees to two men who can only be farmers, their baggy dark trousers stained with earth at the hem, their shirts rolled to the elbow for ease of movement.

'Well hello again, Yanni,' Theo says once he has set down the cups he is holding. Yanni wonders if a reply is expected and if so, what would be appropriate. Babis is shaking hands with two men at a different table and then raises a hand to wave to four men in the front corner of the room, where the floor-to-ceiling windows that look down across the square meet the floor-to-ceiling windows that look across at the corner shop.

'*Yeia.*' Yanni settles for a short greeting that is only just audible. Theo smiles and, picking up a dirty ashtray on the way, goes behind the high wooden counter and busies himself. Yanni can now hear a tap running.

'You know, if tomorrow is my only chance, I should get some sleep.' Yanni sidles nearer Babis. His feet have stopped floating, his legs are now made of lead. They only move with a great deal of effort.

'Two days, Yanni, for God's sake, two days. You think I am going to spend them asleep, my cousin!' Babis pulls out a chair at a free table. Its wooden legs scrape across the concrete floor, the paint worn off the foot rail and stretcher to show the layers of different colours it has been over the years. The pointed toe of Babis' Cuban boot hits the metal leg of the tripod table as he sits down, ringing out. 'Two ouzos, Theo, please. Glasses, not shots. Now sit down, Yanni, and listen.'

Is there a choice? He must keep his focus. He is here for a reason. But he must not be rude. It is kind of Babis to give him a bed; he knows he could not have afforded to stay in paid accommodation. Also Babis has taken him out for food and welcomed him with an introduction to everyone they have met. He could not be a better host. Buying a donkey, this is work, and so everything that buying the animal entails must also be regarded as work. He has never shirked from work. Besides, another ouzo might bring back that floating feeling and, also, from this table he will have a view across the square, Stella and Mitsos' taverna on the left and the sandwich shop on the right. There she is!

Yanni sits down, his legs not quite doing his bidding.

'Right, listen.' Babis moves his chair in front of Yanni, blocking his view. 'Orino Island has become a playground for the rich, yes?'

'What?' Yanni leans to look over Babis' shoulder.

'The yachts at the weekend, the holiday homes for the Americans.' Babis' arms are crossed in front of him on the table and he is leaning towards Yanni.

'So?' Yanni is also leaning over slightly to concentrate on the view behind Babis' head. She has gone inside again. He looks at Babis' face, his youth very apparent at close range. He has rings of dense eyelashes round his eyes which give the impression that he is wearing eyeliner. His cheeks are plump and a little bit saggy, as if his body cannot decide whether to be fat or thin. Dark circles run under both eyes and he has a line between his brows as if he frowns a lot. It is not an unpleasant face, but it is always too close when he talks. Yanni pushes his chair back a little.

'How many estate agents are on the island?' Babis asks

'No idea.'

'No, go on. How many have you heard of? You must have heard who is doing that sort of thing,' Babis insists.

'I haven't heard of anybody, but then, it is not something I would remember.' Yanni stubs out his cigarette. The commercial filtered ones are all right for a change but they are strong and taste of chemicals.

'Do you remember hearing the last time a house changed hands?'

'No. Yes. Kyria Vetta sold her *yiayia's* house when she died, to some American.' Yanni sits back even further as Theo delivers their ouzos. Ice comes in a dish with a spoon so they can add it themselves and there is also a glass of water each and a small plate of cheese on bread cut into squares and slices of sausage on toothpicks.

'And how did the American find out about Kyria Vetta's house?'

'I have no idea. No, wait. The American saw a sign up in her shop window.' He is still watching, but she has not come out again.

'And there you have it: no estate agent.' Babis sits back and slaps the table with the flats of his hands, making the glasses jump. For a moment, the kafeneio is quiet, heads turn. Yanni sinks a little in his seat, tries not to make eye contact with those who are looking. 'The price of houses on your island has gone up and up and up until the locals can no longer afford to buy, isn't that right? Your island, Yanni my friend, is enticing the mega rich with its donkeys and no cars, all those loaded tourists seeking a bit of the old life. You are sitting on a gold mine.'

'I don't own a house in the town.' Yanni watches the lights go off in the sandwich shop and a shadow comes out, locks the door, and walks away into the dark. Until that moment, it has not occurred to him that she might have someone who would walk her home, a husband, a boyfriend. He wishes her no loneliness but he is relieved that there is no one waiting for her. His mouth is dry. He sips some water but his stomach is churning, so he takes a sip of ouzo, hoping the aniseed will have a calming effect. The burn in his throat takes his mind from his stomach. The second sip brings him some relief and he gets the floating feeling again, which makes him smile.

'No, but an introduction fee is two percent. If you find the buyer and the seller, that's four percent. Name your price, let's say it is a house worth half a million, four percent is twenty thousand euros, and for what? Knowing a house is for sale and finding a buyer!' Babis takes a big drink of his ouzo and grabs a piece of sausage on its cocktail stick, which he waves around as he talks. 'Well I can find the buyers, I have a friend who has a friend who can write websites. So we make a website, people email us when they're interested, and we help the sale go through and take the four percent.'

It must be getting smoky; everything is blurred. Yanni rubs his eyes. 'What has this to do with me?'

'You, you are the linchpin, the secret weapon, the eyes and the ears. You put feelers out and find out who is selling what. I'll get you a camera, you can take pictures of the houses that are for sale, we put them up on the website and, bam! We become rich men. What do you say?'

Chapter 10

'To us.' Babis raises his glass. '*Yeia mas*.' Yanni lifts his own glass; it is the polite thing to do. They drink. Babis is grinning from ear to ear.

'I do see a slight problem with your plan.' Yanni has a passing interest in the way his words are coming out, slurred one into another with *esses* and *zeds* thrown in, making him sound Russian or Ukrainian. He leans forward, and with his elbow on the table, he raises his first finger, which begins to wave of its own accord in front of Babis' face. What was he thinking about? Oh yes, going into other peoples' houses, making small talk whilst photographing their private rooms! Could there be anything more distasteful? 'I,' he begins and slowly shakes his head to match his waving finger. 'I ...' he tries again, but the words will not come. He gives up and, looking at Babis, shrugs his shoulders, still shaking his head.

'But why would you not!' Babis exclaims. Yanni shrugs again, smoothing out his moustache.

The men on the next table have begun a game of *tavli*. The sound of wood clacking on wood takes his attention. His baba taught him *tavli*, and the memory twists his mouth into a smile. He loses focus on the room. It was on his return from taking the goats out by himself for the first time. His mama and baba looked up from their work, Mama washing clothes by the well, Baba fixing a handle back onto a pan.

'Here he is, our boy, the man,' Mama said proudly. His oversized trousers flapping around his ankles as he walked. He pulled them up as they sagged over his hips. They were his baba's old work trousers, cut off at the knee and sewn up by his mama so they would fit, to protect him from the spiky bushes on the far grazing ground.

His baba said nothing. Quietly, he put down the pan and slipped into the house, coming out with a flat box. He kicked two buckets over for seats, opened the box, and laid it flat on the ground. It was a *tavli* board. Baba said nothing, just arranged the pieces and waited for Yanni to sit. They played a lot of *tavli* for months after that. A game each time he returned with the goats. The routine was only broken when he began his spasmodic attendance at school.

'Oh!' The exclamation is one of real pain. Yanni turns his attention back to Babis, scanning his hands, his fingers, his face. There is no sign of outer damage. 'Oh no.' Babis lowers his face into his hands, groaning. Aware that the men from other tables are looking at them, Yanni bows his head and sips at his ouzo.

'Babis, what is it?' he asks in a low tone, his head in his own hands, but only so they form shields on either side of his eyes, to make the space between him and his cousin more private, to keep this display of emotion contained.

'Oh God!' Babis pushes back from the table with both hands and throws his head back. He has the attention of the entire room now. Yanni signals to Theo to refill Babis' glass, which he does, trotting over with the bottle, his hair bouncing. He automatically fills Yanni's too. But Yanni is unaware. All he can sense is all eyes on them and his cousin's harrowing display.

'Here, take a drink,' Yanni offers quietly. Babis stops looking at the ceiling, his head lowering until he meets Yanni's stare, whereupon he shakes his head.

'Damn, damn, damn.'

'What, what?' Yanni whispers. The people are still looking.

'Just a minute. Let me think this through.'

'What, what is it? Just tell me?' Yanni's voice impatient, wanting all the tension to go away.

'Will you let me think? Oh God.'

Yanni puts the ouzo in Babis' hand again and he drinks. Yanni waits. Babis' breathing slows.

'Tell me.'

'I have just realized that I have done something really, really stupid. I have blown my career before it is started. I have shot myself before my first pay. I am finished.' With this, he knocks the remains of his drink back. The other men in the kafeneio begin a low murmur of talk amongst themselves and slowly, the attention on Yanni and Babis eases. Yanni takes a quick gulp from his own glass. Not wanting to pry, he says no more but Babis sits and groans quietly to himself until Yanni feels forced to say something.

'This thing you have done, can it not be undone?'

'I wrote on the contract the wrong calculation. The amount that should come to my client on the sale of his house should be more, but I wrote the objective value where I should have written the real value and I have lost him thousands. The difference is not a small sum. He will sue me for sure. No one will ever use me again for such work.' He groans again. Theo trots over again and tops up both glasses.

'Can it not be changed?' Yanni wishes his thoughts would not jumble so before he speaks.

'The contract sits in the Gerasmio's office ready to be typed up and given its official stamp. Once that happens, nothing can change it. It is done. The change of ownership will be registered in the land registry office and that will be that …' He groans again and drinks. Yanni is almost unaware that he drinks, too. The height of emotion being displayed by Babis is making his mouth dry; he can hear his own heartbeat in his ears. If he thought he could stand, maybe he would run. Run like the goats run from the teeth of dogs.

'Stop the dog from biting,' Yanni slurs.

'What?'

'Talk to the seller's lawyer, and you can both go to the notary. Go in the morning and change it before it is typed.' He opens both palms facing upward to emphasize the simplicity of the solution.

'Yeah, right!' Babis snaps. 'Gerasimos is my rival. For years, he has had the privilege of little to no competition. He will have been aware of what I have done when I did it. He did not speak up. This is his opportunity for him to make sure I do not become a rival and at the same time he will save his client a great deal of money. It is all good for him. There is no motivation to change it; his motivation will be to keep the mistake.'

'But if you explain to him?' Yanni cannot understand such a man as the one Babis describes. 'He too was once setting out. Surely he will have some …' The word he is seeking will not come. He looks to the ceiling until he finds it. 'Compassion,' he finally erupts, his head dropping back to Babis' gaze.

'He will laugh. He is one of the big boys, friends with the mayor. He is the one doing the conveyancing for all the houses in the village that will have to be sold. He has no compassion.'

'You know. I heard today that the surveyors have been up to Mitsos and Stella's place and even they might have to sell? It must be the oldest house in the village up there on the hill, and if that isn't safe, none of us are.' The man on the next table leans over to inform them as if he is part of the conversation.

'I even heard a rumour that they have been to Marina's. The village will be a different place without her corner shop,' his companion rejoins.

'But surely not. It isn't long since she rebuilt it?' the first man says. The second shrugs. Yanni closes one eye to stop the two men becoming four. 'Has

Babis told you all this?' one of the men asks. Yanni is not sure if he is being addressed so he tuts his 'no' anyway, just in case.

'They have found a fault in the ground under the village. They are saying some of the houses in the village that lay on the fault are unsafe. Likely to collapse. The local government is saying it is a catastrophe and they will be forcing people to do expensive repairs to avoid their homes being declared unsafe. If they do not do it, their homes will, in the name of safety, be boarded up.'

His companion interrupts. 'The other option is to sell to someone who can afford to do the repairs. There is always someone who will buy, if the price is low enough.'

'Damianos has decided to sell. So has old Maria.'

'No! But where will they go?' The second man speaks as if this is news to him.

The other shrugs. 'What choice have they? Either their houses are boarded up and they have no bed or they sell and they have no bed, but at least they will have a bit of money in their pockets.'

Yanni reaches for his tobacco pouch but one of the men offers a ready-rolled cigarette from the pack on his table. Because it is there, Yanni accepts, offering a light in return, not having noticed the man has not taken one himself. Once his own is lit, he picks up his glass and almost forgets to take the cigarette from his mouth as he goes to drink.

'Drink up!' Babis' head comes out of his hands. His eyes are wide, he is smiling. Yanni wonders what he has missed, where the sudden change in mood has come from. 'Come on, drink up.' Babis stands, energy in his limbs. He finishes his own drink, slaps Yanni on the back, and steps over to Theo, who is behind the counter. Seeing money being exchanged, Yanni stumbles to his feet and fishes into his back pocket to find only a single coin.

'Hey friend, you have dropped your money,' the man at the next table says. Yanni looks at the floor to see his roll of notes unfurling. So much money. More money than he has ever had at one time. All the money in the world. Enough to buy a donkey and get home. Scooping it up, he wonders if his back pocket is the best place to keep it. Perhaps his breast pocket is best. Or his front pocket. He decides on his front pocket.

'Come on, Yanni. We have important work to do.' Babis' arm is around his shoulder again and they step down into the still-warm night.

'*Kalinixta,*' Theo calls after them. A thousand stars twinkle overhead, the same stars that prick the heavens over his cottage. His mama and baba will be asleep now, his own bed empty. He wishes he was in it. Turning to the side road past the kiosk, Yanni can think of nothing nicer than to be horizontal. 'Here we go,' Babis says as a car pulls up. There is not time to even question as the door is opened and Babis pushes him in.

'Where are we going?' Yanni slurs. 'I need to get to bed. Big day tomorrow.' He mustn't say more. Babis puts his finger to his lips; he too wishes for silence, and the taxi drives on. The road to Saros seemed so much longer when he walked it. He remembers none of the corners that throw him against Babis or the door. There are no orange groves to see, just dark shadows and the occasional glare of lights from a house. The car window jolts his head as he leans on it, his eyes closed.

'Out.' Babis pushes him. His head springs upright as he wakes and stumbles sideways from the car and onto unsteady feet. His eyes wide, he looks all around him, finally focuses on Babis, who is paying the driver and then he hears rather than sees the taxi drive away in the blurred darkness.

'Wherearewe?' It seems he has lost control of his own tongue.

'Shh, come around here.' Babis strides round the end of a building into the dark. 'This is Gerasimos' office. Second floor. Look up there. He always leaves that window open because he smokes so much. Can you see?'

Yanni thinks he sees, but a thick bougainvillea vine climbs the side of the building up to a balcony and very little of the dim street light reaches beyond. Above it, the stars are there in their thousands. Thousands of them and one of him. How insignificant his troubles are in the vastness of everything. Nothing is really important, just being alive. He sighs.

'Yes, there, next to the balcony, you see it?' Babis enthuses. At this moment, Yanni decides he would be better off sitting down and does so, on the ground.

'What are you doing?' Babis takes hold of both his arms and pulls. 'I can't do it. I am not fit like you. I have no upper body strength. You are fit as a goat, with the strength of ten.'

Looking from Babis' face to the bougainvillea, to the window, Yanni slowly understands.

'Y' kidding me?' Yanni starts to laugh. 'You's expecting me, up there—to do?' He raises his shoulders, arms outstretched. 'Change the numbers. Which papers. Where.' The words come out mispronounced, word endings merge into word beginnings.

'No, of course not. Just open the door from the inside. I will do the rest whilst you stay on guard.'

'No.' He is done. He wants to lie down.

'What?'

'It's not right.' It is more of a mutter, a mumble. The ground is like water. He is floating on his back.

'It's my life, my future. You want me not to be able to support my mama in her old age?'

In the half-light, Babis' features are unclear. He is in his own shadow, the moon behind his head giving him a halo. Maybe he is dreaming. Maybe all this is a dream and he is sleeping outside up on the ridge. He should go indoors or he will get cold in the early hours of the morning. Yes, that is what he will do, go indoors, sleep well, and when the morning comes, he can tell his mama and baba of this peculiar dream he had. On his feet, he is floating again. Someone takes his hand and puts it on the bougainvillea stem. It feels real, alive, earthy. A cicada is disturbed, flies off the bark, hits him in the face, and flies away. He could be in the pine forest. He must climb the hill to get home. Up, one hand, one foot, up. The steps are steep here. The smell of bark and leaves. Up. It is a sheer climb, it is good that Dolly is not with him. The bark becomes metal, sliding to his touch. It confuses him, so he stops.

'Go over.' He hears. Over, what does the voice mean by over? He must go over the ridge. Over the ridge to the far pasture. Over and … He sits heavily. One foot out through the balcony railing. 'Well done, Yanni,' a voice hisses. Sophia used to say that when they climbed trees together. Sophia, his Sophia. Tomorrow, or is it today now, and he might see his Sophia? See her and … and what?

'Don't just sit there. Get up. The window is to your right.'

She is a sister, a nun. What can he expect? She is not going to pull the headscarf from her head and run away with him.

'Get up.'

The chances are that by seeing her, he will bring his love to the surface, make his life even more painful without her.

'Yanni, get up.'

The best he can expect is to find she has changed. That she is a nun inside and out. Maybe his love will turn to that of the brotherly kind. He can imagine that sense of freedom. Freedom to …

'Yanni, tsst, Yanni. Get up, will you?'

Freedom to talk to his soulmate, who is at this very moment asleep in her bed not so very far from her sandwich shop. He stands.

'To your right. Climb across to your right.'

He would climb a mountain for her. Climb any height to fall into those eyes, haul himself over precipices, grip on to rock faces so he can fall, fall, fall …

'Bravo, Yanni. In there. Pull yourself in there. There's a table on the other side.'

Fall into her eyes.

'You okay? Yanni, can you hear me? Are you standing? Don't turn the lights on. He hangs a torch on the back of the door for when there is a power cut. Can you see enough to see the door? It should be to your right if your back is to the window. Yanni? Yanni? Yanni, if you can hear me, go out the door, down the stairs, but don't go to the front door, go down another three steps. It leads to the back door. Yanni?'

A cat jumps from the bins by the back door as it opens.

'Well done. Bravo. Give me a minute.' Babis grabs the torch from Yanni's grasp and disappears inside.

Yanni slumps to the floor. His legs have gone back to lead, he either needs another drink or to lie flat. There is no drink, so he lies flat. The moon on his face, the cicadas still rasping their love songs. Maybe she will pull off her headscarf. His hand covers his breast pocket, the familiar edges of the book. Maybe if she knows of his feelings, it will change everything.

The poem certainly suggests that was the case all those years ago. He hasn't changed, so why should she?

'Wake up.' The voice is loud. Yanni opens his eyes. Babis' face so close.

'You have done it? That was quick,' Yanni whispers.

'No. I have not done it. I will do it tomorrow.' Babis speaks loudly.

'But I thought you said that, what's-his-name, Gerasimos would not make it possible for you to do it tomorrow?' Yanni sits up, suddenly sober.

'Tomorrow, Gerasimos will jump in the sea if I ask him to.' Babis' smile is lopsided and it does not reflect in his eyes, which are hard and cold. 'Tomorrow, everything changes. I thought I had something to celebrate tonight, what with you being here and my idea for selling houses on the Island. But this, my friend, is even better. Who knows where this could lead?'

He takes out his mobile phone and orders a taxi. Yanni waits for Babis to tell him more, but he is silent, his face set hard. The taxi arrives. When he tries to stand, he finds his body is still drunk. It is hard work getting into the taxi. Once inside, Yanni finds sleep is on him before his head is resting on the window. He is woken when they arrive in the village and Babis helps him to his bed.

He is asleep again before he manages to take his boots off.

Chapter 11

Sunbeams slice through the slats of the shutters. Dust swims in the light, floating, hovering, and unseen currents swirl the specks into mini tornadoes which settle again and drift. Outside, the incessant call of the cicadas rasps the air with their continuous song. A cockerel crows and in the ceiling beams, there is a gecko clicking to its mate. Yanni's legs feel heavy; he still has his boots on. The cockerel crows again. It cannot be very early: the light is too warm, the temperature too heavy. Turning on his side, he finds a litre bottle of water and a packet of aspirin on the small table by the bed. Babis, forever the host. Snapshots of last night flicker though his thoughts. At one point, he was going over the ridge on Orino Island, but it was made of bougainvillea. That must have been a dream. He was not on the ridge, he was in Saros. Why was he in Saros?

He reaches for the water and swills down two pills. The water just gives him a thirst for more. Tipping back the bottle, he watches the geckos chase each other across the ceiling as he drinks his fill. The room has a woman's touch, Babis' mama, no doubt. There are pictures on the wall, prints of flowers, a lace cover over the back of the single chair, long navy curtains. Navy like the skirt of the woman outside the sandwich shop, whose eyes he fell into last night. That cannot be right either; he has not even spoken to her. Not yet. The hairs on the back of his neck stand on end and he gives an involuntary shudder. He is not sure if it is fear or excitement. He knows what Sister Katerina would say.

'*Panayia mou.*' He calls upon the mother of Christ. Today, maybe, he will see Sophia. Scrambling to his feet, he lurches into the main room. It really is a mess. Picking his way through the clutter, he looks around the room for a clock. The cockerel crows again. If it is anything like his cockerel back home, it will be accurate to the hour. It does not feel early but he could be mistaken with the aching of his head and the nausea that is coming upon him. He will just go. His hand fumbles for his tobacco pouch. It is nearly empty. He will ask the way to the convent when he buys some more from the lady at the kiosk. What was her name? Vasso?

'*Kalimera* Vasso.' He greets her, but the day does not seem to be so good. His head is really throbbing, and the thought of battling with the abbess and the general protocol to see Sophia for some reason no longer feels like a joy. Today, it feels like a chore. This fills him with dismay. His own sweet Sophia, why would she be a chore?

'It is hardly morning. Did you get up to the convent?'

'What? What time is it?'

'Nearly five, no, ten to six.'

'In the afternoon?' Yanni turns his back on her to look up towards the sun. Everything is too bright. He turns back to the shade of the kiosk. His breathing has quickened, the nausea has returned. He puts out a hand to steady himself.

'Watch the crisps.' Vasso giggles. 'You make a night of it, did you?'

'Give me some loose tobacco, not that one, the blue packet, yes.' He takes it from her, opens it, and rolls and lights a cigarette before he even thinks to pay her. His hand slips into his back pocket and he turns white.

'You okay?' Vasso asks.

'My … I had …' His hand feels across his breast pockets before delving into his front jeans pockets. He huffs his relief.

'I hate those moments,' Vasso chirps. 'I do it all the time, lose my keys, my purse, my shopping list. It gets boring how often I lose things.' Yanni pays for the tobacco.

'Hello Yanni. Is Babis taking care of you?' It is Stella, with an apron on over her floral dress.

'Er, yes.' But he feels angry. Angry at Babis for not waking him, angry at Babis for taking him out last night. It is one thing to be hospitable, but Babis fills his glass again and again until he has no choice about anything. But mostly, he is angry at himself for not finding the fine line between accepting hospitality and being coerced, bullied. He takes a deep draw on his cigarette at the word *bullied* and Hectoras comes to mind, an image that is too much when his head is being held on by the merest thread.

'He's a one isn't he, that Babis. Blows like the wind from one thing to the next, so much energy, he'll whisk you into things before you know you have agreed. All the makings of a lawyer.' Stella takes a step closer to Yanni and says more quietly, 'Take some advice, my friend: set your course and don't let Babis take the rudder.' Her smile is so open and warm, and something about her reminds him of Sister Katerina.

'Truer words were never said,' Vasso agrees. 'Not a harmful bone in his body, that young Babis but, my, he has energy that takes him this way and that. What can I get you, Stella?'

'I just want some matches. You heard they came up to our place, I guess,' Stella says, a tremor in her voice.

'The surveyors?' Vasso's eyes grow wide as she hands over the matches. Yanni is held fixed to the spot, his legs too heavy to move. His throat has tightened and his eyes are stinging, moist. How can he have overslept when it was so important? He never oversleeps for the goats, or if he has a job arranged hauling stuff from an early boat. Why now? Why? His hand creeps over his breast pocket, feeling the edges of the book.

'Yup, they say it does not look good, but we must wait for the report. Mitsos will be gutted. His family have lived there, well, forever and a day.' Stella's voice rings with compassion, her eyes dart with fear. Worry for what they will do, perhaps.

Yanni smooths his moustache and draws on his cigarette. He wants to wrap his arms around himself and cry, but instead he keeps his back straight and his chin held up. Without a word, he flicks away his cigarette and then, with no warning, his stomach growls so loudly, Stella and Vasso stop talking, turn and look at him, and giggle.

Yanni can feel the heat in his cheeks.

'Come on,' Stella says to him. 'The chicken is done, the chips are hot, and you are hungry. *Yeia sou* Vasso.'

They take the few short steps to Stella's eatery side by side. They find no reason to fill the space with words.

'You want sausage with your chicken and chips?' She asks. Yanni shakes his head. 'Lemon sauce?' This time, he nods and takes the same chair as the last time he was there. The sandwich shop is lit but there is no sign of the woman.

'Oh Sophia, what is happening to me?' he whispers to himself in hushed tones. 'My second day here and all I have done is drink.' He lets his head sink into his hands. 'And the price, Sophia my love, is not seeing you.' He takes out the book from behind his tobacco pouch in his breast pocket and it falls open on the oft-read words. He traces them with his finger. Maybe to turn up after all these years is a cruelty to her. In all his self-indulgent moments, he has never once considered what impact contacting her after all these years might have on her life. Maybe she will have no dilemma, her marriage to God unshakable. But maybe the sight of him will ignite her love again. But, then again, maybe not enough to set her free, just enough to present a divide, a tear, an abyss between the life she has and the life he offers. Surely she would curse him for that. Then she will be condemned to live her life as he has lived his, a life that is everything he wants except that one niggle, that single thorn that twists when he least expects it, just often enough to remind him that he is not completely content.

That would be an unthinkable thing to do to her. He would wish that on no one. He turns to see if anyone has appeared in the sandwich shop doorway and sure enough, she is there. His heart leaps into his mouth, his breath is sucked from his lungs. He tries not to stare.

The aspirin begins to have the desired effect.

'Okay, enough.' He snaps himself out of it. 'Be logical.' His brow creases. But his internal answer asks how can he be logical about affairs of the heart, and through the shadows of some dim memory, Sister Katerina recites a poem they read somewhere together:

It is well to be happy and wise and it is well to be honest and true, it is well to be off with the old love, before you are on with the new.

'I do not wish to cast Sophia off,' he hisses under his breath. He can feel the woman's eyes on him. He turns to look at her, but a customer approaches and she goes into the shop.

There has been too much swaying about. He must stick to his plan. He must go to Sophia. If she does not let him go then he will not let her go, either. He will fight for her until either she is his or he forces her to cruelly reject him and so extinguish his love for her. 'But if she lets you free, then you can go to the girl at the sandwich shop. '

'Sorry, did you say something?' Stella puts a hot plate in front of him.

Chapter 12

The food restores his energy but not his mood. To deliver Sister Katerina's letter and to face Sophia, he will now have to wait another three days. He can fill one with the buying of the donkey, but the other two? And what of his goats and his baba's strength, his mama's worrying?

'*Panagia mou.*' He drops his fork heavily onto the empty plate.

'Problems?'

Yanni turns in his chair to see an old man sitting in the shadows. He grunts and looks back at his empty plate.

'Come,' says the old man, 'I will tell you a story, and it may be of use to you.'

The exchange has drawn a glance from Stella, who has come to clear his plate and ask him if there is anything more he wants. The way she looks from him to the old man suggests she knows him. Not wishing his bad mood to affect Stella's business, Yanni pulls out his chair and turns it to face the grey-haired old man's direction. In this, he can no longer keep an eye on the sandwich shop door.

Stella, who has taken Yanni's dirty dishes inside, returns with a plate of sliced, honey-covered fruit, which she puts on his table.

'Compliments of Mitsos,' she says and puts a small jug of wine and two glasses in front of the old man on her way back inside. The old man pours a glass which he pushes to the very edge of the table towards Yanni. The second glass, he keeps hold of himself.

'I hear Babis, our budding new lawyer, is your cousin,' the old man begins, raising his glass and indicating for Yanni to do the same. When Yanni hesitates, the man frowns a little. 'Go on, it won't bite. Do yourself a favour and relax a little, and take some advice from an old man.'

Yanni shifts a little on his chair, leans forwards, and reaches for the glass from which he takes the smallest sip. He is not going down this route again. The wine is cool and the old man smiles broadly.

'So.' His faces creases into weather-worn lines and he settles a little in his chair, as if to become more comfortable. He puts one old boot on top of the other, his knees fall outwards. He has soil dust around the bottom of his trousers. 'I will tell you a little story about a lawyer and a policeman, and you can judge for yourself.' He clears his throat but there is a falseness to the cough, a clichéd beginning, and the outer corners of his eyes crease as his mouth curls up into a flicker of a smile. It is all part of the performance. 'It concerns a lawyer. A lawyer with a fast car. It was inevitable that one day, he was pulled over for speeding on the road to Saros.' He looks down the road that leads out of the village and waves his hand vaguely in the direction of the town.

'The policeman who stopped him checked all his documents of course, and found various irregularities. Probably his insurance was not up to date, and the vehicle did not have an emissions certificate, a light didn't work, that sort of thing. It doesn't really matter, the point is that the combined fine was rather steep.' The old man pauses to drink and to refill his glass. He looks over to Yanni's glass too, but it is still full, and he puts the jug back on the table with a sigh.

'So anyway, our lawyer friend has to present his papers at the police station within a week, along with the pink slip detailing the offences, and if he does this, the fine will be reduced a little. So he goes in his best suit, hoping to intimidate the police officers. He is a lawyer after all, and all lawyers think they are better than the rest of us!' The old man chuckles at this, clearly enjoying the telling of his tale 'But the policeman at the station is not impressed. He will not be intimidated, and his hands stay on his side of the counter; he does not take the lawyer's bribe that he tries to slide across the desk. He is poker-faced, and he fills out endless forms, and then, just as he is about to print out his report, he finds that the printer has run out of paper. He calls across to the receptionist to get some more paper, but she is on her mobile phone and she swivels her chair so her back is to him. He has no choice. Reluctantly, he goes off to the storeroom to get some more himself. "Wait here," he says to our lawyer friend, who has resigned himself to paying the fines by now.' The old man pauses again to drink, and this time, he finds the jug is empty. 'Stella!' he calls and waves the empty vessel in her direction.

'Now where was I?' he asks, but with a grin, as if this too is part of the show. 'Ah yes, our policeman stepped out to get the paper. So, as the lawyer is sitting there waiting for him to return, he picks up the pink slip, for want of something to do, and he notices that it is all filled in apart from the space for the reduction in the fine. Quick as you like, he picks up a pen and fills in the space with a very modest number and puts the slip back on the policeman's desk. The policeman returns in a few minutes, and as you can imagine, all hell breaks loose. The lawyer swears blind that the policeman filled in the sum, and the policeman curses the lawyer and calls him all manner of names. The secretary is called as a witness, but she was on the phone to her boyfriend and didn't see anything, so the policeman swears at her too, and she returns the insults. You get the picture. This goes on for a while, but soon they all calm down a little. But a solution is needed! The pink slip is an official form, and this is an embarrassment for the policeman. He looks to see if he can add a nought on the end, but there is no space. What can he do? He does not want to lose face in front of the lawyer, and he does not want to admit to his superiors that he left official documents on his desk while he left the room to get the printer paper. Nor does he want to admit that his own secretary would not run the errand for him. The lawyer lets him stew for a while, and then

114

he comes to his rescue, offering a bribe again. "I will pay the fine that is written there, and you will take this fifty euros. And now that you have taken it, that can be an end to this matter". This is a solution for the policeman, of course, and he accepts. And perhaps that should be the end to my tale?' The old man looks over his glass at Yanni, chuckling and grinning. 'Eh? Do you think that is the end?' Yanni shrugs.

'For you to be asking, I guess it is not,' he replies, cautious, but curious too.

'Of course it is not the end! We are talking about a lawyer here!' The old man laughs out loud and coughs violently, going red in the face. Mitsos comes hurrying out, puts the jug he is carrying down, and pats him of the back before pouring a drink and putting it to the old man's lips as if it is an everyday occurrence. Mitsos tuts and smiles before he returns indoors.

The old man manages to compose himself, and he continues.

'So as I said, the lawyer is a lawyer, and in the top pocket of his shiny suit is a little tape recorder. And he takes this out now, and as you can imagine, the policeman's face goes white. A tape recorder! And he has just accepted a bribe. Now, the lawyer is with the upper hand, and he snatches back the fifty euros and, without paying his fine, he stands to leave. As he goes, he waves the tape recorder at the policeman, who is still just sitting there. "I trust I will hear no more about this", he says as he marches out. It's clever, yes? But then, he is a lawyer, and lawyers are clever and sneaky.' Having finished the tale, the old man sits back in his chair and his shoulders relax, and he regards Yanni gently now, sipping from his glass.

'Why have you told me this?' asks Yanni.

'Because I have dealt with lawyers too, and perhaps you can save yourself some trouble, if you are not too proud to take advice from an old man…'

'Well,' says Yanni, 'I appreciate your concern, but you know that Babis is my cousin…'

At this, the old man sits up straight and looks Yanni straight in the eyes. 'And who do you think the policeman was? I tell you, he was the lawyer's brother!' And having delivered this line, he stands, drains his glass, chucks a handful of coins on the table, and begins to walk slowly towards the square. He turns as if he has forgotten something. 'Be careful,' he says, and at that moment, Stella comes out to clear his table and he tips his hat to her with the slightest of bows.

'He's a character, isn't he?' She smiles at Yanni.

'Is he a farmer?' Yanni asks. Something about the soil dust on his trousers did not fit with his manner.

'Well, everyone in the village has land and trees, but he is retired, used to be a policeman.' She finishes wiping the table. 'You want anything else?'

'No, thank you, Stella. That was a good meal.' He stands and leaves some notes on the table and a couple of extra coins for a tip. If he goes to Babis' house, there will be no ouzo, no beer, early to bed and then tomorrow he can at least go see the donkey man. Damn Babis for not waking him.

Putting his shoulder to the door, it pushes aside some jackets that have fallen off a hook on the back. Scooping them up, he rehangs them. How is it possible for a place to get so jumbled? Picking up a couple of abandoned plates, he takes them to the kitchen. The sink is full. He looks around for soap and a sponge. Leaning against the kettle is a note from Babis.

'Left early, didn't want to wake you. Gone to Athens. Hope to return with exciting news. Can you make a bit of an inroad into clearing up? There's a washing machine in the back room. B.'

'Didn't want to wake you!' Yanni exclaims and, balling the paper, throws it with force into the sitting area. It lands in the remains of a pizza in a box on the sofa just as the back door opens.

'Have I got some news for you!' Babis enters, holding a cardboard file triumphantly above his head. He stops abruptly and looks about the room. 'Oh, you've not made much impact here, have you? Anyway, that's all secondary now. Come on, we have work to do.' He turns on his heel and waits for Yanni to follow.

Yanni stays where he is.

'Come on, this is going to be great!' he enthuses.

'You know what, Babis. I thank you for the hospitality, but I only intended to come for a couple of days. I arrived only yesterday and during the time I have been here, I have spent more time drinking than any other time in my life and the result is that my baba is left to deal with the goats for a couple days longer than I told him to expect. It is too much for the old man. I think it best if I just stay here now, do what I have to do, and then go.' Yanni turns away from the sink.

'Ha! I think that is the longest sentence I have ever heard you say. Maybe the mainland is loosening you up a bit.' Babis grins. 'Come on, I need your support on this.' He waves the files. 'I mean, let's face it: you're not doing much good round here are you?' He indicates the unwashed plates in the sink and on the kitchen table. 'But as a bit of support, a bit of muscle, as a witness even, you will pay me back tenfold for your bed.' He steps close enough to put a hand on Yanni's shoulder.

Still Yanni does not move.

'Look, I promise.' Babis squeezes his shoulder; the muscle does not give at all in his grip. 'No bars. No ouzo. Just, please, I need you to be with me when I face Gerasimos.' His eyebrows arch in the middle and, just for a moment, Yanni is reminded of the young boy who came to stay with them for a few weeks all those years ago. He was told it was just until his mama found her feet because his baba had walked out. But Babis told him the real truth when they were out checking rabbit traps that his own baba had laid.

'Look, there, came straight out of its hole, it would not have felt a thing.' Yanni's fingers carefully worked the wire off from around its neck, and he stroked the limp form before gently putting it in his sack. Babis had been with them two days and in that time, he had not said a word. 'You can do the next one,' Yannis offered. Babis' sadness was like a wall around him. It must be hard to have your baba leave and never know when or even if he was coming back. Yanni tried to imagine the weight of responsibility for the goats and all that needed doing around the place solely on his young shoulders and just the thought made his knees buckle. He put his arm around Babis' shoulder as they walked on. After some minutes, a faint squealing could be heard. Babis' eyes grew wide as he looked up to Yanni.

'I guess the wire hasn't fully tightened. Poor thing will be in pain. Let's find it and put it out of its misery.' Yanni released Babis and started to check along a line of burrows. Babis went along another line.

'Find a rock,' Yanni advised, 'so if you find it, you can stop its misery as soon as possible.' The lay of the land made the sound of the squealing rabbit echo; it was not easy to pinpoint the source. But just as Yanni thought he knew where it was coming from, the inhuman shrieking grew wilder and wilder. He wanted to put his hands to his ears and he turned to see if Babis was all right. He was standing rigidly, the wire trap in his hand, the rabbit dangling and squirming, it rear legs thrashing, its spine snaking to get free and the wire digging deeper and deeper into its neck.

119

'Quick, put it on the ground and hit its head, it is suffering.' Yanni leaped towards Babis. But Babis turned his back and put a hand out to stop Yanni from getting near to the rabbit. He watched it writhe some more before Yannis pushed him to the ground and with a quick, sharp blow, the rabbit lay still.

'What on earth were you doing? It is one thing to eat; it is another to make an animal suffer!' Yanni yelled. Babis, who for a moment lay prone, began to shrink in upon himself, his legs tucking up to his chest, his arms around them, his head between his knees, and he was crying.

Yanni can remember the feeling of horror of such an open display of emotion. He wanted to step backwards, then turn and run. Instead, he crouched by his cousin's side and put a hand on his shoulder.

'Babis?' he asked and the small boy sprung upon him, his head buried in his neck, crying in great sobs as if he would never stop. 'Are you upset about the rabbit? It is okay now. He is at peace,' Yanni tried to console the boy. But Babis just kept crying until slowly he quietened and the feeling that passed through Yanni when Babis looked him in the eye, he never wanted to feel again. He said prayers in his head to stop what was coming next but somehow he knew, he wasn't sure what he knew, but he knew it was bad and he knew he was not going to be spared from hearing it.

'My baba, he did not leave.' Babis begun. Words that should have filled Yanni with glee sent shivers down his spine. 'I came home from school. There was a sandwich on the table. Mama always left me a sandwich on the table; she changed sheets in a hotel and always got back after me.' Yanni resisted the urge to cover his ears with his hands. 'I sat and ate my sandwich, but there was something wrong with the house.' Babis' voice was flat, the words coming out staccato. Yanni was transfixed, looking into his cousin's eyes, the black lashes silver with tears. 'I washed my plate and put it away, and by the sink was a note asking me to tidy my room, "love, Mama", it said.' A single tear trickled down his face. His arm lifted and wiped his nose, the tear smudged across his cheek. 'I took a step to my bedroom. There was this feeling, like someone was watching, and then I smelt this smell and I looked and I saw his boots. Mid-air. Through the open crack of their bedroom door. The smell so strong and under the boots, on the floor, brown, and I wondered why my mama had not cleaned it up and I wondered how boots could be suspended, and even though I was retching, I pushed the door open to see.' It came out in one breath, his face drained of all colour. 'They were half-closed but one eye looked at me and one didn't and his head was not on his shoulders properly. His mouth was black inside.' Yanni knew what he was hearing was not good, but nor did it make sense. He just wanted Babis to stop talking, go back to where he had come from, leave him alone. But he did and said nothing. 'The silence began to roar, my legs had no bones, I fell forward, my hands in the brown, my head hit his boots, and he began to swing.'

'Stop.' Yanni said the word so quietly. His arms wrapped around Babis' head and he pulled him gently into his own small chest and rocked him until the light faded and they returned to the cottage. There was no more conversation. They shared his bed—there was no other that Babis could be in—and then Yanni hugged him as he imagined he would like to be hugged and waited for Babis to cry himself to sleep before he allowed his own dreams to take him as well.

After that, Yanni kept Babis by his side every day he was with them. When Babis' mama eventually sent for him, the boys made a silent farewell. There was no way to keep in touch, and besides, there was nothing to say. Yanni never spoke of it until a couple of years later when he spent time with Sophia. It was a brief conversation, but she understood, and it was his turn to be held and rocked.

Hard enough for a boy to lose his baba at any age, but when he was so young and in such a way?

'We go just to face Gerasimos?' Yanni asks.

Babis nods, his hair falling over his forehead into his eyes.

Chapter 13

Yanni rolls onto his side. His legs feel heavy and a twitch of his feet lets him know he still has his boots on.

'Oh no.' He groans and rolls onto his back. His hands clenching, expecting to grasp Babis' guest-room bed linen, but there are no sheets. His fingers fold around looseness, like earth, but softer, drier. He lifts his hand to see what he has hold of, but his eyes will not open yet. He waits until he surfaces more. There is a very familiar smell. The muscles around his eyes relax, softened daylight chases away sleep.

He is not at Babis' house. Above him are beams and crossing laths. The sunlight slides between the lines of concave red roof tiles, lighting up many plumes of cobwebs that have caught dust and dirt. The webs hang in festoons and sway in the breeze that blows under the eaves, hissing and hushing. The walls are stone, windowless, and at either end of the barn is a closed wooden door, a gash of daylight at the bottom. He releases his grip and the crumbled goat droppings fall to the compacted mud floor. The barn is empty and the dryness of the floor suggests it has not been used for animals in some time. Yanni struggles to sit up.

'Where the …' he whispers, unwilling to disturb the stillness of the place. The light between the tiles takes on an orange glow but where some are broken or missing, shafts of brilliant sunshine spotlight the floor. Yanni draws in his leg that rests in one such shaft of light, because the sun is fierce; it must be around midday. Did he drink—again? Is he waking in the afternoon—again?

He rolls onto his knees and stands. He does not feel particularly hungover, nothing a drink of water wouldn't wash away. He brushes off the earth and dried dust of the crumbled goat droppings. No wonder it was a familiar smell.

Two paces take him to one end of the barn to push open the door. It does not give. He must have come in by the other door. With three strides, he reaches out with his fingertips to push open that door, bracing himself for the brightness of the day, the sudden heat. It does not give. He applies more pressure; still, it does not move. His shoulder has no effect either and so he grips the wall on either side of the door and gives it a strong kick. It does not even rattle.

Marching back to the first door, brushing the cobwebs from his face, he repeats his effort, but this too shows no signs of opening. The gaps beneath the doors show sunlight, but squatting down and leaning over only allows him to see the grasses growing outside, blocking the view.

If he got in, he must be able to get out. Did he fall through the roof perhaps? But there is no break in the beams, only a few small gaps between the tiles. Then it stands to reason that he has been closed in by someone from the outside. Babis?

With his back against the rough stone wall, he sinks to the ground and pulls his tobacco pouch from his pocket.

'So we went into Saros, to the office of Gerasimos.' He sprinkles tobacco onto a cigarette paper, trying to gather his thoughts. 'Babis talked to him.' Just a little bit more tobacco. 'Gerasimos got angry, they screamed and shouted, Gerasimos went red, Babis laughed. We left.' He pockets the pouch and puts both hands to the cigarette paper. 'Oh no.' He groans as he begins to roll the cigarette 'We did go to a bar.' He licks the paper edge. 'Babis was talking. What was he saying about the mayor and Gerasimos? Something about the houses.' He remembers times when his brain did not want to think in the early days of learning the Greek alphabet with the Sister. Now it feels the same, but he knows if he persists, it will come. 'Oh yes!' He finds the recall he seeks. It is almost beyond comprehension that anyone could be so underhand and dirty. Bogus surveyors enlisted to say the houses are unstable! It takes him a moment to believe it is all true. Shaking his head, the reality of it all sinks in. But it doesn't explain why he is locked in this barn.

'I had only one drink, one beer.' He puts the cigarette in his mouth and searches for his lighter. 'There were those two men, the ones that made Babis feel uncomfortable, the way they were watching him so…' There is a slight delay as he remembers. 'We moved to the next bar.' His words come out muttered, his lips not moving around his cigarette. He takes the cigarette from his mouth and continues his search for his lighter. 'Babis ordered drinks all round and made friends with that girl and they left through the side door.' He finds his lighter but continues to use his cigarette to orchestrate his words. 'I did not touch my drink and I left through the front door and …' He sparks his lighter. A mouse runs across the dried floor and into a dark hole in the wall. 'I took the road to walk back to the village.' He puffs and then puts the lighter away. 'Back past Gerasimos' office, past the army barracks, the orange groves on either side and …'

He raises his free hand and curls the ends of his moustache before running his hand from forehead to the back of his neck to smooth his hair. He winces. He touches again, tentatively, just his finger ends exploring. He must have fallen. Maybe that's why he has no memory of coming into this barn. He leans his head carefully back against the wall and smokes. Maybe he could climb up the inside walls and break through the laths. The tiles will move aside or fall off easily.

He stubs out his cigarette and stands, searching the wall for a foothold.

There's a noise outside, an engine draws close and stops. Voices. Running to the door, he opens his mouth to call out but something stops him. He knows that voice from somewhere. He pauses to listen, the hairs on his arms raising. He shivers involuntarily.

'Why is he in there?' a low voice asks.

'He just collapsed, so it seemed like the best idea.' Plaintive, lighter.

'What do you mean he just collapsed?'

'You know, I coshed him over the back of the head so he wouldn't put up too much of a fight...'

'And he collapsed?'

'Well, basically, yes.'

'So you hit him too hard.'

'I guess.'

'And what was your thinking carrying him here?'

'Well, you cannot really teach a guy a lesson if he is unconscious, can you? So I brought him here so we can wait till he wakes up and then we can frighten the life out of him.'

'Is he awake?'

'I don't know. I came down for you. '

Yanni creeps away from the door, sits on the ground, and then lies prone. At the sound of a bolt being shot, he tries not to react as the heat of the day and the sunlight streak across him.

'Who the heck is that?'

'The guy you told me to beat up, the lawyer.'

'Does he even look like a lawyer?' This voice's pitch is rising, the words spilling out faster.

'It's the guy you pointed out and besides, his friend put his arm around his shoulder and called him "lawyer" as they passed our table, you know, when he looked at us.' This voice, too, now sounds agitated. Yanni keeps his eyes closed as he tries to put an age to them, assess if he can rush them both before they have a chance to shut the door.

The door closes with a bang.

He opens his eyes.

'The guy that spoke was the lawyer. You idiot.' The voice only slightly dulled for being outside.

'But why did he call the other guy "lawyer" and look at us?'

'Maybe the lawyer was not as stupid as he seemed? Maybe you are the stupid one.'

'I don't understand. Did you or did you not point to this guy?'

'No, I pointed to the guy next to him.'

'The one that called this man "lawyer".'

'Yes! Look, this is not so difficult to understand, you got the wrong guy.'

'So what shall we do, open the door, let him wake up and just wander away?'

'No. Maybe we can use him. If he is a friend of the lawyer's, we might be able to get out of this okay. It depends what Gerasimos says. Can you get a signal up here?'

'Not usually. Better from over the hill there.'

'Okay, wait here.'

Yanni can hear the sound of footsteps growing distant and someone on the outside of the door settling down, sitting on the floor maybe.

There's only one of them now. Maybe this is the best advantage he will get. Stretching and yawning loudly, Yanni stands and walks to the door.

'*Yeia*, anyone there?' he asks, tapping at the boards.

There is silence. The wind blows under the roof, lifting tiles gently as it sighs and grows still again. Far away, a sheep bleats and further still, a dog barks.

'Please, I need some water.' Yanni leans against the door, his voice sounding even more imploring than he meant it to. That's a good thing.

Silence.

'Please my friend, my head hurts where you hit me and I am dehydrating.'

Silence.

A small sound.

A bottle of water is rolled under the door.

'Thank you.' It could be fear he is feeling, but it does not hold him still. His chest expands, he has a strange sensation of power, maybe it is excitement. A challenge.

He takes a drink, not taking his eyes from the door.

'It's hot in here.' Yanni leans his head against the door.

'It's hot out here,' a voice replies.

'I'm Yanni.'

Silence.

'You planning in letting me out sometime soon?'

Silence. There is a whisper of tiny running feet beside him, a movement in the bit of straw in the corner. Even the smallest of animals take shelter from the day's heat.

'I imagined not, so I'm Yanni.' With his fingers, he combs a web, whitened with dust, from his hair.

'Spiros.' The voice on the other side of the door relents.

'You like the smell of goats, Spiro?' Yanni asks. His baba would often start a game of *tavli* with a tactical opening, the move itself needing the following move to make it make sense. It always caught him off guard.

'What?'

'Well. Do you?'

'Not really. Bit strong, gets in my throat.'

'Mine too. It's very strong in here.' Yanni coughs. 'A little air would help.'

There is no reply.

The last of the cool water runs down his throat and he rolls the empty bottle back under the door. His hands are wet from the condensation on the outside of the bottle. He wipes them dry on his trousers.

'The day before yesterday, I had never been off Orino Island. Never seen such cunning.' Yanni speaks slowly, almost as if talking to himself.

'I think it is best if we don't talk. Takis will be back soon.' Spiro's words come out in spasms, as if the effort is too much in the heat.

'You scared of him?' Yanni asks, but he does not expect a reply. He remembers his fear of Hectoras, but he would never have admitted it at the time. Sophia standing up for him, offering to be by his side diluted that fear. It showed him that he was not the weak animal Hectoras suggested. It gave him his pride back. Maybe offering to stand by the side of Spiros will give him the incentive he needs to open the door. Yanni continues, 'I've been bullied, too, when I was at school.'

'He doesn't bully me. He helps me.'

'What, like getting you this job? Is this a job of choice for you then, beating people up, holding them against their will?'

There's a cough, a clearing of the throat.

'So of all the jobs you could do, this is the one, is it?'

'Well ...'

'Oh.' Yanni relaxes his throat, tries to make the conversation sound casual, friendly. 'So what would your first choice be?'

'Sheep. I like to take the sheep to feed.'

'You got a herd, then?'

'No.'

'Shame. If it is what you like to do, you should be doing it. I have a goat herd.'

'Really?'

'Yes. Take them to the far pasture morning and night if I can.'

'You are making this up so I will let you out.' A hard edge to the voice now.

'I could, that would be smart, but I am not. So this Takis, he looks after you, does he?'

The light in the barn is gentle, the stone of the walls show chisel marks here and there from when they were split, which are heighted by the shadows. The mortar is mud. Some insect has made one patch its home, turning the mud into cells where young have long ago hatched. They are now empty and, in one, a spider has made its home spinning a tunnel of web along the wall.

'So now Takis has me in his web, what will he do? He will expect you to beat me up because I am not a lawyer, I guess. He won't do it himself, will he?' Yanni picks up a twig and tickles the web. The spider comes out to investigate before sinking back into its hideaway. 'Or will Gerasimos come along with his big stick and beat you up for getting the wrong man?' He leaves the spider in peace and explores the bump on the back of his head again. It makes him wince. He draws his hand away and puts it in his front pocket around his roll of money.

'You know about Gerasimos?' Spiro's voice is tight.

'You might be surprised what I know. You know why Gerasimos wants to scare the new lawyer?'

'It is not my business.' But his words raise in tone at the end of his sentence. It is almost a question.

'You live round here, Spiro. Have you any family in the village?'

'What has this to do with anything?'

'Humm, this smell is really hurting my throat. It's like acid. And the bump on my head.' Yanni groans.

'What's it got to do with my family?'

Yanni groans again. It sounds fake to him, but maybe it will fool Spiro.

'Ah, you are bluffing. Playing games because you're scared.' His voice gains assurity.

'So you have family in the village. You have a house there?'

'You know nothing.' The voice sounds distant, as if he has turned away from the door.

'I know you will end up with no house. Have the surveyors been around yet?' Yanni leans against the wall.

'The surveyors?' the voice is nearer the door again.

'You want to know? Give me some air, a wet cloth for the damage you did to my head.'

'What do you know of the surveyors?' The sunlight from under the door is blocked. The toes of a pair of trainers shuffle in the gap.

'I know that the surveyors are being paid. I know there is no fault under the village. I know someone who has papers to prove it.' Yanni speaks slowly, allowing each sentence time to filter through the man's thoughts. He digs his own toe into the dust, twisting it, making a little pit.

'But why?' Spiro's voice sound incredulous.

'Why?' Yanni looks at the back of the door, his mouth drops open slightly, and he shakes his head. 'Why do you think?' The pit his toe is digging in the crumbled animal droppings is down to the compacted earth. Yanni removes his foot and watches the dust cascade down the sides.

He waits.

'I don't understand. If the surveyor comes to your house and says it is on the fault, you must drill columns, put in metal, fix it up. You mean Gerasimos is taking a cut of that?'

Yanni smiles, twists the ends of his moustache, and with a sweep of his foot covers over the hole.

'And what price does the firm qualified to do this work quote?' Yanni looks up at the sunlight filtering between the tiles.

'Well, I understand they don't. They give you a basic minimum and then it depends on what they come across as they work.'

'Aha,' Yanni agrees. 'A limitless amount, and who is going to agree to that? Who can afford to?'

The man outside is shuffling.

'So their alternative?' Yanni asks.

'To sell, and Gerasimos can arrange that ...' Spiro's words come out quickly.

'There is more, but I cannot talk any more in this heat. I need some air.' Yanni speaks through the door. 'Come on my friend, and I will tell you all about it.' He inclines his head towards the door. There is a scratching on the other side. Fingernails around the bolt?

'Spiro, what are you doing!' The voice sounds angry.

'He says my family will lose the house.'

'What are you bleating about?'

'Yanni, he says it is Gerasimos that is up to no good.'

'Yanni, who's Yanni? Ah! Well he would, wouldn't he?'

Yanni stands and puts himself flat against the wall by the door. For the briefest of moments, his mama comes to mind, the fear for his safety that she showed when they parted. His dismissal of her worst case scenarios and Sister Katerina talking of irrational fears, not justifiable fears, such as two men holding him against his will. The pulse in his temple throbs, he puts his hand over his heart. His body is trembling and yet he finds he is smiling, waiting for them to open the door. He does not recognise himself. His fists clench in anticipation. He is ready.

Chapter 14

Sweat runs down Yanni's forehead.

'Come on, let him out. It sounds like Gerasimos is doing some dirty moves that will affect everybody,' Spiros pleads. Yanni listens as he looks to see if he can break off any of the laths. It might be useful to have a weapon, but there is nothing within reach.

'We have been paid to do a job.' Taki's voice is lower, gruffer.

'But not on this man,' Spiros says.

'Excuse me?' Yanni taps on the door. The men outside go silent. 'You've been paid? How much? Maybe I can beat his price.' His hand slides into his front pocket where his coil of notes nestles.

'What did he say?' the gruffer voice asks.

'He says he will beat Gerasimos' price Taki. There, you see, I told you he was a good guy. We can get paid and keep our homes.' The tension in Spiro's voice has eased a little.

'Have you the money on you?' Takis asks.

'Yes.' Yanni takes out the roll and looks at it. It is not a good plan; he cannot afford to lose the money. His breathing quickens, his heart begins to race again.

'Push it under the door then,' the man called Takis barks.

'And what guarantee does that give me?' Yanni addresses the door.

'None, but you have no choice.' Takis again.

'It is you who has no choice, not me,' Yanni says.

No one says anything. The wind is still gusting through the eaves, sighing and heaving as if the old barn is alive, breathing, waiting. Yanni looks down its length to the far door. He paces it out quietly: five strides. He is fast on his feet, but is he fast enough?

'Okay, so here is a solution.' Yanni returns to speak through the door. 'Spiros can be at one door and you can be at the other. I pass the money to Spiros and you open the door. No open door, no money. No money, no open door.' The adrenaline running through his body is making his movements sharp, fast.

He hears one of them mutter something and their voices fade as if they are stepping away from the barn. He presses his ear to the door to listen.

'You will leave the area and never come back, understand?' Taki's gruff tone commands.

'It will be my pleasure,' Yanni assures him. One of his hands creeps over his chest and covers the pocket where the book Sophia gave him lives, feeling the corners, caressing the edges, but the images in his head are of the woman in the navy skirt at the sandwich shop.

'Right. Spiro, go the other end. Tell me when you can see the money. You inside, can you hear me? When I unlock this door, you march out and just keep going, don't look back or we may have to give you a beating anyway, you understand?'

Yanni nods. 'Understood.' He doesn't trust this Takis, and there has been no discussion about the amount he will give. But there is no choice, and he draws out his money. All the money he has in the world. His new donkey, his fare home, everything.

'Can you see it, Spiro?' Takis shouts.

Yanni pokes the roll under the door. Cobwebs curl around his fingers, a black beetle scuttles in out of the sun's harsh rays.

'Yes.' Spiro's voice sounds to be right by his ear.

'Just remember your family house,' Yanni says quietly. 'I can help you.'

'Okay take hold and when you have it, tell me and I will unlock the door. If he pulls the money back, I will lock it again. Ready?'

'Yes, I have it.'

The sound of the bolt being drawn is louder than Yanni expected. The door opens a crack, he lets go of the money, and in five paces, he is out of the door and running around the outside of the barn. He catches Takis before he has reached Spiros. For the briefest of moments, Yanni hesitates. The man is a lot older than he expected. He is also rounder and shorter.

Yanni's right hand raises to the side of his own ear, his elbow cocked and with a twist in his wrist and a sharp extension of his arm, he cracks Takis on the side of his head, feels the give of his ear. As he staggers out of balance, Takis' hand reaches out to the floor to take the impact as his body follows. Before Takis has time to draw breath, Yanni leaps to straddle him, locking him between his knees, like a sheep ready to be sheared, an arm around his neck, pulling tight. He watches as the man's face turns first red and then takes on a blue tone, his tongue extended, his eyes bulging.

'Stop! What are you doing? You'll kill him.' A man, slightly younger than Yanni himself, but taller and bulkier, with a shallow forehead and hair that does not lie flat runs at him, bowling both of them over. A stone digs in Yanni's back, they roll, Spiros exhales in his face—garlic—then round again. Yanni throws out his leg to stop their momentum; everything becomes still. Spiros wriggling out from under Yanni, breathing in big gasps, struggling for air.

'Breathe slowly and deeply,' Takis says, as if this is ritual they have been through a thousand times before. Spiros is wheezing. 'Asthma,' Takis clarifies. Yanni stands and backs away. The men eye each other warily, but the tension is passing. 'Spiros, come here.' Doing as he is commanded, Spiros shuffles across the ground. Takis holds his hand out and Spiros gives him the roll of money. 'Right, come on.' He looks up at Yanni, 'There is no need for us to fight; we are all men here. We could have left you in that barn to die, but we didn't. So be reasonable and I will be reasonable too. Here.' He peels of a few notes from the tightly grasped wad and holds them out to Yanni.

Yanni's ears buzz, his fists clench, his whole frame begins to tremble, and with a step, he is standing over this cockroach of a man who dares to negotiate with him with his own money, the cost of which was Dolly's life, the money that will ensure his family's future.

With an open hand, he slaps the man across the face, the shock and fear instantly registering in the man's eyes. Yanni has never struck anyone before this day and he wonders if his own shock registers as clearly. He tries to unpeel his fingers; his fists have automatically clenched. If he has to strike again, it must be with an open hand. He will use fear, not force. From the look on Taki's face, it is clear who has control now. Yanni's spine straightens, his shoulders drop back, tensed, his chin lifts.

'Here's what we will do.' Takis stumbles a little as he stands. The strength in his voice is forced. 'We can split this and call things even.' He holds up the money. 'Then you and I …' He takes a step toward Yanni, slowly, unthreatening.

Yanni's voice comes out like the breeze through the barn, hissing, suggesting its power, the damage it could do if it gained any strength. 'Don't you talk to me about what "we" are going to do.' Takis stops moving and blinks rapidly. Yanni holds out his hand, palm upwards. Takis looks sadly at the money and slowly hands it over. 'Now go.' Yanni can hear the growl in his voice, like a dog. He is surprised at his resolve, the emotion behind it.

Takis, looking at the ground, shakes his head and turns towards a battered truck parked at the side of the barn, which until this moment, Yanni has taken little notice of. 'Not the truck,' Yanni says.

'But it's a good few miles back to Saros. I am not such a young man.'

'If you get into this sort of business, you must be able to take the consequences. Throw me the keys.'

Takis fishes keys from his pocket. 'But how will I get back?'

'Use your feet. And Takis, unless you want me to come find you and give you another slap, I suggest you stay out of sight for the next couple of days.' Takis throws the keys to land on the ground at his feet.

Behind him, Spiros stands and shuffles forward as if to follow Takis.

'Not you, Spiros. You have had enough bullying.' Yanni watches Takis turn off the rough road and takes a footpath that cuts straight down the hill, but out of the corner of his eye he can see Spiros. At first his eyebrows arch, worry lines across his forehead as he watches Takis leave. Then his look of concern relaxes and slowly, he begins to grin. Finally his shoulders pull back and he shifts to stand alongside Yanni, his chin lifted high. They watch until Takis disappears behind the curve of the hill.

'Right, drive me to the village.' Yanni bends to pick up the keys and throws them at Spiros, who fumbles the catch and drops them.

'Me? I cannot drive. They told me I was too stupid to learn.' His eyes shine as tears rush them, his shoulders dropping in an instant.

'Well, one of us has to and I have never even sat in anything more than a bus and a taxi so Spiros, it is time to learn.' Yanni pats his shoulder before walking to the old pickup truck. His stomach grumbles. Lower down the hill are orange groves, and the thought of their sweetness, their juiciness makes him suck in his moustache in anticipation.

The truck shudders as the ignition is turned. Spiros experiments with the pressing of pedals. They shoot off quickly, to stop just as suddenly. Yanni remains patient, remembering the hours Sister Katerina sat quietly opposite him as he struggled to twist syllables into words. There is no rush. If he grips the chair and braces himself against the door and gives Spiros some time, he will get it. The truck bucks and stalls as they begin to crunch down the hill.

'A little too much speed perhaps,' Yanni suggests. 'Tell it to stop.'

'It's not a donkey; there is no telling it. It is pedal or a lever,' Spiros shouts over the noise of the grinding gears, his feet lifting and pressing. Their speed decreases. 'Ha!' he exclaims. The driving becomes less erratic and they bump along down to the bottom of the hill and onto the main road. Yanni leans from the window to grab oranges off the trees as they pass, leaves and thin branches coming, too.

'Turn to the village. We need to see Babis.' Yanni peels an orange and hands half of the segments to Spiros.

The truck half-mounts the pavement by the kiosk, but it attracts no interest at the kafeneio. Several trucks and many motorbikes are huddled in around the square wherever they can. One moped is leaning against the fountain, a truck is parked alongside a car, the two vehicles taking up half the road. If anything is in the way, it is not such a hard job to find the owner as he sips coffee and argues politics. Yanni cannot help but look to the sandwich shop, but there is no one outside; not even the stool is there.

The door to the house needs a shove; the coats have fallen again. Babis is sprawled on the sofa eating a cheese pie, a can of beer balanced on the arm of the sofa.

'Ah there you are,' Babis says, but his eyes remain fixed the television. Yanni is not sure what he expected to return to. He didn't know what to expect, but with the sight of Babis lounging on the sofa and his casual 'There you are', he finds his fists clench. Whilst he has been locked in a barn, his life threatened, Babis has been drinking beer and watching the television!

'Do you know …' The ordeal he has been through is pressing to be released. But he hesitates. It has happened; he is no longer in the barn. How will making Babis aware of it change what is going on? But his teeth grind and he begins again. 'Whilst

143

you've been sitting here. ...' But Babis does not even look away from the screen. Yanni takes a few laboured breaths. There's no point in feeling sorry for himself, he has suffered nothing compared to what the families of the village will suffer if their homes are taken from them. He must focus on looking forward, what needs to happen, that is the question. What needs to happen next.

'Have you been to see the mayor?' Yanni finally barks.

'The mayor? Why would I go to see the mayor? Awww!' He cries this last sound and throws one hand in the air, 'Would you look at that? They cannot give a free shot for that!'

Yanni's fists tighten again, his forehead knots, his eyes narrow. Can Babis really be so dim? Need he explain it? No, because Babis was the one who explained it to him. Maybe he has not understood properly?

'From what you told me, what the mayor is doing is not only criminal but inhuman. These are peoples' homes we are talking about.' As Yanni, speaks Spiros puts his head around the door. Babis stops looking at the television now, his face becomes rigid, his jaw clenches. Yanni makes the introduction. 'Babis, this is Spiros.' Babis looks from Spiros to Yanni, fear in his eyes. 'Oh it's alright Babis. He is with us now.' Yanni reassures but at the same time wonders how Babis would know that Spiros was ever even a threat. With his words, Babis' face does not immediately relax, but he manages to compose himself.

144

'*Yeia sou* Spiro.' He says his welcomes slowly and loudly. Spiros gives a little wave and smiles. After prolonged eye contact, Babis turns from him back to Yanni. 'Look Yanni, Gerasimos is dethroned, which leaves plenty of room for …' He stops to think of how to express himself. 'For things to change.' He grins. 'So let the mayor do what he will and let us do what we will.' He lifts a six pack of beer from the floor and holds it out to Yanni. 'Beer?'

Yanni steps to the television and pulls out the plug.

'What did you do that for?' Babis wails.

'If you only think about how things will change to improve your life, then how does that make you any better than Gerasimo?' Yannis asks. 'Have you no *filotimo*? No decency, no pride, no honour, no higher thinking?'

Spiros picks up a photograph in a frame on the sideboard, a picture of Babis' mama and baba when they were young.

'Put that down,' Babis says. Spiros gently replaces it. 'Look, I have to do what I have to do. My mama has no one else. From a young age, I have done what is needed to pay the bills and put enough food on the table. It is a dog eat dog world over here, Yanni. We are not all family like on your island. The mayor is a big shot with plenty of influence. If I step on his toes, there will be no work for me even if there is no one to take my place.'

'I, of all people, know your history.' Yanni pauses and looks him straight in the eye. 'But you cannot use that as an excuse not to do what is right. If you do nothing, you are stepping on everyone's toes in this village and then what life will you or your mama have when her friends turn their backs on her?'

'Can I ask a question?' Spiros says quietly. 'What has the mayor got to do with this? I don't really understand what is going on.'

'I don't think you understand how wide the mayor's influence goes,' Babis says, but with little assertiveness.

'What has the mayor got to do with my house?' Spiros asks.

'You will, just a minute.' Yanni answers Spiros quickly. 'Babi, once you know something, you cannot un-know it. I know what I know and my conscience will not let me walk away. Too many people's lives rest on this. We are going to the mayor. If you come, then you will be seen to be standing with us. If you do not, how will you be seen?'

Babis stands and throws his arms into the air. 'You come over here and you poke your nose in where it is not wanted. You talk about rights and wrongs of something you don't really understand and then you give me ultimatums like that. It was you, after all, who broke into Gerasimo's office in the first place. Without opening the door for me, we would never know what we know. So if you go to the mayor, you will have to own up to breaking and entering. The judge in Saros is a friend of the mayor's, and they will throw the book at you.'

'He's my uncle,' Spiros says.

'I broke into Gerasimo's office?' Yanni asks.

'Yup! Up the bougainvillea and in through the window.' Babis smiles now.

'Onto a balcony?' Yanni sits on the armchair, recalling dream-like images.

'Yup.' Babis opens another beer. 'You want one, Spiros?'

'No thank you.' Spiros remains standing by the door.

'You opened the door. I went in to change the numbers on the contract and by chance, I happened to find on his desk the proposal to the mayor from the German firm, and Gerasimos named as his legal representative. It just all fitted together. A quick flip through his address book led me to the surveyors in Athens. Gerasimo's business card and a little legal pressure got me the information I needed from them, which was enough to make Gerasimos run. Which he has. His office is empty, his car has gone, opening up Saros and the surrounding area to me. The mayor, on the other hand, is a much bigger fish. But the bottom line is it was you who did the breaking and entering.'

'You okay, Yanni?' Spiros asks. 'Does my family get to keep their home?'

'So I say to you, you choose, Yanni. How do *you* want to be seen?' Babis plugs the television back in.

147

Chapter 15

As the door slams behind him, he hears the coats falling onto the floor on the other side. His feet carry him away from the square, up the hill, wishing he was on the ridge, goats by his side. Sister Katerina said a lot about fear and denied that there were demons. It seems to him that fear gives life to demons. Since stepping on mainland soil, his fear of not being a good guest has taken solace in an ouzo bottle. He has drunk so much, his memory has failed him, he has fallen asleep in company and even broken into someone's office. He has become involved in politics and the ways of the world that he has spent most of his life trying to avoid. He has been kidnapped, gambled his money for his freedom, and he has beaten up a defenceless old man who, in all fairness, had kidnapped him. While he has been busy doing all this, he has left his poor baba to cope by himself and, if she is not already, then very soon, his mama will be worrying why he isn't home.

The problem isn't how he will be seen; the problem is who he is becoming.

The houses are below him now, the road peters out into a path and the rough land leads up to a clump of pine trees that top the hill. A cockerel crows somewhere in the village. The vegetation thins and is replaced with a bed of pine needles that deaden his footsteps and add to the hush of the wind that whispers through the tree tops.

Is it because he is a solitary, reticent creature that he cannot be amongst men and carry out three simple tasks? Buy a donkey, deliver a parcel, and maybe visit an old friend. Is he such a fool, such a simpleton? Has he learnt nothing in his studies with Sister Katerina? What did all that learning give him?

He sits to look over the village spread before him, at the whitewashed walls and red tiled roofs surrounded by orchards of olives and oranges that spread as far as the eye can see, all the way to the foothills of the faded purple mountains that surround the plain. There, to his left, almost entirely hidden by the hill he sits on, is the sea lapping at Saros town, the sparkling blue that stretches a finger towards the village, making it the ideal spot it is. He drops his weight heavily to sit, leaning back against a tree, his feet pulled in, arms resting on his knees, his hands dangling. There are houses dotted across the plain as well as in the village and within each house, there will be a family, each most likely with a mama and a baba, and *papous* and *yiayia* maybe, and children who will get married and the cycle will go on, generation after generation. Even the most uneducated man manages to keep this cycle going.

What did all that learning with Sister Katerina give him? He knows now what it didn't give him! It didn't give him the peace he seeks. It was not the desire to speak foreign languages or to 'better' himself, whatever that means, that motivated him. In fact, he does know what it gave him because he has found the same thing in the bottom of an ouzo glass! It gave him an escape, a sense of doing something to avoid actually doing something, an anaesthetic. As long as he was learning, taking steps to decode Sophia's poem, he had his excuse to remain a recluse. Withdrawing away, like a monk, on the top of an island rather than getting out there amongst men and finding himself a wife—and a life. Bottom line: He is nothing but a coward. Fearful and hiding.

No, the question is not how will he be seen but who has he become.

He is not proud.

A donkey brays and Dolly comes to mind. He sighs and takes out his tobacco. His fingers linger around the book, his heartbeat quickening. To be brave, fight his fears head on, how different would his life be? Would he have found Sophia already? Would he have talked to the woman in the navy skirt? Maybe his life would have been even more complicated.

How is he meant to know what to be reticent about and what to be brave about? Maybe that's why there are social rules. Maybe they help?

Trying to help this village, surely that is something he needs to be brave about, put himself second. What does it matter how he is seen if the villagers keep their homes? But then again, what does he really know of the mayor of Saros? The mayor on Orino Island is shifty and out for himself, but everybody knows everybody's business on the island; there's not much the island mayor can keep hidden. But here, maybe the mayor is a bigger fish, maybe he will be able to just bury the whole affair even if they confront him with it. If that is the case, Babis will not come out of it at all well and then how will Babis and his mama cope? Perhaps keeping himself to himself is the best course after all. Perhaps he should just get his donkey, deliver the Sister's parcel, and leave. Getting involved in other peoples' business is never a good idea, maybe even seeing Sophia is a bad idea.

'Oh why is it all so complicated?' He stands. 'I just want to be quiet.'

He looks down at the houses in the village, aware that getting rid of the mayor's lawyer, Gerasimos, is not enough. Every last one of the houses will be declared unsafe, including Babis'. Every last one of them will be bought up cheaply by the company that fronts the mayor's dealings. Then the whole town will be sold as a job lot to the German firm and turned into a walled holiday destination, boasting its own coastline. The mayor will get rich beyond his wildest imagination. The tourists will be bussed in like cattle and trapped in their individual holiday homes, herded to eat at the tavernas provided, drink at the kafeneios run by the organizers, buy their sunscreen at the German-run corner shop and the people who have lived there for generations will be displaced and forgotten about, all for the sake of this inhuman theme park.

Apparently, Babis said, the same German firm bought an onion field on the coast just outside of the village a while back, built a hotel on it, and are raking in so much money, it will fund the entire project.

One man's get-rich-quick scheme of selling his onion field could be the downfall of the entire village.

'Why do people not work for the good of the whole?' he asks the breeze, which answers by lifting the ends of his moustache. He twists them to a point and then flattens his hair with a stroke of his hand.

'And her house too, the woman in the navy skirt, where will she go?' But the breeze does not answer this time. 'It's a business that relies on fear,' he tells it.

He knows what Sophia would do. She did it for him. She stood up for what she believed in without a thought for herself. No fear.

Before he even realizes he has made a decision, he is marching back down the track to the road, to Babis' door. With each step, his breaths come deeper, his movements more certain. He does not knock; he shoves hard with his shoulder.

Babis is sitting on the sofa, Spiros is still standing, but each with a beer in their hand.

'You asked me a question,' Yanni starts. 'You asked me how I want to be seen. That was the wrong question, The question is "who do I want to be".'

Babis stands and picks up a beer, opens it, and holds it out to Yanni. 'Couldn't agree more, my cousin.' But Yanni is prepared for a fight and hardly hears him.

'I cannot be the man who stands by and … sorry, what did you say?'

'Exactly, my friend. I have thought it over and decided you are right.' Babis tires of holding out the opened beer and turns to offer it to Spiros, but Spiros raises the one in his hand, so Babis puts it on top of the television. Yanni looks from Babis to Spiros and back again.

'You've changed your mind quickly. What about your fear of the mayor and his friend the judge?'

'The judge …' Spiros begins.

'Yanni,' Babis says quickly, taking his attention, 'it is every man's duty to think of the people around him and the village he comes from. What a small sacrifice my career will be for the good of the people. Where would all these villagers go if this terrible scam were to bear fruit? It is my duty as a fellow villager, as man amongst men, as a lawyer for the people that we stop this plan right now.'

Yanni frowns and looks back to Spiros, who is shifting his weight from foot to foot, decidedly unsettled about something. Babis stands and steps between Spiros and Yanni. 'When a man is right, he is right. There is no arguing with that.' Babis lifts his beer to salute him.

'What am I not being told?' Yanni asks.

'Oh look Spiro, a cartoon,' Babis says and Spiros, with a turn of his head, becomes absorbed by the television. 'Be happy that I have seen that you are right, Yanni. Not afraid of being right, are you?' Babis asks. He should say something, but what should he say? Babis agrees with him. They will go to the mayor, so how come he doesn't feel settled?

'Come on then,' Yanni says at last.

'What, now?' Babis looks back to the television where the match has started again.

'I have a donkey to buy tomorrow and a nun to visit the day after and then I plan to go home, so yes, now.' Yanni picks the coats off the floor and hangs them up again.

Babis takes a last look at the screen. 'They are losing anyway.'

'Spiros, you want to come?' Yanni asks. Spiros takes a last sip of beer and puts the can down on an empty crisp bag.

'Oh yes. We need Spiros.' Babis laughs, but the sound is hollow and neither reaches his eyes nor his throat. 'And we can get something to eat and have a little drink on the way.' He pulls the door shut. 'Or not,' he mutters, looking at Yanni's face, 'if you are not hungry.'

Babis insists on calling a taxi, and the truck is left abandoned in the square. The road to Saros almost feels familiar now to Yanni, but as they pull into the town's main square everything seems a little too big, the buildings large and made of cut stone, their doors too tall and ornate and there are many people, all who seem to be rushing.

'His office is on the first floor.' Babis presses the button to call the lift. Yanni walks past him and begins to climb the stairs, Spiros in tow. Babis hesitates and then runs up behind them.

To the left of a pair of ceiling-height double doors on the first floor is a brass plaque that reads *Mayor*. To the right of the doors is a neatly ordered desk and an empty chair, no secretary in attendance. Stuck to the double doors with sellotape is a piece of lined paper with a torn edge upon which is written, 'Back tomorrow'.

'Excuse me,' Yanni asks a man with several files under his arm waiting for the lift. 'Do you know where the mayor is?'

'Same place as most people.' He takes out an oversized handkerchief and mops his bald head and then the back of his neck. He is wearing a suit. 'Up at the convent, for the open day.' The lift arrives and he pulls the concertina doors closed behind him.

'Thirsty work, this,' Babis says.

'We'll go there then,' Yanni states.

'Where?' Babis asks, a glint of hope in his eyes.

'The convent.' Yanni is already at the top of the steps. Babis' smile fades.

Babis sits in the front and chats away to the driver. The road to Saros is now etched onto Yanni's mind and the green of the trees and the watering systems under them, in the shade, is no longer a marvel to him. This time, he looks around the taxi itself, at the cluster of icons hung on the rear-view mirror competing with those stuck onto the dashboard. Saints to protect the journey, to give wealth, to give friendship, to protect his family. There is also a picture of a baby on the flipped-down sun visor, the corner of which lifts and drops in the breeze of the air conditioning. Despite the air conditioning, it's hot inside the taxi, and a plasticky smell permeates. The orange groves give way to houses and they drive straight through the village square and out past fruit trees again. The road begins to wind up a hill and the cultivated land becomes scrub. Ahead, a high wall and a gathering of many cars, two buses, and a couple of donkeys suggest they have arrived.

The arched wooden doors set into the wall are open. Three steps take them into a great marble-flagged courtyard with a church in the centre. Around the edge of the open space, windows set into the walls suggest cells and corridors and the living area that must be behind them. There is a bustle of people and the few benches dotted here and there are crammed with women in ironed blouses, pleated skirts, and shoes that look like they have never been worn. None of these women seem relaxed. The men loitering around them lean on their crooks and look beyond the walls to the hills. Children run round in their frills and white, young mamas trying to calm them. Today, both nuns and villagers alike will celebrate the saint's day that the nunnery is dedicated to.

A nun approaches them. Yanni swallows. He looks around and sees more nuns, coming in and out of a room opposite the church doors.

'Welcome,' the nun approaching them says as she glides past them, now addressing a priest in his long black robes and pillar box hat who came in behind them.

She could be here. She must be here! Yanni looks from face to face of the nuns, but they are too far away. He begins to walk toward the doorway that is the centre of all movement. Babis is crossing himself as he follows, Spiros behind him.

'Yes, good idea, He is bound to be in there,' Babis says, but Yanni is looking more intently from nun to nun the nearer they get.

'Sorry boys, this sitting is full. If you wait, they won't be long,' a wrinkled face wrapped in a black *apostolnik* informs them. Yanni looks at her blankly. 'Don't worry,' she says. 'There is plenty of food for everyone.'

'Do you know Sister Sophia?' The words just come out, followed by the fear of the answer he will receive.

'You know, I think I saw her in there.' She points to the doors with all the commotion.

The stone room is hot, hotter than outside. Trestle tables fill the space, each seating eight or ten people, everyone talking and everyone eating, the nuns staggering between with plates laden with food, smiling as they go.

'I can't see him,' Babis says.

'Who?' Yanni asks. There is a nun whose movements suggest she is not so old serving at an end table, but he cannot see her face.

'The mayor.' Babis sound incredulous. '*Yeia sou* Stella. Mitsos,' he calls. For a second, Yanni's attention is taken as Stella calls back.

'*Yeia* Yanni, Babis.'

She is sitting next to Mitsos, who is next to Theo from the kafeneio. Theo has a woman beside him whom Yanni has not seen before, and he is holding her hand. Vasso sits opposite and next to her is the woman in the navy skirt, only today she wears a dress, also in navy. Next to her, a woman with blonde hair who does not look Greek. But Yanni's eyes only touch on her, as they are drawn back to the woman in the navy dress and he tries to swallow but his need for breath comes first and he starts to choke. She looks up at the sound and their eyes meet.

Chapter 16

At the end of the hall, a plate smashes and the nun young enough to still have energy in her limbs bends to pick up the pieces.

The room is oppressively hot and the small windows do not let in much light. There is a haze in the room, a mix of dust and smoke from the wood burning stove in the kitchen. Yanni cannot understand the appeal of sitting and eating in such a stifling atmosphere.

'Come on.' Babis is growing impatient. 'If we get this done, we can sit and eat, too.' Spiros has a hand on his stomach as he watches plate after plate being brought out from the kitchen, steaming and aromatic—tomatoes, garlic, and oregano. Yanni, bending backwards slightly, still can't see her face even as she stands; the side of her headscarf has dropped forward. Another nun, older, stouter, who is helping her to pick up the pieces, gets in his line of sight. He leans the other way. A man at another table stands to shuffle his chair in, momentarily blocking the view of both nuns.

Above the joyful chatter of the throng, the scraping of wooden chairs on the stone floor, and the clatter of knives and forks against plates Yanni hears a voice in his ear.

'Would you gentlemen mind waiting for the next sitting outside,' a middle-aged nun requests, with a rather stern expression on her face. She seems fazed by the number of people in the room. 'It's getting a little difficult to move in here.' She presses up against Yanni, muttering her apologies, as another nun pushes past her with a jug and glasses. Yanni only glances at the nun talking, and the one who pushes past for a second, but when he looks back to where the plate pieces were being cleared up, the younger nun is gone. He scans the room; she is nowhere to be seen. Looking from corner to table, he scans each of the nuns who are serving and those hovering, eager to be of service around the tables. In his search, he makes eye contact with the woman in the navy dress again, who now has a sadness in her eyes. She holds his gaze for a fraction of a second and then breaks the connection by looking down at her food. She is not eating. Her food sits untouched, her hands in her lap. Without thought, one of Yanni's feet lifts to take him to her.

'Yes, I'm hungry,' Spiros says and Babis pulls on Yanni's sleeve, breaks his trance, and with a determined tug, they leave the room together, Yanni's legs moving mechanically. As he walks, he looks behind him; it is Spiros who leads. His hand is over his breast pocket, over the book given to him by Sophia. His mind's eye creates pictures of the woman in the navy dress but his thoughts are focusing, sharpening on getting him home, leaving this madness behind. The whole emotional situation is too much. It would be simpler to be alone the rest of his life, on the top of the ridge. Alone with his goats and away from these things that torment.

'There he is,' Babis announces.

The smell of incense wafts out of the chapel before Yanni's attention is grabbed by the shimmer of the thousand lit candles reflecting on the gold surrounds of the icons. Next to the *manoulia*, glittering with its tiers of prayer candles, stands a big man in a dark suit, his chest puffed out as he talks to a priest. The holy man only appears the taller of the two due to his black pillar-box hat. There is an insincerity in the suited man's voice and he does not look the priest in the eye as he talks. Instead, he gazes far away at the ideas and aspirations he vocalizes. He has his arm around the priest's shoulder. The mayor speaks loudly and laughs strongly. Next to him is a slim man also in a suit, but his is a pale grey, of thinner material. This man's eyebrows are formed as if he is permanently surprised and there are smile lines around his eyes. His arms dangle by his side. In one hand, he holds a candle as if ready to be lit, to say a prayer. It gives the impression that the thin man came in to kiss an icon and the two of them being there together is a coincidence, although they are standing close enough together to suggest they know one another.

The priest shakes the big man's hand and departs.

'That him?' Yanni asks. Babis nods but seems to hesitate. Yanni's mouth sets hard as he jerks his head, encouraging Babis to make a move. Babis stands rooted. Yanni gives him a last hard stare and turns to go to the man himself, which creates a reaction in Babis.

'Leave it to me.' Babis puts a restraining arm across Yanni's chest as he steps forward. 'But we cannot talk of such things here in God's house.' Yanni opens his mouth to say something as the big man notices them and steps towards them.

'Ah, the new lawyer,' he says loudly but as he does so, his focus flicks across to Spiros, his eyes darkening, his smile wiped away for a second and his bottom lip twisted. He recovers quickly.

'Lawyers.' Spiros adds the plural. It is Yanni's turn to glance at Spiros, but the mayor speaks.

'Might be needing you, my friend. What's your name again?' His voice fills the domed room, echoing off the gold leafed frescos. The faces of saints look down on them, smoke from the hundreds of flickering candle swirling upwards.

For a second, Yanni watches Babis falter, a smile on his lips at the thought of being needed by the mayor, perhaps? Yanni steps closer to him. Spiros comes around his other side, in between Babis and the thin man in the light suit who smiles broadly at him.

'I think we need to talk.' Babis regains control of his smile, his brows knot, but his resolve seems shaken. Yanni steps even closer, so his shoulder touches Babis'.

'Any time, my boy, any time. My door is always open to you, and like I said, I might be needing you to help me with a little project.' He leans towards Babis to say more quietly, 'Could be very interesting work. Interesting in many ways perhaps.' He straightens and resumes his booming baritone. 'Gerasimos was going to look at it for me but his mama has taken ill, you know. He has been called back to Thessaloniki.' He laughs from his stomach, spittle coming white in the corner of his mouth. It seems inappropriate after talking about a sick woman.

'That's the very thing I, or rather we,' Babis looks at Yanni and Spiros, one either side of him, 'wish to talk about.' Yanni can see Babis is ever so slightly trembling. He puts a hand on his shoulder, squeezes it briefly to let him know he is there, to give him some confidence.

'Good, good.' The mayor eyes Spiros again, who has been distracted by the gold leafed icon painting on the *templon*. He looks from one to the next, his mouth open slightly.

'Perhaps not so good,' Babis regains the mayor's attention, 'but I do not wish to say all your sins here in the sight of God.' Saying this seems to harden his resolve. In any case, he stops trembling. 'Sufficient to say I have enough evidence for you to need to say your prayers tonight. We can meet tomorrow.' Babis' own chest puffs out with these words.

The colour drains from the mayor's face and it takes on a waxy sheen. There is a pause and no one seems to know what to say or do next.

'How are you, nephew?' the thin man, who Yanni had completely forgotten about, says kindly to Spiros.

'Oh Yanni,' Babis is suddenly animated, 'you haven't met the new judge of Saros, have you?' Babis introduces the thin man, who holds out his hand to Yanni.

'You are this man's uncle?' The mayor's voice is not so loud now as he addresses the judge. His forehead is speckled with beads of perspiration, each drop reflecting icons and candles, giving the effect that he is almost on fire.

'Is something amiss, my boy?' the judge says and puts an arm around Spiros, declaring an affiliation to him.

'I think I need a glass of water.' The mayor pushes past them out into the courtyard.

'He knows we know,' Babis says, an edge of triumph from his voice. 'We will see him tomorrow!'

'It all sounds very intriguing,' the new judge says, his words light, calm. 'I suppose I will get the hang of everything eventually. Oh, look, there's your aunt, Spiros. I'd better go to her. I said I would only be a minute.' With this, he quickly lights his candle, plants it in a sand tray that is illuminated by a hundred others, crosses himself, and strides outside to a woman who is beckoning him to hurry. By the surge of people going in through the doors opposite, it's clear the second sitting has been called.

'So, there we go. There is no turning back now,' Babis says. 'You happy now?' There is a smugness in

164

his voice and energy in his limbs, one hand rubbing his stomach, perhaps in anticipation of food he might now be able to go and eat.

Yanni's face is like stone, and Babis takes a step back, a puzzled look on his face. 'What is it, Yanni? I thought you would be pleased …' Without warning, Yanni's fist drives towards Babi's face. Spiros leaps between them and the blow glances off his shoulder, sending Yanni reeling into the chairs that line the side of the little church. Spiros recovers first and puts his hands out to help Yanni up, brushing him down as he stands.

'What the …' Babis holds back the expletive and crosses himself for his thoughts. 'Now what's wrong with you?' He holds his arms out towards Yanni in submission and takes a couple of steps to put himself behind the *manoulia*, adding distance and solidity between them. Spiros is standing with arms open, first facing one of them then the other, clearly confused by the situation.

'When exactly did you know the judge was Spiro's uncle?' Yanni spits as he speaks.

'I told him when you went for a walk,' Spiros is quick to say, turning to Yanni. 'He was badmouthing the referee on the television and saying everyone who is in a position to judge judges badly, so I got cross and told him my uncle was the new judge, which he seemed to like and he gave me a beer.' The words rush out.

'So that speech of yours that you gave me when I came back from my little walk, how did it go? "It is every man's duty, blah blah blah. What a small sacrifice my career will be blah blah, as a lawyer for the people and so on". All those flowery phrases that you met me with when I came back were because you knew Spiro's uncle was the judge.' Yanni clenches his fists.

'Well obviously it had some bearing …' Babis looks quickly to the door, but Yanni moves to block his exit. 'But I am not sure why that would move you to strike me, cousin?'

'So as soon you knew the judge was not in the pocket of the mayor, as soon as you knew he was the uncle of someone on your side, as soon as you know you are safe, then and only then do you think to act on the peoples' behalf?' Yanni is so cross, flecks of spittle leave his mouth as he tries to speak without shouting, 'And you haven't even got the decency to say so. Instead you put on that little performance about being the lawyer of the people. A performance to me! Me, of all people! Who are you really trying to impress? Yourself?' He draws the tone down at the end of the sentence; he has finished. Babis' eyebrows raise as he shuts his mouth. 'What's more,' Yanni hisses, animated with new thoughts, 'I saw you hesitate to speak out in front of the mayor just now. I saw your hesitation when he said he "needed" you.' Yanni sucks his teeth in disgust. 'You would have stepped into Gerasimos' shoes without a care for anyone if you thought you could get away with it.'

'Yanni, the ways of the world are harsher than you think ...'

'The ways of the world are as you make them ...'

'That's easy for you to say. You have two parents back on your precious little island. Your memory is short, my friend, and you have forgotten the things that happened to me here in the real world ...'

'I have not forgotten,' Yanni says, more quietly now, 'but that is no excuse to make the world a worse place.'

'But I am not. We are not. We are going to face him.'

'Only because it will further your career now. Have you no *filotimo*, Babis?' Yannis uses the last of the air in his lungs to spit these final words. He turns his face away and takes a lungful of incensed air. A teenage girl comes in, assesses the situation in a glance, and walks out again.

'I don't think with you both being lawyers, you should argue in the house of God,' Spiros whispers loudly, his eyes wide and uncomprehending.

'And where did you get the idea I was scum like him?' Yanni explodes. 'I am no lawyer.'

'But, he said you were.' Spiros points to Babis, who is waving his hands as if to stop him. 'That night that we ...'

'When?' A stillness has come over Yanni.

'When we first saw you in the bar. I asked Takis which was the one we were to beat up, which one was the lawyer and Babis looks up, he must have heard me, he pointed to you, and then when you left, he called you "lawyer" again.'

Babis backs away from Yanni, his eyes on the door, the only exit. 'Look, I am sorry, Yanni. I just thought you would deal with them better than me. I am not athletic like you.' Babis' eyes shine as if tears have filled them. 'Gerasimos is known for his hard-handed approach, and the way they were looking at us,' his eyes flick to Spiros, 'but really I just thought someone like you could brush them off.' His voice is pleading, the sweat stains on the armpits of his shirt growing rapidly, the smell over the incense just discernible.

'Did I do something wrong?' Spiros asks.

Yanni watches Babis shrinking and turns to Spiros. 'No. You can be proud.' His emphasis is on the word *you*. His step is sure and controlled as he walks from the church.

The nun who asked him to wait outside comes trotting as fast as she can across the courtyard.

'I have saved you and your friends a place.' She smiles through the words.

Yanni's moustache twitches but he holds back the words and searches his pockets to draw out the folded and string-bound missive Sister Katerina gave him.

'Please, would you give this to the abbess for me?' He keeps it short and turns to leave.

'But she is just there, you can give it to her yourself. Where are you friends? I will call them to eat.'

'Please, just give this to her for me.' He pushes the note into her hands and marches toward the exit.

'But your food. I have saved you a table,' the nun calls after him. Yanni knows he is being rude, but he has no control over the surge of emotions within him. He could well start to say one thing and something else may come out. Best to say nothing.

The air is somehow fresher outside the convent doors. The walls, the candles, the incense, the crowded refectory, the nuns themselves felt stifling. He keeps walking. The paved area in front of the convent narrows back to a road. Was he too harsh on Babis? The look of sadness on the sandwich shop girl's face is all he can picture, that and the side of the young nun's head. Clenching his fists, he chooses some harsh swear words and mutters them under his breath. Maybe he was too harsh with Babis, maybe he lost control over his frustration in finding and facing Sophia. Maybe Babis had no part in this anger at all. And why did the girl from the sandwich shop seem so happy to see him when first their eyes met, and so sad the second time? He should not have been so hard on Babis. He recalls rocking him after he spoke of his Baba's death, and then it is him being rocked and Sophia doing the rocking, and then it is him rocking and the sandwich shop girl is in his arms.

'Stop!' His feet halt and he shouts out to the skies. His mind never raced like this when he was with the goats. Is it the mainland that stirs his thoughts, or is it the woman?

'Damn them all.' He thrusts his hands in the front pockets of his jeans and, looking down to his worn cowboy boots, bought cheaply one year because they were no longer in fashion, he measures his pace as if he is up in the hills with the goats. 'That's a decision, then,' he tells himself. 'To hell with them all. I am happiest alone.' He looks down to the village, and as he descends the hill, his panoramic view of the fields of orange trees changes until he is looking up at individual trees to see the oranges now as big plums but still hard and green.

It does not take him as long as he expected to reach the heart of the village and after brief enquiries, he is on the road that brings him to the donkey breeder. Alone on the final stretch of road, the light changes and a pinkish hue covers the world, making everything look magical and soft. He thinks of his mama. He will be pleased to see her again. It is just before twilight when he finds the cottage tucked under olive trees and a familiar smell of manure greets him.

As he passes the truck parked at the end of the house, heat comes from it, shimmering off the engine. It turns out that the breeder has also just returned from the convent.

'I would have gladly given you a lift had I known you were coming my way.' The man introduces himself as Thanasis. His calloused hands are rougher even than Yanni's. His suit shows the wear of years and his shirt is clean but a uniform grey. He discards his jacket with relief and, rolling up his sleeves, he invites Yanni into the enclosure next to the barn.

With donkeys and hinnys around him, Yanni's heart begins to beat to a gentler rhythm, a sanity seems to return to him, and a quietness settles which he has not felt since he left the island. Thanasis is a man after his own heart and even when his new donkey has been chosen, a really pretty thing with big nostrils and long dark eyelashes, and the deal has been done, Thanasis urges him to linger a while. They drink tepid water together, eat what is left of a spinach pie and a *tavli* set is brought out. Thanasis suggests he stay the night, in the cot in the barn, and travel with the animal tomorrow on the truck and save himself the bus fare back to the boat that will take him to Orino Island.

Yanni allows him to win at *tavli*.

Looking up through the holes in the barn's roof, Yanni sees the same stars that are visible from the cottage up on the ridge. Tomorrow night, he will be there. His mama and baba, Suzi and Mercedes. It seems a bit of a long name for the new beast, but seeing as Thanasis has taken the time to sew it into her brow-band in beads, he will probably keep it. Anyway, the point is it will be just the five of them. It's enough.

Part II

Chapter 17

'This heat wave is just not relenting ...' Stella wipes her face and then her hands on a cloth which she takes from a hook by the grill before going through to the room with the tables. Her eatery consists of two small rooms. There is a long counter going almost the full length of the first room with a small gap left to squeeze behind it at one end, and this is where Mitsos is most often found, wrapping takeaway meals in aluminium trays for collection, taking the money and tuning the radio into *rebetika* stations with the cling-film-covered knob. With a turn of his heel, he can attend to the open charcoal grill and the chip fryer on its makeshift table at the far end. The back of the grill and the back wall itself create another corridor of space. Here, mirrored and glass shelves collect grease and dust as the years pass, and the floor has proved impossible to keep clean because the storage of buckets of lemon sauce and bottles of water make mopping a time-consuming affair. At the far end in this dingy area is where Stella will be if she is not serving, her back to the world, washing dishes and glasses in the stained marble sink.

Mitsos is not in yet today. Work has not fully begun and Stella stands for a second in the doorway that connects the two rooms. Gay plastic cloths cover the four tables, each with a different design; one shows dogs, tails up, running around the edge followed by men in red coats on horseback, another a trellis of flowers, the designs on the tops faded white where the surface has been wiped again and again. A blue glass bottle holding a single plastic flower has been placed at the centre of each. The far corner of the room is partitioned off with a sliding door, screwed to which is a cast metal plaque of a young boy peeing into a bowl.

Before she sits, Stella wipes over a glazed photograph of a donkey wearing a straw hat that hangs on the far wall, the intense red bow of its bonnet sharp against the green walls.

'Absolutely relentless! I'm having to water my garden twice a day already. My water bill is going to be enormous for this quarter.' Juliet scrapes her straw around the froth on the inside of her glass and pushes her chair onto its back legs.

'Mitsos is the same with all the geraniums. I said we should plant them out. They are hardy enough, but he likes them in the pots. He says the back yard has had them ever since he can remember.' She laughs briefly. 'I told him he must have a short memory because when I moved in, there was nothing but empty pots.' She wipes a hand across her forehead. 'Actually, I need water myself. Do you want some?' She stands again and turns to the drinks fridge.

'Yes please.' Juliet looks out the open door, across the road to the sandwich shop, and waits for Stella to sit.

'Did you want ice? It's cold anyway.'

'Don't mind as long as it's cold.' Juliet takes a sip. 'You know, why would someone want to open up a sandwich shop directly opposite you?'

'Oh I don't think it is competition. It has its own trade.'

A man comes out of the bakery two doors up from the sandwich shop. He carries a crate in front of him, leaning back against its weight as he crosses the road. Like enormous brown eggs, the rounded ends of loaves peek from the wooden box. Stella stands and goes through to the grill room where she meets the man and takes her day's staple. She returns to Juliet eating a chunk she has just pulled off one of the loaves.

'You want some?' She holds out the remains. Juliet shakes her head. She points with it to the sandwich shop. 'The farmers use it before my grill has heated up. The kids buy a pie or sandwich there to take to school. I mean, you could hardly eat chicken and chips in the school yard, could you?' They both chuckle.

'True. I just wondered if it took any of your trade,' Juliet says. Stella shrugs.

'I don't think so.' She sits and extends her legs in front of her with the abandon of a teenager, belying her age. 'You know, I think about half of my business is from the women of the village who can't be bothered to cook.' She gnaws on her bread, crumbs falling and rolling down her floral print dress.

'You're kidding?' Juliet sound genuinely surprised. 'All the women in the village seem to talk about is what they are cooking, or what they will cook—or what they cooked yesterday.' She pauses. 'I think it was one of the first verbs I learned in Greece. *Mageireuo*.'

A dog sniffs its way along the road. It is the dog that guards the sheep in the barns just out of the village, recognisable as it is larger than most dogs that wander the village streets. Its wide leather collar is worn where it is chained up when it is working. But for now, it is free and the smells to be found are enticing. It looks up briefly as it approaches the shop. Stella throws the remains of her bread out onto the road in the dog's path. It sniffs and eats, but with no real relish. This is one of the more spoilt working dogs. Well-fed and given its freedom when his sheep are out in the pasture. It is one of the dogs that does not need to be called when it is time to return to work, eagerly reporting for duty.

'Market days are a good day for me,' Stella continues. The dog continues its journey, turning up a side lane out of sight. 'When all the women go into Saros to buy veg but don't get time to cook, the phone rings off the hook.'

'Unbelievable, and there I was chastising myself for not being more domestic.'

Stella takes a serviette from the metal holder on the table, pulling at one. They all come out. 'This heat helps, too. No one can be bothered to cook.' She wipes her neck and, keeping hold of the used serviette, she stuffs the others back in the holder. 'Shall we sit outside?' The used tissue is thrown in the small bin by the door.

'It's funny, isn't it? You can never really know a business from the outside.' Juliet stands to follow, taking both her frappe glass and her water. Sitting at the table nearest to the tree which is wound around with fairy lights, she stretches out her legs and kicks off her flip-flops. The golden colours in her hair take on a brilliance in the sun.

'Talking of business, how is your translation going?' Stella straightens the painted wooden chairs around the next table—their raffia seats face outward towards the road—before pulling out her own chair to join Juliet.

'Good, good. I have more than enough work. In fact, I have been taking on books recently—bigger jobs. Lump sums, which come in handy. This year, I'm treating both the boys to a holiday to come over here.' She pauses. 'If I didn't, I don't think I would ever get to see them.' She smiles but there is a sadness around her eyes.

'Are they doing alright?' Stella stretches even more, and as her legs extend, her feet point inwards, childlike. 'Has Thomas actually bought the engagement ring for Cheri yet?'

'Yes. Bless them. But their careers are still all they talk about, so I don't see the wedding happening any time soon.'

'And Terrance?'

'Terrance is in Peru of all places at the moment, as part of his PhD. Still set on changing the world, one sewage works at a time.'

'I don't understand all these things they can study now. It seems you can take a course on anything you like in England.' Stella finishes the water in her glass and pours them both some more. The plastic water bottle is empty. She crushes it vertically, concertinaing it from the top down on her knee before replacing the lid to make it hold its compressed shape. She leans sideways, aims and throws it in the small bin by the door, smiles, and nods at her success. Juliet rolls her eyes.

'I think it's even worse in America. I've heard of some of the most bizarre courses. Princeton used to offer a course in "getting dressed".'

'No!' Stella's laugh is light but heartfelt and after a moment, she wipes tears from her eyes. 'The world is a bit mad, I think.' Her laughter reduces to a giggle until it simmers to nothing. 'Have you got anyone studying with you at the moment?'

'No, why? You want some more lessons?' Juliet says in English.

'Ha! Thank you but no, not for the moment.' Stella replies, also in English.

A tractor putt-putts up towards them, the gears grinding as it comes to a stop in the middle of the road between the taverna and the chip shop. The farmer slides from his seat and the dog that was following the tractor stops and watches him enter the sandwich shop. After a second, it flops down in the shade and waits patiently, panting. The farmer comes out, shouting something back over his shoulder to the woman inside the shop, and climbs back aloft. The tractor splutters to life, gains momentum, the dog breaking into a trot to follow. It turns the corner of the square and the noise fades away.

'Who owns it anyway?' Juliet asks.

'The sandwich shop? A guy from Saros. He's got three in the villages around here.'

'Oh, so it's not the woman who works there, then?' Juliet heaves a sigh in the heat.

'No, she's only been there for a couple of weeks. It was someone else before that. Do you not know her?' Stella asks.

'Who, the woman who works there?' Juliet wrinkles up her eyes, peering into the dark of the shop opposite, but the contrast with the bright sunshine makes it impossible to see anything of the interior.

'She'll be over in a bit, when the breakfast trade has gone. It's nice to have some company when business is slack.' Stella lets her head drop back, the sun on her face. 'India this year.' She yawns.

'Hm?' Juliet, distracted by the children gathering at the bus stop across the street.

'Mitsos. He's taking me to India this year,' Stella replies without opening her eyes.

'Wow, lucky you.'

'Didn't you have a friend from there?' Stella asks.

'Pakistan.' Juliet offers the one word, looks up to the square, to the wall around the palm tree where two Asian-looking men sit as they speak.

'Oh yes, that's right.'

'He's in England now. Got a job there.'

They watch a car draw up outside the sandwich shop, spilling out a couple of school children who go in and come out laughing, their mouths inside paper bags, gnawing on *bougatsa* and croissants or whatever their choice has been. They join the group waiting at the bus stop as the car drives off.

'Is your grill burning?' Juliet asks. 'I can smell something.'

Stella jumps up and skips indoors, coming out again in a second and sitting down.

The woman in the sandwich shop comes to her door and looks up and down the street, arms folded.

'Still hot,' Stella calls.

The woman looks across and nods, and one lazy foot takes a step into the road. As she gets nearer, her hands relax and fall by her sides, swinging easily. Her dark chestnut hair is tied in a high ponytail, short, untamed wisps forming a halo around her head, particularly around her ears. Her countenance is open and her eyes inquisitive, moving quickly, taking everything in. There is a containment and a contentment about her.

'This is Juliet from England. She lives here now, bought an old farmhouse.' Stella introduces as she points vaguely in the direction in which the farmhouse can be found. The woman holds out her hand to Juliet.

'Juliet, this is Sophia. She i …' She corrects herself with a smile '*Was* a novice up at the convent.'

Chapter 18

'Hello.' Juliet's face is animated.

Sophia takes a seat, tucking her skirt under her and sitting gently. '*Kalimera*,' she says.

'You think this morning's rush is over?' Stella asks her.

'Hardly a rush.' She notices Juliet's reaction when she speaks. No one expects the husky character to her voice. It's soft and low, and outside the hushed corridors of the convent, she might need to learn to speak a little more loudly. Juliet leans toward her, turning her head slightly to one side. 'Breakfast for fifty hungry nuns, now that's a rush.' Sophia speaks up. When she laughs, that same warm tone that makes her voice resonate has an infectious quality.

The abbess was the first to draw her notice to it. Sophia stood mutely staring at a rather bad painting on the back wall of the sister's office. It was of the mother of Christ and her acrylic indifference seemed to back every word the abbess said. The sermon droned on for what seemed like hours. The subject was Sophia's purposeful intent to lead the other nuns astray with her irreverent humour. The painting gave her a focus. The perspective was wrong and the hands too small. Its awkwardness held her attention until the black-clad sister banged a book on her desk.

'Have you been working long at the sandwich shop?' Juliet asks, pulling her back to the present.

'These last two weeks. But it is getting difficult. I am still living up at the convent until I get something sorted.'

Juliet looks at Stella with a slight frown.

'Sophia's left the convent,' Stella explains.

Sophia doesn't mind the assessing look Juliet gives her; it shows no sign of judgement. If anything, taking time to assess someone must be a good thing, shows an enquiring mind. Perhaps, as a foreigner, Juliet's mind is more open anyway?

'It was time.' Sophia answers the question she suspects Juliet wants to ask.

'So you are halfway between worlds?'

'As long as I need it, the convent is offering me a bed. But getting there and back doesn't make life easy.' Sophia finds speaking loudly all the time takes effort.

'It's a long way. You're not walking every day, are you?' Juliet blinks in the sunlight.

'Anyone want a frappe?' Stella stands. They both nod.

'No. I rely on lifts. I don't like that, to be honest. The first week, I was a novelty and people offered and enjoyed it, but now I feel I am becoming a religious duty, which is exactly what I don't want.' Her voice has become quiet again, but if she keeps trying, it will become a new habit, just like speaking softly became all those years ago.

'I suppose it depends how long you need to do it for. Do you have any plans?' Juliet is so different to anyone she has talked to before. She has an accent, but it is not strong, and there is an assurity about her. As Juliet rubs one of her bare feet on top of the other, Sophia notices the length of her dress. She pulls her own skirt down even though it almost reaches her ankles. The length of her hem is one of hundreds of new decisions she will have to make. Long skirts are impractical, and hot, but after years of being covered up, she feels exposed just showing her ankles. A knee-length skirt would be so much cooler, but then again, her legs are not hairless like Juliet's.

'Yes. My plans are forming.' She answers Juliet's question, but she can see Juliet is waiting for more.

'Here you go.' Stella carries all three glasses clasped together in her small hands. As she puts them on the table, one slides from her grip and both Sophia and Juliet reach out to save it. Juliet reaches it first and she offers it across to Sophia with a smile.

After two weeks of passing food over the counter to customers all day at the sandwich shop, this gesture has a kind quality that touches Sophia. She accepts the glass with a smile and they make eye contact.

'My mama died,' Sophia offers and half-raises a hand to Juliet's unspoken sympathies. 'It was a mercy. My baba died ten years ago and life has been a struggle for her ever since. But it means we inherit what there is, so it seems like the perfect time to change course.' She takes a sip of her coffee and begins to chuckle. 'Besides, Abbess thinks it is "for the best".' Her voice takes on a different quality, as if she is mimicking someone.

Stella giggles and says, 'I met Sophia one time when I went up to the convent. It wasn't an open day, was it Sophia? What was it?'

'I think it was our saint's day. Yes, because we had decorated the church with flowers.'

'Oh yes, of course. Anyway, I went up with Mitsos, and most of the village was there. Mitsos was talking to everybody and, well to be honest, I got little bored, so I wandered around until I heard behind this closed gate someone laughing.' Stella points at Sophia, as if Juliet had not realized who it was. 'Such a laugh, I wanted to know who it was. So I pushed the gate and it opened onto a big vegetable plot. And there in the middle, a spade resting against her legs, was Sophia and she was juggling potatoes, dropping them mostly, and laughing to herself. Can you imagine? The hem of her habit covered in earth, her sleeves rolled up, juggling potatoes and laughing.' Stella throws her head back and laughs herself, her hair softly falling back over her shoulders. 'I think that was it, eh, Sophia? Instant friends?'

'I have to say you were a lot better than me at juggling,' Sophia says through her own laughter. Juliet smiles.

A car pulls up outside the sandwich shop. Sophia hastily puts down her drink and trots across the road to serve. Once she has given the man his coffee, sandwich, and his change, she trots back again. The man does not pull away immediately. He sits in the driver's seat and arranges his drink and food on the dashboard. A taxi turns the corner onto the main street and when it draws level with the car, it comes to a stop. Sophia stands again, ready to move, but no one gets out. The back window of the taxi buzzes down.

'*Yeia*,' says the man from the car, and a voice from the back seat of the taxi repeats the greeting.

Sophia sits again. For a minute, they watch and listen. It's all part of the day's entertainment.

'How's it going, Babis?' the man in the car asks as he gets out.

'Good. Better than good.' Babis also gets out and the two shake hands.

'You hear about the mayor of Saros? Ill, they say. No warning.' He offers a cigarette to Babis. The taxi driver wanders round to join the pair, pulling his trousers up from where they have sunk over his hips. He too accepts a cigarette.

'Ill, they say, do they? I heard it was his mama that was poorly?' Babis sniggers. All three click open their own lighters. 'I don't think that man has been sick one day in his life.'

'His deputy won't hold the reins for long, that's for sure. There'll be a scramble for that seat.' The taxi driver joins in the conversation.

'I heard a rumour that you had something to do with that, Babis?' the car driver says.

'Pah!' Babis exclaims. 'Anyway, come by when you have a moment. With that new baby of yours, perhaps we need to talk over your will again, perhaps? Anytime, okay? See you.' Both he and the taxi driver grind out their cigarettes underfoot and climb back in the taxi and, with a toot of the horn, they pull away. The car driver takes his time to finish his cigarette and drops it down a drain by the curb before getting back into his own car and driving off.

'So the mayor's stepped down, eh?' Juliet says. 'I wonder what all that is about.'

'It won't be straight, that's for sure.' Stella dismisses. 'Whoever is mayor next needs to sort out this problem with the houses. Have they been to your house yet, Juliet?'

'No, and they can stay away as long as they like.'

'They'll be at the convent next,' Sophia adds without a smile and Stella makes a little snort.

'Not likely,' says Stella. 'The Church keeps all the best spots for themselves – the tops of hills are all covered in little churches. It's an amazing view from up at the convent!'

The three of them sit in silence. A dry clonk is heard, followed by another. The first goat into the road comes running, with others following, until the lane is flooded. Stella stands and goes to the edge of the pavement, her arms wide, keeping the goats from knocking the tables.

'*Yeia sou* Sarah,' Stella calls to the shepherdess who follows her slowly moving flock into the square. The woman wears a floaty, plain-coloured dress, her

187

hair is combed back into a ponytail and, most surprisingly, she is wearing lipstick. Something Sophia has not often seen on the farmers' wives who visit the convent. The shepherdess smiles her hello.

'Hi Sarah,' Juliet says in English. The woman with the crook moves with ease, a laziness that suggests contentment. In fact, she has the look of someone truly satisfied. Not just content, but actively happy. Sophia sighs at the sight of her. If one person can live their life in such a state of bliss, then so can she.

The goats stay mostly on the road but when they pass the kiosk, Vasso comes out waving her hands at them, slapping one on its rump when it gets too near her rack of crisps.

'Can you not take them the other way?' she shouts at the shepherdess, who smiles and waves in return, calling out '*Kalimera*' as if she has not heard Vasso's request.

'If you can teach English, then you can teach Greek,' Stella says to Juliet. 'Sarah could be your first pupil.'

'You teach her, Stella. It would do your English good, too.' Juliet tips her head back, the sun on her face.

Sophia wonders how much call there is for a private teacher. It is a possibility that she has not considered. That would give her an income without having to go out into the world too much. It is something worth thinking about.

'Anyway, give her a minute to find her feet first. She's only just moved here.' Juliet stretches as if she has had a hard morning.

'Who's next, that's what I ask,' Stella says.

'Next for what?' Sophia asks, just loud enough to be heard.

'These English taking over our village.' Stella leans towards Juliet and nudges her with her elbow, encouraging a response.

'I have read of villages down in the south of the Peloponnese where there are now more Germans then Greeks,' Sophia says, watching Juliet's face, not sure of how she is reacting.

'They also say there are more Greeks outside Greece than in it,' Juliet returns without emotion.

'I guess people come and go these days, like your friend that rented your room,' Stella says.

'He didn't rent it exactly,' Juliet replies.

Stella raises her eyebrows and looks directly at her. Sophia watches the interchange and expects Juliet to respond, defend herself, but she doesn't, she gives Stella a blank look and turns to watch the last of the goats leave the square. Sophia crosses her legs towards Juliet. It takes someone very sure of themselves not to have the need to defend their honour.

'Do you rent the room now?' Sophia asks.

'No.'

'Will you?' Juliet turns to her slowly as she takes in her meaning. 'Just for a while, a few weeks, until I get on my feet?' Sophia expands.

Juliet does not answer immediately. Stella goes in to check the grill and comes out again.

'I don't think I would rent it; it gets too complicated with the tax laws,' Juliet says after a pause. 'But if you want to stay, for a week or two, you can.'

'Thank you. I appreciate your offer but I would have to pay,' Sophia replies and Stella gives her a swift, non-comprehending look. 'To be honest, I am looking for independence, not charity now. I feel I have had too much of a hand-out being a nun.'

'It's not a hand-out. The people who donate to the church do so to clear their own sins. It's a very important job you do.' There is humour in Stella's voice.

'Did.' Sophia puts it into the past tense.

'Are you good with plants?' Juliet asks. Sophia nods. Stella mimes juggling and giggles. 'Perhaps you can give me a hand with my own vegetable plot in return for a bed.'

Sophia looks Juliet straight in the face, reads her features to see if she is genuine.

'*Kala*,' Sophia says.

Juliet holds out her hand and they shake.

Chapter 19

Looking around the cell that has been her home for the last twenty years, its containment makes the outside world seem very large. Her personal things sit in a small box on the bed. There's a lot of empty space in the box. A last glance and Sophia steps into the corridor. It is the corridor she has walked down a thousand times before, the floor she has swept and mopped, the walls she has painted, the icons she has dusted. There is a numbness building inside her. A sister hurrying along the corridor stops to hug her with a warm goodbye. She tells her she will be missed. But for Sophia, goodbyes have really all been done, and anyway, she will be back once a month to check in with the abbess until she has found her feet.

The abbess is at the main gates and she wishes her, 'Go to the good,' as Sophia steps out over the threshold. With a last goodbye and a turn on her heel, her breathing becomes a little less shallow. Walking to the car, she looks over the plain laid out before her, the village settled under the small hill tufted with pines not far away and then it comes, her first full feeling of the day, and it is one of freedom, and she takes a deep breath. She wants to drop the box and throw her hands in the air and thank God, which seems a little ironic. According to the sisters, it is not a happy day for Him. But surely for her to feel this much joy at the sight of the world and to be this happy that she is in it can only be a good thing. She grips her box tighter. The convent door closes with a thud behind her.

'Is that it?' Juliet asks, peering into the box as she puts it on the back seat.

Sophia shrugs and smiles.

'No, I suppose why would you have anything at all, really?' Juliet looks again at the box, which holds a navy skirt and white blouse, a hand-sewn bag full of her underwear, a bundle of letters, some official papers, and a crisp-looking Bible.

'I guess we will need to go shopping.'

'What for?' Sophia cannot think of anything she needs.

'Well, a purse or bag to keep your money in for a start.' Juliet starts the engine and pulls away from the convent. 'You might want some sandals as well. It's too hot for shoes. Aren't your feet hot?'

Sophia looks down at her flat shoes and thin, short socks.

'I've never really thought about it, but now you come to mention it, yes, they are.'

'Take them off, then.' Juliet grins and changes gear.

'What? Here, in the car?' She must have misunderstood.

'If you want.'

Sophia looks at her feet again. They can stay hot for a little longer. The box on the back seat is a red-hot coal sitting behind her, a solid reminder of what she has done, and the road ahead stretches forever. Her feet really don't get much of a say at this point.

'Anyway, get settled in at my house first; give yourself a bit of time. Things will come to you without having to make decisions.' Juliet glances over to her and back to the road several times.

'I hope so.' Sophia cannot make her voice very loud right now.

They drive down the hill in silence. The scrubland gives way to orchards, houses appear between the trees, and soon they arrive in the village square. Juliet turns to pass in front of Theo's kafeneio and then turns again down a street which opens into a small, unpaved square. She pulls in to a very narrow lane at the far corner of the square. It feels a little unreal and twice, Sophia turns to look at her box, her only anchor right now.

Through a metal arched gate covered with wild climbing roses, the tyres change their sound, crunching on gravel, and they scrunch to a stop.

'What a peaceful spot,' Sophia exclaims. An L-shaped house encloses a patio shaded by a pergola covered in vines. There is a table and chairs at one end and a sagging old sofa covered with throws and cushions at the other. Two wicker chairs face the sofa, with a battered look of age and the wickerwork broken down the legs as if an animal has been scratching at them.

'You thirsty?' Juliet steps off the gravel onto the patio, where she kicks off her flip-flops.

'Not really.' Over the boundary wall are two hills, the one that can be seen from anywhere in the village, and even from right up at the convent, with the pine trees at the summit and a second smaller hill behind it with a rocky outcrop on top. Between the two sits a house where the land hangs down to the top of an olive grove. Inside Juliet's boundary wall, pomegranate trees break up this more distant view. On the patio, plants are arranged in pots. Underfoot, the flags are dotted with lichens. There is so much at which to look. Sophia turns around. The sofa invites her. Behind the sofa, a blue-shuttered window hangs open. A bougainvillea in a pot, bursting with flowers, drapes over one arm of the sofa. She puts her face in her hands and closes her eyes.

'You okay?' Juliet asks.

'Fine.' Sophia sniffs as she draws her hands down her face.

'Fine but crying.' Juliet sits in one of the wicker chairs. The way she does it, slowly and consciously, invites Sophia to sit too, and she sinks gratefully into the sofa. It gives more than she expects and she rolls backwards, her feet lifting from the floor.

'Oh.' The shock is followed by a laugh. 'Deep, isn't it?' She wriggles to sit up and a cat winds around her ankles. 'Hello, cat. Has it got a name?' she asks, but she is not ready to lift her face yet. The tears are wiped away once more.

'That one's Aaman.'

'Amen?'

'No.' Juliet chuckles. 'Aa-man. It's a long story.'

The cat jumps onto Sophia's knee and turns around twice before sitting down and tucking its head and tail in.

'So that's it. You are part of the family.'

Sophia tentatively strokes the cat.

'Can I ask you something?' says Juliet.

'Of course.' Sophia looks up now, her countenance open, ready to be of help.

'How old were you when you joined the convent?'

'Thirteen.' Sophia strokes the cat again.

'Just a child!'

'Well, I was only a novice. I lived there and helped with the chores and went to church and Sunday school.' Sophia leans back, allowing her spine to bend, her uprightness gone.

'Still, very young even to leave your mama.'

She shrugs. Juliet seems to wait.

'I had four sisters and no brothers. On a small island, that's a problem.'

'Oh, where are you from? Not from round here?'

'Orino Island.' She looks up at the same sun that shines there too. 'It never occurred to me that it was a problem. It was a bit of a squash, I suppose, but even that was just how it was. Vetta, Sotiria, Angeliki, Sada, and me. Do you have any brothers or sisters?'

'No.' Juliet is very still.

'It was fun at times.'

'Orino Island is so beautiful. The first time I went there, I didn't believe there were no cars or motor bikes. But once you see how the houses are built on that steep hill above the port and how narrow the paths are between the buildings, you realise that only feet or donkeys would work. Did you live near the port or higher up? Everything is counted in the number of steps to it there, isn't it?' Juliet asks.

'About halfway up the town, past the point of counting steps, I'm afraid.' Her stroking of the cat becomes mechanical and her eyes glaze over slightly as she speaks. She hasn't really thought about home for years. Too far away, perhaps. Too removed from her reality. Vivid pictures return now and the sound of laughter of her and her sisters.

'The house was traditional. You know, where the sleeping rooms have double doors, one leading into another. I suppose they don't build them like that any more. That's how ours was, upstairs anyway, the four rooms in a line. Vetta had the far end room, Sotiria had the next, then the room that had a door to go down the outside stairs was Angeliki's, and then the largest room, I shared with Sada. I say it was the largest room because it had Mama and Baba's old double bed which Sada and I slept in, but it was no bigger than the other rooms.' She gives a little laugh. 'The trunks with our clothes were downstairs.' Her hand pauses over the cat's ears, and it wakes and lifts its head to meet her touch, encouraging her to continue stroking. 'Our room led to the inside stairs that went off and round at an angle.' She uses one hand to vaguely indicate the setup. 'I think it was added on to the main house at some point. We would drive Mama crazy running up one set of steps and down the others, chasing each other in circles.' She takes a deep breath and lets it out slowly before gaining some energy to say, 'But you don't want to hear all this.' She hasn't talked like this for, well, a very long time. It certainly was not encouraged at the convent and, after a while, it seemed sort of pointless. No one was ever going to meet her sisters and she wasn't going to go back. It was just a dream, a distant sweet memory, a contrast to her reality, and after a while, it was as if she lost her will to think of such things.

Juliet, who has been sitting listening without moving, now sits up a little and crosses her legs.

'When I first came to Greece, years and years ago, I fell in love with the place. It took me a long time to make the move to live here and I often wish I had done it sooner so I could have seen so many of the ways people used to live that are disappearing now. Like your rooms that led one into another. So many of the old houses have been pulled down to make way for the new. In Saros town, I have seen timber-framed houses with hand-made bricks that must have been hundreds of years old just bulldozed down in a couple of hours so profit-making flats could be built. I can see the need to make a living, but I think one day Greece will regret it.'

'I don't think much will change on Orino Island. They have strict rules about what can be built and what can be changed. But I imagine, behind closed doors …'

'What was the point of the double doors?'

'I have no idea, just communal, I suppose. We would leave them open and talk to each other although Vetta, being the eldest, would often close hers.'

'Where did your mama and baba sleep?'

'Oh, we had two daybeds downstairs, but they were up first and last to bed, so I never really saw them sleep. Except, sometimes, Baba would fall asleep under the tree in the garden if he had been out all night.' Sophia looks from one of the pomegranate trees to the next. It's nice talking about her family, remembering her closeness to her sisters before the convent, the love, the laughter.

'What did he do?'

'Fisherman. Not the best job with five girls. I mean, it's a useful job if you have a growing family, I think a day did not go by that we did not eat fish soup.' What she would give for a bowl of her mama's fish soup right now. She was too nervous this morning to eat breakfast. 'But it does not make much of a living and they struggled to find us each a dowry.' She looks back to the cat on her knee. The sun has found its way through the leaves and Juliet shifts her chair a little, back into the shade.

'There, you see, dowries. For me, it's hard to imagine anyone, let alone someone younger than me, having a dowry.' Juliet uncrosses her legs, stretches them out. Her full skirt hangs between them.

Sophia notices grey hairs hidden in the blond, the slight sagging to Juliet's face and ever such a tiny hint of a jowl beginning to form, but she cannot age her. She could be anywhere between forty and fifty, maybe even older. How do you tell?

'In the end, they only needed three. For Sotiria, Angeliki, and Sada,' Sophia says.

'Of course, with you going into the church, but what about … Sorry, I have forgotten her name.'

'Vetta. She's the oldest. They did have a dowry for her, and she had her own chest of linen and so on. She dreamed more than any of us of being married. I think it was partly to get away from us all.' A mischievous smile accompanies this last sentence.

'She was the person in the house who did the sewing and mending. She learnt how to make lace and put edges on things.' She wrinkles her nose. It is not so much a look of distaste but of lack of comprehension. 'Anyway, they found a boy and made arrangements and the introductions and within weeks, from being a happy person she gained this gloom, a lack of life. I found it scary. She spent as much time in her part of the house as possible with the doors closed.' She grows still. Maybe talking this much about her family, things from the past is not such a good idea.

'You know, I don't think I have talked this much since, well I don't know when. All these memories are just flooding back like they happened yesterday.' Admitting it makes her feel more easy.

'Well, you are starting a new life, so I guess you will be adjusting. You have only so much experience from which to judge things. It's a big change. Are you hungry, by the way? I have fresh bread from the bakery and some feta. We could pick a tomato or two.' She stands and goes inside, from where she calls, 'I have local yoghurt and olives. That will be enough, won't it?'

'Sounds fine.' Sophia has to wriggle to get her weight forward enough to stand up from the sagging sofa. The cat gives a look of disgust and jumps onto the chair Juliet was sitting on and lies with its legs overhanging at one end and its head lolling over the other. 'Where do the tomatoes grow?' At the end of the house, by the gate and up against the stone building next door, some plants grow in lines, bamboo sticks here and there, and as she gets nearer, she sees the tomatoes between some beans that do not look like they are doing very well. 'Got them,' she calls back. The vegetable plot faces the end of the house, and beyond opens into a garden. There is a pergola creaking under the weight of thick vine stems next to an area of lawn surrounded by an abundance of flowering bushes, geraniums, and more tropical blooms. A passion flower vine covers part of the back fence. Fruit trees are dotted at random on the lawn, offering shade, and a gnarled and crooked olive tree in the centre has a curved bench around it.

'Did you find the tomatoes?' Juliet calls from the front.

'Oh yes. Coming.' She picks and pockets as many as she thinks they will need and returns to find Juliet has laid the table on the patio. 'Beautiful garden.'

'It was a mess when I moved in. Some help getting the vegetable plot in order would be very much appreciated, though. The beans are very sad.' Sophia takes the tomatoes from her skirt pockets. Juliet takes them inside and returns with them glistening wet. They sit down to eat.

'So what happened to Vetta, then?' Juliet asks, tearing off some bread.

'She shut the doors to her room and refused to come out. There was a big fuss about what to do with her. To cut a long story short, she ended up hiding away in Baba's net storage room by the port, to get away from the pressure, I suppose. She's still there now; she turned the top into her home and the bottom into a shop and she sells her lace. Never married.' Vetta always knew her own mind, she was the strongest of all of them. Mama and Baba found more suitors, and with one, it even looked like a match could be made but after walking out with him, it was all over. Her lace-making grew in complexity, she was asked to make things for other peoples' weddings, and as time passed, it seemed her business became more important than her desire to be married.

'And your other sisters?'

'Well Sotiria was the looker, always in front of a mirror. She married a man from Athens and lives in America now. Angeliki loved to cook and she married the son of a taverna owner. There were only a couple of tavernas on the island in those days, so it was good business then and still is today. Now their sons are the waiters. Angeliki is still doing as much of the cooking as she can. And Sada, well Sada married Aleko, a fisherman like Baba, but not like Baba.' She crosses herself three times. 'He drinks, he smokes, the front yard of their house is a tangle of nets that need repair. He goes fishing only when the bills that need paying press him and Sada, and poor Sada takes comfort in a Czechoslovakian piano player from the jazz bar, and everyone knows it except her husband, who is mostly too drunk to care.' Sophia stops talking to bless the food. Juliet pauses in her eating but does not close her eyes.

'So just the three dowries,' Sophia says with a smile.

'And then there was you.' Juliet passes her an earthenware dish of yoghurt.

'Yes, and then there was me.'

Chapter 20

'Yes, and then there's me.' Sophia's voice is quiet. She puts the yoghurt down and does not look up from her food, pushing an olive around her plate with a chunk of bread. After a moment or two, she lifts her head. 'Your garden is amazing, I saw a peek of it when I was picking the tomatoes.'

Juliet seems to melt into her chair. 'It's my oasis,' she replies and the talk turns to plants and soil. When Sophia uses technical terms in Greek, Juliet takes out a notebook, asking her the meaning and scribbling it all down. Their plates empty and their talking slows. The cat jumps onto a chair and begs for crumbs from the table. After a final heavy sigh, they both push their chairs out from the table, laughing because it happens in unison. Juliet stands slowly and offers to show Sophia her room.

'It's off the sitting room here.' Juliet lifts the latch and opens the wooden door. It is a simple room, with a single bed, white sheets, white walls, and a cupboard set into the thick stone wall. It is not so different to her convent cell but there is a jar of flowers on the bedside table and a framed, brightly coloured print on the wall. It is more friendly somehow, lived in.

'There isn't anywhere really to hang your clothes; that's the only problem. Only a hook on the back of the door here with a coat hanger,' Juliet says. The coat hanger, of shiny wood, has a little bag hanging round the hook. She reaches out to touch it. 'Do you like lavender?' Juliet asks. 'It grows by the gate and last year, I dried a load and made those. Pretty, aren't they?'

Sophia leans forward to smell it. 'Lovely.' Sada made little bags like that and put them in the chests. It seems everything is bringing back memories of her life before she entered the convent. She takes a breath as tears prick.

'I am going to lie down for a bit. This time of day gets way too hot for me to do anything. Do nuns take a *mesimeri* sleep?'

'We have a quiet time in our cells. I know I used to sleep.' Sophia keeps her eyes busy looking around the room, holding back the tears, the emotions, the memories, the waste. She crosses herself at her thoughts.

'Right then, see you later. There's a portable electric fan you can take from the kitchen and there's a plug by the bed head if you want it. Let me know if you need anything else.' She heads across the sitting room to a corridor that leads into what looks like an older part of the house.

As it happens, Sophia does not see Juliet until much later. The best solution to the tears stinging her eyes, the emotions bubbling to the surface, the

204

lurking horror to think the years have been wasted is to close them. When she wakes, there is no sign of Juliet. The double doors to her bedroom are closed and so, leaving a note, Sophia sets of for the village square, to work. She took the morning off for her move but must be back for the late afternoon shift.

Few customers venture out in the heat and the afternoon is slow. Across the road, a group of farmers are bantering with Stella. Along with her voice, there is a new noise and after focusing in on the sound, Sophia sees an air-conditioning unit that was not there yesterday. She is pleased for both Stella and Mitsos. They work hard and it must be so hot by the grill. The farmers' laughter grows wilder and louder as the afternoon changes to evening and as the day begins to cool, more villagers emerge. Mitsos spends most of his time behind the grill listening and mopping his brow. From her doorway, Sophia can see him smiling at Stella's words, occasionally turning his head sideways, presumably to look through the interior adjoining door when Stella says something that particularly amuses the farmers. Everything in the way he moves and listens and turns his head betrays his admiration, his love for Stella.

How wonderful it must feel to have someone love you like that. Sophia folds her arms across her chest. To have this empty yearning, this fidgety drive not lurking, sitting, waiting to be ignited by a thought, or a dream, or a word. The feeling has become so much a part of her, sometimes she no longer notices it until her shoulders ache and the realisation comes that she has been tensing her shoulders to her ears, or her jaw is sore and only by opening her mouth can she unlock the stress she has been holding there. To feel at peace, truly content, what that must feel like! Something she never ever found on her knees or in church no matter how much she concentrated, or if she did, it lasted a fleeting second, just long enough to make this hollowness feel worse when it returned.

Mitsos must have sensed her staring. He looks over to her and smiles. She smiles back, her hand lifting to wave but not quite making it. He laughs and turns his head, his attention back on Stella.

At the far end of the square, a priest crosses the road to the corner shop. His long black robe hanging from his rounded stomach, he rocks his weight from foot to foot, leaning forward to climb the few steps to the doorway, pressing hands on knees. The sisters would fuss so when a priest came to visit the convent. There would be a flourish of cleaning and polishing, biscuit baking and a general alteration to their routines. For a while, she was quite excited by such visits, the anticipation of something different. In more recent years, she resented the change in routine, the jolting out of the meditative state that carried her through her days.

It feels like a dream of years gone by but in reality, that was her life just hours ago. Now she is just an ordinary citizen. The thought makes her eyebrows raise. An ordinary citizen. It doesn't sit properly. It's a nice idea, but she feels far from ordinary. Ordinary people live full time in ordinary houses doing ordinary jobs. She is never going to manage that. There seems to be a skill to being social that she just doesn't have anymore. It exhausts her to think what to say at the right time and then remember to say it loud enough for people to hear. She can imagine spending a lot of time on her own in the future.

Back at school, she was social. She would speak out all the time. She didn't have to think, she just did. It was the easiest thing in the world. But then again, maybe it was not the best thing. Maybe Mama was right, maybe that was the problem. Maybe if she had thought more, many things could have been avoided.

Speaking before she thinks. Twenty years in a convent has ironed most of that out.

A car stops by the shop. It's cooler inside, where she makes the driver a frappe and puts a cheese pie into a paper bag, his change on the counter. He leaves it behind as a tip, says he has just got a job, grinning, his legs jiggling as he walks, expending the energy of his excitement.

And how do people cope with the instability of working for other people? The possibility of being unemployed at a moment's notice, no money coming in and no way to bring money in? She too is in that situation now, the convent doors closed firmly behind her. Her shoulders tense and raise. What if the sandwich shop does not make a profit, if she cannot make a living, then what? Her jaw stiffens.

A shriek of laughter comes from the taverna. Mitsos has the sausage tongs in his hand and he is wiping his eyes with the back of his wrist, laughing so much, he is crying.

That's the other side of all this uncertainty perhaps. What she would give to abandon herself and laugh like that, like she did back at school. The fridge rattles as it reaches temperature and the motor switches off. She needs to give the fridge a bit of a clean. Now would be as good a time as any. Keep busy; it is one answer.

The heat of the afternoon gives way to a softening of the light and a slight breeze. A pink hue over the village announces the evening drawing in. The children pour from the bus, coming home from *frontistiria*, the cramming schools where they have exhausted themselves to keep up their grades. They pour into the shop in a tired exuberant mass, buy the last of the cheese and spinach pies. The sausage rolls are gone and there is only one piece of *bougatsa* left.

The lady who owns the house next door to the shop comes out to sweep the dust from the road in front of her house, her white apron stark against her mourning black. She stops just to have a word. She talks of God and the strength He gives her, her eyes drawn to the lone cream-filled pie.

'Thirty years ago, my husband died. You are a nun, you know how to live alone. I do not. It is lonely for me.' Sophia can hardly bear to hear, nods without listening. She cannot think of anything the lady will want to hear so she says nothing.

'You are wise,' the woman informs her. 'I have a daughter. She is a good girl, don't get me wrong, but

208

she is out all the time, making her own life. Which is as it should be. But it is the love I have for her that makes it so painful. My selfishness wants her to stay at home with her mama.' She puts a flat hand on her chest. 'Which is selfish.' The hand lifts from her chest a fraction, her fingers pinched together, and she taps the smallest sign of the cross onto her rib cage, her eyes again wandering to the *bougatsa*. 'But it is God's will that must be done. We manage on what little money I have.' She makes a huge dramatic sigh and rests one arm on the counter.

'Can I offer you the last of the *bougatsa*?' Sophia breaks the ensuing silence and takes the well-worn path behind the counter to put it in a paper bag.

'Oh no, no, no, I couldn't,' the woman protests, her hand outstretched to receive it. 'Things are not that bad. I am just not very good at being lonely.' She takes the bag and Sophia wipes the crumbs from the counter and folds the cloth, putting it in the sink.

'Is anyone?' Sophia asks.

'Ha!' The woman barks her laugh. 'With belief like yours, everything is possible.' She forgets her broom as she walks back to her house with the paper packet. Sophia waits until her front door is closed, then she takes the broom and puts it inside the woman's gate. Back at the shop, she counts the change in her pocket from her tips to pay for the *bougatsa*.

There is nothing left to sell now until the delivery comes in the morning.

Everything is cleared and clean. She makes a note of what sold out first and what they need to order more of, then counts the day's takings and locks the till. A man stops and asks if she is closed, buys a can of beer, so she leaves his money on top of the till with a note so she will not forget what it was for tomorrow.

Outside, she takes a second to admire the fairy lights all lit up round Stella's tree. Is that a vanity, wrapping lights around a tree? It looks pretty, whatever it is. She pulls her stool inside and shuts and locks both the door and the window. The chain around the drinks fridge outside gets stuck under one corner of the door and for a moment, she wonders if she will have to call Mitsos over to help, but it suddenly frees itself. The chain and padlock seem unnecessarily thick and heavy to protect some cans of fizzy orange and colas.

When all is secured, she stops to think, looking up to the smeared grey of the Milky Way. She cannot remember who will be giving her a lift back to the convent today. She puts her hand over her stomach as it turns with a little panic and then she smiles, her hand drops, she pockets the keys, and strolls looking at a million stars in the dark sky, heading towards Juliet's.

The men in the *kafeneio* briefly glance her way as she passes, but all eyes are on a basketball match showing on the television that is balanced in the window of the café, facing out to the square. Tables and chairs have been pulled outside into the cool of the evening and Theo is trotting backwards and forwards across the road with coffees and ouzos. His halo of frizzy hair bobs as he moves, and he is smiling. Always smiling. She has heard that he too is loved but the woman refuses to marry him. The luxury of such a choice.

Her arms and legs feel light and floaty. No abbess to face, no hours of evening prayers in the church that manages to be cold at this time of night even in the middle of summer. No hushed silence in icon-lined corridors.

The front of Juliet's house is lit up with soft orange lamps. It glows in the dark, inviting. Her feet slow and she savours the approach, a ripple of excitement running through her chest.

'Hi,' Juliet calls from the sofa where she is lying with a book. She looks so comfortable.

'Don't get up.' Sophia sits in one of the wicker chairs. The cat that was pinning Juliet's arm jumps off the sofa and up onto her own knee.

'Was work alright?' Juliet puts her book face down over the arm of the sofa and takes off her glasses to put them on top.

'Oh yes, thank you.' It feels a nice question to be asked. 'How is your book?'

'It's a bit dry. It's about Greece, the role the church has played in its history.'

A little of the charm seems to drain from the moment and just for a fleeting second, Sophia experiences a feeling she cannot quite recognise which is aimed at Juliet and her choice of books. Reason states that Juliet's choice of book has nothing to do with her, but the feeling persists, and it dawns on her that the feeling is anger. Her lips part and she makes the smallest of gasps. Her hand flinches, never completing the movement to raise to cover this reaction, but the twitch is a tell-tale sign. Her cheeks glow a little warm and she looks at the floor.

'You okay?' Juliet asks.

'Oh yes, sorry.'

'No, you are not. What is it?'

She cannot blurt out that she is angry that Juliet is reading such a book. How ridiculous that would seem. Besides, what difference does it make to her what book Juliet chooses to read? She takes a moment to let everything settle.

'Walking up here.' She turns to look at the arch over the drive to indicate what she means. 'It all looked so perfect, so peaceful, so inviting that I forgot about the church.'

'Oh, I see. I think …' Juliet sits up a little, moves her book and glasses to the table beside her so she can lean on the arm of the sofa. Something in the way she looks around the patio without really seeing suggests she is going to say more, which Sophia would be glad of. She opens her mouth to unlock her jaw.

'Tell me, did you always know you had a calling for the church?' Juliet's voice is not loud but the question slaps hard. Her head jolts back and her eyes grow wide. 'If you don't mind me asking,' Juliet adds on, but it softens nothing.

Chapter 21

The cat jumps off her knee, trots across the patio, up onto the wall and over the other side, gone. Its absence from her lap, the warm spot suddenly exposed to the breeze leaves her feeling naked, vulnerable. Juliet is not all she seems. Of all the questions she could have asked, she chose the one that cut straight to the heart of the matter. In her one question, she has suggested opening all those closed doors in her mind and her heart to let her life fall out. She can imagine the pitiful contents spread in a thin, transparent layer and there, staring back, exposed for the world to see, the worst sin of them all: her wasted life.

'Sorry, I didn't mean to pry,' Juliet says. But she does not move, she does not break the spell. Nor does Sophia want to let it go. She just needs the courage to speak. Start with one word. Just one, and let what follows follow.

'No,' is all she manages. Her breathing is shallow, there's a knot in her stomach and a tightening in her throat. A film of cold sweat across her brow gathers and a dribble of sweat runs down one temple. She wills herself to say more. 'I never chose it.'

'Oh.' The exclamation from Juliet is light, surprised, inviting more. 'How old did you say you were?' It's an easy question to answer.

'I was thirteen.' It seems like yesterday, so much rushes back at her. 'Vetta was living in the storeroom with the nets down at the port, much to my mama and baba's horror and the gossip of the island. Stamatia had married Yorgos, the half-American, and they had moved to Athens. Angeliki was engaged to Miltos by then and cooking alongside his mama every night in their taverna, and everyone was trying to keep Sada away from Aleko and his bad moods and never-ending bottles. It seemed the island was always talking about us for one thing or another and I was the last straw, I think, for my mama.'

'You? They were talking about you?' Juliet asks.

'Yes, especially about me.' Although it crosses her mind from time to time, most days, she hasn't thought in detail about it for years. It would be preferable not to think, but her past is crowding her thoughts, demanding to be spoken out loud, and Juliet's calm presence makes it feel safe enough to speak. Once, as a nun, she had a pain. It began under her tooth, just a niggle, nothing really, a dull pressure. Her body wishing to rid itself of some minor infection. Ignoring it seemed like the easiest option and sure enough, it went away. Well, sort of. It turned into an earache, only slight, nothing that anyone could do anything about surely? Then it went away all together. It was forgotten about until a lump appeared on the roof of her mouth. It wasn't exactly painful but nor was it pain free, and it affected the way she spoke and the things she ate and it was all she could think about. But still she did nothing, hoping it would come to a head, burst, and let the poisons drain. But that wasn't what happened. After some days, the lump left her mouth and it was natural to believe she was in recovery. Maybe it had popped in her sleep, who knows? The good thing was it was gone. But then the pain started in her throat. It grew worse and worse until she could neither speak nor eat, her limbs lost power, and a doctor was called She was on a variety of tablets for weeks. She spent many days in her unadorned cell looking at the arched ceiling, too weak to do anything else. Sister Maria was her designated aid and she came a couple of times a day with food and to pray with her. Other than that, she was left alone.

'If you had said something sooner, it would have been easier to treat,' the doctor scolded her. 'If the lump was still on the roof of your mouth, we could have drained it, got rid of the poison, and you would have recovered quickly. But now the infection is in your system. It will take time.' Then he packed up his bag and left her to two weeks of silence and solitude and boredom.

This feels the same, but she is not sure which stage of the process she is at. Wherever she is, though, speaking now, draining the poison must be the right choice.

'There was a boy, Hectoras, who was also a cousin, but distant, through marriage. If you look hard enough, nearly everybody is related to everybody on the Island.' There, not so hard. 'I had seen him around all my life but I first really had anything to do with him at school. By the time I had reached thirteen, he showed some interest.' Not hard at all.

'You mean in you?' Juliet asks.

'Yes.' It's getting harder. 'He would come to the house on errands from his aunt. She was a second cousin to my mama, also though marriage. She wanted fish. My baba was a fisherman. Did I say that? With my mama, Hectoras was very polite, correct, but always spoke down to her. One day, when she was out, he sent my sisters away on little jobs.' Speaking the words is becoming painful now. Sophia forces herself on. 'I begged them not to go but he had declared his intentions by then and they thought it was all part of the courtship. His ways were not right. His words were crude.' She looks away across the drive, memories of his bitten fingernails scratching her skin as he pinned her to the wall, his hands forcing their way up her skirts until she kicked him and Sada returned. 'I told them he was not right but I did not want to get into trouble again. I told Sada, and she understood. After that, she did not let him alone with me again.'

'Didn't you tell your mama?'

'She did not believe me.' She looks at Juliet, who has developed a small frown, her shoulders lifting a little, asking for more information. 'I have always spoken out about things, ever since I was small. It is

216

almost like a compulsion. If I see wrongs, I have to speak out. But it has been held against me.'

The smell of the headmaster's office, the stale smoke, the damp walls, the faint odour of ink returns to her nostrils as she begins to tell of that memory. Her mama was called to the school because Sophia had spoken out about an event that was not just and the accused had not liked it. This was her first crossing with Hectoras—Hectoras the bully. All the children knew who he was. They all thought Sophia brave for standing up to him but as it turned out, Hectoras was not only a bully but also the son of the mayor's brother and, to play out his defence, he was also a very convincing actor.

'She's lying.' Hectoras brought tears to his eyes. His father in his new white shirt looking sympathetically at her mama in her Sunday dress, now a little tight after years of wear.

'I am not!' The accusation stung Sophia like a bee. 'He had Yanni pinned on the floor and he spat on him.' Sophia can remember her fists clenching so tight, her nails dug hard into her palms. Her jaw was so clamped, it hurt to speak afterwards.

'I would never do anything so disgusting! What a mind you have,' Hectoras threw back, calm, controlled, condescending, the tears still glistening. He was good.

'Children, children,' the headmaster soothed.

'Perhaps we could ask this Yanni,' Mama suggested. Her own tears were real.

'He is away with the goats now, won't be back … well, my guess is, probably this year.' The headmaster shook his head at this futile line of enquiry.

'We do not teach our sons to spit in my family,' the mayor's brother said. 'If we had such manners, how would my brother have been elected mayor?' The question hung in the room, waiting for an answer, but none came. Sophia knew at this point that the argument was lost and she stared out the window up to the hills, up to the place where Yanni might be, and she wished herself up there too. 'May I suggest that this young girl, Sophia is it?' The smooth tones broke through her reverie and she looked into Hectoras' baba's eyes as he bent to meet her gaze, on her level. He smelt of coffee and a chemical-based perfume. She wanted to cough, put her hand across her nose but did not want to appear rude. 'That Sophia was mistaken.' He straightened himself and addressed the adults. 'Boys will be boys and he comes from a strong family. Maybe what Sophia saw was a little game of rough and tumble and her imagination did the rest.' The headmaster sat down at this point behind his large desk and shuffled papers that looked like they had not been moved for a decade. Her mama glanced at her sharply and Sophia noticed her mama's stomach relax outwards, straining her dress, as though she had given up making the effort to hold it in. Hectoras' baba, sensing his victory, slapped his son on his back, made his excuses, and they marched from the room, leaving an awkward silence between Mama and the headmaster. Sophia's disgust came as bile into her mouth and she ran from the room. Her mama caught up with her halfway home and lectured her about taking a firmer grip on the real world and to stop making such trouble. She was nine years old, and her mama did not seem to believe anything that she had said after that. Sophia prided herself on her honesty, for standing up for what was right, and it stung, her mama's disbelief.

'That's harsh,' Juliet says as she finishes speaking. This is the first time she has had the courage to tell her story to anyone besides Sada and Yanni, and it comes as a huge relief to hear that a stranger can recognise how unfair it was. Of course, in the totality of the world, it is and was a small event, but it was one to have devastating consequences for her later on.

'So that was why your mama didn't believe you later on?' Juliet clarifies. Sophia's arms lay lifeless in her lap, her legs without movement, her whole body slumped in sadness.

'Yes,' she answers softly, readying herself to lance the root of the poison.

Chapter 22

'I am scared to tell you.' The words come of their own accord.

'Don't tell me anything you don't want to,' Juliet advises

'No, I want to, but I don't want you to hold these images in your head, to live with this horror that I have lived with.' Sophia is not sure she intended to say these words but now they are out, it seems only fair to warn Juliet. She waits for a response.

'You know, I have lived through some horrors myself.' Juliet seems unperturbed. 'And I have talked about them.' She exhales as if remembering the times. 'And I thought, maybe even hoped to some degree, that the horror would be transferred to the other person so I would not be alone, so that I could really share it. But the truth is, no matter how graphically you tell it, you can never express the depth of the impact that it has on you. The other person can only guess how it felt for you by relating it to the horrors of their own life.' She takes a breath. 'I may not feel what you felt, Sophia, but it will awaken my own memories and in doing so, I can get as close as it is possible to get without actually experiencing it myself.' She looks from one of Sophia's eyes to the other. 'But you and I will be safe,

Sophia, because it's not happening now.' After a pause, she adds quietly, 'But you don't have to say anything you don't want to, of course.'

The silence that lays between them is like a silk blanket, billowing and shifting as their thoughts flow through them, each in their own world but both waiting.

'I was in the house.' It seems like a safe beginning. 'Mama and Sada had gone down to the port to see Vetta. Baba was out fishing. Angeliki was using the chance to go and see Miltos, at the taverna. The one she married. Sotiria was already married and in Athens. So I was alone.'

Juliet settles more deeply into the sofa. The evening has become night. The moon is full and hangs over the stone barn next door, big and round and glowing white, with coloured rings around it that disappear as Sophia looks directly at them. The sound of animals scratching leaches round the end of the house from the garden. A moment of squealing is followed by quiet.

'Pine martens.' Juliet dismisses the disturbing sound, encouraging Sophia to go on.

'I think it's only fair to say in defence of my mama that I was quite full of myself at thirteen.' In the early days at the convent, she spent hours on her knees telling the Greek Orthodox God the secrets of what seemed like her puffed-up pride and over-sized ego. Even though they concerned her, once in church, they always seemed so petty, trivial, compared to the horrors of the world which the sisters made her aware of and told her she should be praying about. But her attitude before her entry into the sacred walls continued to bother her once inside those quietened chambers and in the end, she sought a private interview and broached the subject with the abbess. The result was a lecture on vanity and the forms it can take. That Sunday, the abbess suggested her focus should be on vanity through prayer, and as a result, she forced herself to stop thinking about such things. She pushed her worries away as weaknesses, things to be overcome by silence, and her prayers, over time, became nothing more than hollow recitals.

Sitting here in the evening, opening up this subject that for years she has pushed aside feels cathartic. Surely even a nun, or now an ex-nun, has to be whole herself before she can be useful to others? The thought drives her on.

'I found school easy. I had picked up English very easily and as a consequence, enjoyed it and studied as much as I could.' Her poor mama, how hard it must have been for her, one daughter living amongst the nets, another playing with fire in the form of Aleko the drunk, and a third rubbing her nose in her ignorance whilst making herself unmarriageable. As Mama herself had said, 'Who amongst the islander's sons wants a girl whose head is full of books and learning as a wife? What good will she be if a rabbit needs gutting, a chicken needs plucking, or a puppy needs drowning?'

Her answer at the time was, 'If there is a man here on the island who would want such a woman as a wife, then that is the husband for me.' So slick, so cocky. Her mama must have despaired. She overheard Baba say to her mama on a couple of occasions, 'Take her in hand.'

But what could she do, really? Her arrogance came from her intelligence, everything coming so easily, how could Mama undo that? But now, if she could, Sophia would do anything to take all her attitude back. Now, when her mama and baba are both dead. Now that it is too late. Then again, over time, who really suffered most?

She unclenches her hands and continues, Juliet listening.

'For example, when I was about twelve, an English professor came to the island to give a talk on Nineteenth century poetry. Only about three islanders attended, the rest were Athenian academics who had come down specially. But I was there, the only child, pretending I understood what I heard. In reality, of course, I was out of my depth. He discussed one English poem, explaining its structure, what it meant. A woman with her hair so perfectly tied in a twist at the back of her head, smelling of soap, shared her book with the verse in it with me. She talked to me like an equal. The conversation thrilled me and she told me to keep the book. It was the most precious item I have ever owned.' She stops for a second, letting the memory of the precious book sink in. 'The fluent English, the in-depth discussion, the new words. I was in heaven. My mama was horrified I had gone. But the horror seemed to me to

223

be fear. Fear of who I was, what I would become. I probably flaunted my learning in her face. I was cruel.'

'Part of growing up,' Juliet offers softly.

'Anyway, that was the situation between us. She didn't trust me and she certainly didn't understand me. They were tense times, and she spent as much of it ignoring me as she could. She wanted me married and gone.' Sophia sniffs, but all she can feel is a cold, hard core grow rigid inside her at the memory. 'On the day I was going to tell you about, she was down in the port seeing Vetta. I was alone in the house and there was a knock on the door.' She looks at Juliet, who appears composed. 'I opened it. The house had a big courtyard, walled all the way around, very private. It was Hectoras, and I was afraid. He asked who was in.

'I told him they were down at the port and to come back later and tried to close the door, but his foot was wedged against it, his chest pressed up against the opening. He said to me something like, "What I want is right here". And I remember noticing that his pupils dilated and he did this funny movement with his tongue. It sort of came out and back really quickly, but it half-turned over as it did. It left his lips glistening with saliva.

'I stepped back, away from him. Which was the wrong thing to do.' The pulse in her temple grows stronger, she crosses her legs, uncrosses them, wraps one foot behind the other as her breath quickens in the telling of the tale. 'He used the gap to come into the courtyard, took the door from my grasp, and shut it behind him.'

'I was firm, Juliet.' Her hands are sweating; she pats them on her knees. 'I did tell him. "I want you to go", I said. I looked to see if I could make a rush for the door and go myself. But he stood before it with his arms outstretched as if he was herding chickens, smiling as if it was a game. I had forgotten to breathe and I suddenly took in a depth breath, the oxygen rushing to my brain making me feel dizzy.

'"We are to be man and wife, you and me, Sophia", he said, or something like that, and I felt my stomach recoil, the food inside heaving, wishing to make a quick exit. "I have asked your mama and baba and they say yes. Why do you think she took Sada to see Vetta with her? She knows I am here. She knows I am come courting. She wants you married, Sophia. I want you, Sophia". And his tongue made that darting, twisting movement, his lips left overly wet, shining in the sun.

'I stepped back further, toward the house. If I could get in there, I could close the door on him. He took another step, his tongue darted again, and I ran, slamming the house door behind me.'

Juliet lifts her head a little as if coming up for air.

Sophia needs some space to breathe, herself. The emotion leaves her voice as she recalls the layout of the house.

'The main room is the full length of the four bedrooms above. Under the floor is the *sterna*, a water holding place, a tank if you like, that collects rainwater from the roof all winter. It was built beneath the stone floor to help keep the house cool in summer. But the *sterna* does not reach the full length. It stops before the kitchen so this part drops lower, a step down takes you into this little room.'

She twists her fingers on themselves in her lap. She has surfaced long enough to continue, and the tension returns to her voice. 'I backed down into the kitchen.' With these words, the moment returns as if it were real.

Her heart was in her ears, the pounding in her chest shook her ribcage. She gasped once for air and then held this breath to be silent, to listen. The securing latch on his side of the door was dropped, shutting her in. Then his feet slid, grit on stone as he took the outside steps, one by one, up to the door that opened into Angeliki's room. Sophia dropped to her knees, her hands together as she prayed that Angeliki had shut the door, bolted it from within, but she knew her prayers would not be heard and sure enough, the door upstairs creaked open. Her heart beating in her ears competed with the rush of blood. There was no door to the kitchen, nothing to close, nothing to bolt. Quietly, each step tentatively placed, she crept back out of the kitchen and pushed as quietly as she could against the downstairs door but it was jammed from the outside too and it would not open. Sweat ran in rivulets down her back, her mouth so dry she could not swallow, strands of her hair plastered to her sweating face.

Bare boards made up the floor of the rooms above, over wooden beams set in to the thick stone walls. With each step he took, the old wood creaked in complaint, gave a little. His steps were slow, as if he was looking around as he moved. He was in no hurry. When his steps reached Sophia's room at the end, they paused. She wished she had been tidier, put her comb into the drawer, closed the book she was reading—a book of poetry lent her by an English woman who lived in town. She shivered at the thought of him touching her bed, his fingers on her nightgown. Then the stairs in the end room creaked as he came down. Step by step down to the ground floor.

The walls in the kitchen were nearly as thick as the length of a man's arm, to keep the house cool in summer. Silently, Sophia struggled to reach the window catch. Even if she could reach it, the window was too narrow to allow her hips to pass. From the corner of her eye, she saw him enter the end of the room, silent, black in the shadowed interior. All the windows small, to keep out the sunlight, the heat. The long room in gloom. His silhouette advancing.

She retreated into the darkest corner of the kitchen. Her hands reaching out, finding support, keeping her legs from collapsing. Her fingers feeling until they touched her baba's big fish gutting knife on the chopping board. They closed around it. Her grip was sure. He stood in the kitchen doorway. With one move, she flashed the blade in front of his face. His tongue darted and then he chuckled. She waved it at him again as she came out of the corner, but he seemed to have no fear.

He did not see the step down. One foot caught behind the other. His head leading, his shoulders following. His legs trailing. It was a lunge that looked like an attack. But really, it was a fall. All Sophia could focus on was his darting tongue. Her hands raised in defence. They lay on the floor together. Sophia wriggled and kicked but found little resistance. As she pulled herself free, there was a strange gurgling sound. She could see nothing in the dark. Her legs took control. She ran to the other end of the house. Two stairs at a time, past her bed to Angeliki's room. Door flung open. Hand against the whitewashed wall, two stairs at a time down to the courtyard. No one following. Eyes focused on the door to the street. But behind the house door, the sounds inside quiet but alarming. Her heartbeat did not slow but it changed its rhythm. The adrenaline coursed, but for a different cause. The sounds from inside were like tiny waves trapped in pockets of rock, or donkeys drinking, their noses submerged. It was a sound that should not be coming from a man. With quivering fingers and legs ready to take flight, Sophia unbolted the door, expecting to find him still on the ground. He stood tall, legs stiff, arms by his side. For a moment, nothing made any sense. His shirt had a red streak down it. He was grinning, or so it seemed, his mouth partially open. His tongue darted, half twisting, half not, truly reptilian. He struggled to form her name 'Ssssooph…' The rushing through her ears defended her. The blade of the knife piercing the roof of his mouth. His twisting tongue divided. His jaw forced open. The sun reflected off the blade behind his teeth. The fish knife handle coming from under his chin. The blood coursing from there down his neck to the opening of his shirt.

He shook his head as if to pity her, his eyes only leaving her to see the door in the walled courtyard open and Sophia's mama come in.

'Oh my God what have you done?' Mama rushed to Hectoras as he chose that moment to sink to the floor. Sada was behind her mama, her own mouth open, unable to move.

'Don't talk. For goodness sake, don't talk.' Mama held Hectoras as best she could as he sank further to the ground, his head resting on her knee. 'Sada, run, get the doctor.' His shirt was reddening more rapidly now, his face whitening. 'Oh my God, Sophia, what have you done?' Mama shouted and held his head, rocking back and forth. No words would come from Sophia.

'But he looked at me, a glint in his eye as if he was enjoying himself. I hated him with such a force at that moment, I thought I must be the devil himself.' She looks up abruptly. 'I think I need some water.' Sophia stands.

Juliet's head moves but her eyes are unfocused.

'Yes please,' she says, as if surfacing from a trance.

The water refreshes them both.

'Did he die?' Juliet finally finds her tongue.

'The doctor came and I told them what happened.' She tosses her head back and sucks her teeth as if it was pointless to have related anything. 'The doctor nodded wisely and gave Hectoras some injection which seemed to make him go even more floppy, and then he pulled the knife from his throat. I saw the blade end pass through his mouth before coming out under his jaw. The doctor muttered something like, 'Thank goodness the knife wasn't serrated.' Sada fainted, so I dealt with her. When I turned back, Hectoras was lying flat out on the floor with his wound stitched up. Mama was staring at me wildly and the doctor was gathering his things.

'He'll live,' was all the doctor said as he left and then all hell let loose.

Chapter 23

'What in God's name did you do?' Mama screamed at Sophia. In that moment, her world fell away, she felt so alone, so utterly abandoned. Having just experienced the most petrifying event of her life, she now needed her mama to hold her tight, to tell her she was all right. In the kitchen, a puddle on the flagstone floor marked where she had stood as he walked towards her and all she needed now was reassurance that she was safe. But what she got was her mama's arms flying around as she screeched at her.

'Here he is, a fine boy,' she shouted, waving her hands over Hectoras in his drug-induced sleep where he lay, still on the courtyard floor. 'He comes courting you and what happens? You attack him with the fish knife. Are you mad? Has all that book learning scrambled your brains?' she yelled, not caring who could hear them over the courtyard wall. The tears welled in Sophia's eyes. She would have run to Sada, but Sada was lying down, recovering from her faint. Sophia needed someone, right now anyone, who would put their arms around her and tell her she was all right.

'Mama …' she began.

'Don't you Mama me!' She backed away from her youngest daughter, her arms extended towards her, palms out, warning her off. 'You are no child of mine. You are the devil's spawn.' The dam burst and Sophia's thirteen-year-old tears ran down her face. The world was suddenly too big and scary; she wanted to hide like an infant in her mama's bosom, be lulled by her words, be comforted by her love.

'And now you cry as if you have emotions? You had no emotions for this boy as you stuck him with your knife, did you?' Her mama's eyes were wide, the whites showing around her irises. This too was terrifying.

'But Mama,' Sophia began again, her whole being surging up into her throat and coming out in these words.

'He was here, willing to marry you. You who have filled your head with such nonsense that no one would want you, you that walks as if you are better than all of us, but still, Hectoras was willing to court you. If you didn't want him, why could you not just run and live amongst the nets like Vetta? No, you have to even upstage her. There will be no keeping this quiet, Sophia. You have gone too far, you are done for. No one will have you now. You will die an unloved old maid.' And with these words, she left the courtyard, the door left swinging on its hinges behind her.

'I looked at his body lying there, stitched up, the wounds on display. If I had not decided to fight back, my wound would have been invisible. No stiches to show. No horror to illustrate his actions. No slander would come his way. Instead he would gain a wife, a subservient, scared wife, who would be his servant for the rest of his life.'

Hectoras lay there, a bloody wound under his neck and with his wound and the lies he would tell to accompany it, he held any future Sophia may have had in his bullying grasp. She watched him breathe, part of her wishing each was his last. At least then, there would only be her side of the story told. But each breath was followed by another until her mama returned, bringing with her Hectoras' father and some other men who carried him away as he slept on. Sophia's mama held her eyes to the ground and never spoke a word. No one looked at Sophia. When the door in the courtyard wall closed, Sada came out of the house.

'What happened?' she asked, her hand on the wall, still not sure on her feet.

'Your sister here will have to spend the rest of her life on her knees to make amends for the sin she has committed.' Mama spat, grabbing at a broom to sweep the crushed, deep pink, bougainvillea leaves from the spot where Hectoras had laid.

'What happened, Sophia?' Sada's words came out kindly.

'He pushed his way in ...' Sophia began.

'He pushed his way in ...' her mama mocked. 'He would not have had to push his way in if you had had the sense to invite him in. His uncle is the mayor, you know. It was a match most girls would die for.

You are done for, Sophia. You must ask God to forgive your wicked ways. No one else will listen to you now. Maybe even He will turn his back on such an evil deed. What on earth possessed you?'

'Sophia?' Sada questioned, but it seemed pointless for Sophia to tell her side of the story. Her mama had made her mind up.

'So you see nothing but evil in me then.' Sophia ignored Sada's question and responded to her mama's jibes. The world was devoid of all joy and in that moment, Sophia wished she was dead. She wished she was up in the hills with goats. She wished that she was anywhere but where she was.

She turned on her mama. It was her turn to shout; she had nothing to lose. 'If I read, that is evil. If I think, that is evil, and if I don't want to be married to a bully like Hectoras, I am evil. Nothing I do pleases you. What do you want of me, Mama? You don't want me to be me, so what do you want? I have cut down the amount I read because it makes you unhappy that I know things. I don't speak out when I see injustice take place because you don't want me to bring attention to the family. I hardly ever go out anywhere for fear of shaming you. But still you are not satisfied. Do I have to become a nun before you think any good of me? Is that it? Is that what you want, you want me to be a nun? Then fine. I'll be a nun.'

And with these flippant words, she ran up to her bedroom, pulled her precious poetry book from under the mattress, and ran from the house up to the pine trees and beyond. Up to Yanni, the boy Hectoras had spat on all those years before. Yanni, who was kind and caring. Yanni, who did have a brain and did not need an uncle as a mayor to make him interesting. Yanni, her friend. More than a friend even, in her heart at least, and she knew where she would find him.

He was there collecting firewood. At first, Sophia could not talk to him, she was so upset. She knew that what had happened was not going to go away easily and something would come of it. More than anything, she wanted to be climbing the trees with Yanni like they did the year before, free of any worries. She also wanted to be in the lecture room with the woman with the perfect hair, talking about poetry. She wanted to combine the two. How could she explain to Yanni how learning made her feel as if she could conquer the world? Was there any way to explain that there was a life beyond de-scaling fish and cooking and being a wife? If she could explain that to anyone on the island, then he was the one person who would understand, but with all the emotions coursing through her, she didn't know how to find the words.

She held the book of poetry to her chest and looked in his eyes. He asked nothing, he just stayed still with her. Eventually Sophia opened the book. She thought if she read the verse she had learnt about, he would understand everything. But when she looked at the words, they blurred behind the tears. Something terrible was going to happen because of Hectoras and there was no way to avoid it. She suspected it would be a while before she would see Yanni again. At the very least, she would not be allowed out unescorted. At the very least.

Taking a pencil from her apron pocket, she drew a ring around the verse that had given her such pleasure, that had filled her heart and set her free even if for just a brief moment, and then she gave the book to Yanni for safekeeping. Then without a word, she turned and ran. She left what was good and pure safely in the trees and she ran back down into town to face head on whatever was coming her way. All she could hope for was that Yanni would read the poem and realise her love for him. If she was betrothed to him, maybe it would save her. Of course she could not ask him. She had to wait for him to ask her. The intellectual jump necessary to escape that tradition was beyond even Sophia.

By the time she returned home, what had happened had already been gossiped around the town, the story changing on its journey, the crime becoming an increasing form of amusement, the events more comical until by the evening, there was such shame in the event for Hectoras, the story being told—that he was gutted like a fish by a child not even old enough to be called woman—was so demeaning that his uncle, the mayor, sent a rumour out amongst the town that Sophia was to be tried for attempted murder, which certainly stopped the sniggering but only fuelled the gossip.

236

Sophia's mama and baba were distraught, and even Vetta came up from amongst the nets for a night. Baba told Mama to go and plead with the mayor not to press charges, to say that she would send Sophia to go to live for a while in repentance in Saros convent. Sophia overheard her baba and protested most strongly, which only made them more determined. The more she protested, the more adamant they became.

The next day, before it was fully light and certainly before the mayor could give his answer to the proposed solution, Sophia was taken by fishing boat all the way up to Saros and from there, she walked with her mama's priest up to the convent. As they planted one foot in front of the other, climbing the hill to the convent, Sophia was given to understand by the priest that once the whole thing had died down and people had mostly forgotten about her, she could probably return. He rapped hard on the convent door and they were both quickly ushered to the abbess, where the priest requested that Sophia be taken in as a form of mercy.

For a while, Vetta wrote and even suggested in one letter that that the mayor never really intended to prosecute anyway, that he had said what he had said to stop the people laughing at his nephew and really, he thought their mama's course of action was an overreaction. It gave Sophia hope that she would return home soon. But her mama, on the other hand, wrote, using Vetta's hand, only the once. Her letter made it clear that she was convinced sending Sophia to the convent was the best thing she could have done and that Baba agreed. There was no mention of Sophia's return.

As Sophia finishes telling Juliet her history, she does something that surprises even her. She kicks off her shoes and becomes lost in the deliciousness of the evening breeze blowing its cooling wind between her toes.

'That's a really, really bad reason to become a nun. How come you stayed?' Juliet asks.

Sophia snorts.

'I was thirteen. You have no say in your life at thirteen. The nuns were so warm and friendly when I first arrived. They had lots to tell me, mostly about how they saw life, and for the first few weeks, it felt like a warm place full of things to learn and I kind of liked it, although I missed Sada and Yanni. But when I discovered I was not allowed out of the boundary of the convent walls and it dawned on me that I would not see my sisters or Yanni probably for weeks, months maybe, I became at first very upset and then uncontrollable. I felt my life was being stolen away. I got angry and my temper would explode over the least little thing. The sisters prayed for me and then one day I was called to the abbess' office. She explained nothing. I just stood there and the phone rang. It was my mama. Just for the briefest moment, I thought I was going home and then the abbess explained to my mama that I had a demon within me and that she had been wise to take the action whilst I was so young because it gave them a chance to put things right and perhaps it was best if I did not return immediately.' Sophia's head drops forward as she recalls the event.

'It's beyond imagination,' Juliet says and they sit in silence, each with their own thoughts.

'Do you know you cannot prove yourself to be sane?' Sophia says at last. 'I was watched by all of them. They reported back to the abbess. Some of the nuns were kind, others appeared to be kind, but they threw a skew over things when they reported back. Others were plain mean.'

'You were told what they said?' Juliet asks.

'Oh no, not individually, but I was given a summary every so often and it was easy to work out who had said what. For example, I would only tend the vegetable garden with Sister Evangelia so when the abbess related back that the energy and aggression I used when I dug could only come from deeply held anger, then it was obvious who had done the reporting. But I couldn't win. If I dug with energy, the demon was showing its face. If I dug with lethargy, the demon was draining my spirit. It was the same with the mending. We had rotas to darn and mend things. I am not a seamstress and I hate sewing, so this was the demon in me. If I put in some energy, that was the demon trying to trick them. I tried so hard to be perfect so I could go home. If I managed it, I would hear the whispers, the demon was dormant, biding its time, waiting, the nuns should be more aware and then they would socialize with me less and less until I could bear it no more and I would cry and ask them why they were being so mean. This was met with even more caution, as if it was a trick until I would finally not be able to hold back my frustration any longer and I would shout at them not to be so unkind, and it was as if the whole convent breathed a mutual sigh of relief, as if to say "Ah, there is the demon. Now we can see it again". And the nuns would be kind and considerate again and show me affection. It became a terrible cycle.'

'It sounds unbearable,' Juliet admits. A frown flits across her brow. 'I was married for years to a guy called Mick. Irish. We had two boys. Well, starting when they were ever so young, Mick would find things to complain about. Like why there was still washing up in the sink when he got home, that sort of thing. I would try to explain that I had had a heavy day with the boys. He would scoff, tell me that every other mother could manage their children and the washing up, so what was wrong with me, and it slowly became his phrase. "What's wrong with you?" So if I was even just tired, he would ask, "What's wrong with you?" like an accusation. If he asked his mother round to baby sit with no warning and then told me to get ready to go out, if I said I didn't want to go, he asked "What's wrong with you?"' Juliet sighs, as if, even though it was years ago it still exhausts her.

'It was insidious. And after a while, six months or so, I started to believe that something really was wrong with me and I went to see a doctor. He said there was nothing wrong with me and why did I think there was? I thought his next words were going to be "what's wrong with you?"' She stops to smile at her own joke but quickly continues. 'I told Mick the doctor said I was fine and he sneered and shook his head. "You don't get it, do you?" He made me feel I was crazy. I got more and more tense around him and in turn that made me do stupid things, become clumsy, forget things, overreact. And each time, he pointed it out as evidence. I really thought I was losing it. Eventually I accepted how useless I was and so I stayed with him, thinking I was in the safest place for someone like me.' Juliet lifts her chin, looks beyond the wall up to the far hills. 'So although I have not experienced what you have experienced, Sophia, I know what it is like to be convinced you are crazy and how that can keep you from moving forward. But you were so young, it's amazing you didn't actually go crazy.'

'I think I probably did a bit.' She looks at Juliet, seeking signs on her face of her own life's ordeals. But her features are open and kind and she looks back, waiting for Sophia to say more. It would be nice to hug Juliet to take away any remnants of her hurt. Why not; she would not feel any worse with someone else's pain on top as she does now.

Sophia finds her face is wet. She sniffs. Juliet springs from the sofa and, within seconds, she has returned from inside, placing a box of tissues on the table between them as she sits down again. She takes a tissue herself and pushes them nearer Sophia, looking at her intently, listening.

'I just counted the days until I would be eighteen,' Sophia says. 'I was nearing my fourteenth birthday when I arrived at the convent. It was near my fifteenth birthday when I overheard the telephone conversation to my mama. So I started to count the days until I would be eighteen and I could leave. It was all I could think to do. Mama had stopped writing. Sada had enough problems of her own with Aleko, and Angeliki was all about her marriage. Only Vetta wrote occasionally, and I had no stamps to reply.'

'Yanni?' Juliet asks.

'Ah, Yanni.' Sophia takes another tissue. 'I planned to leave the convent when I was eighteen and they could not stop me. I wanted to get married. I desperately wanted to have lots of children that I could love and care for, to show them the love that children should have, make their worlds safe for them. The days dragged longer and longer as the time drew near. The seasons in the vegetable garden helped me through. Then my birthday was just a month away, so I took a big step and I wrote to Yanni. He was the only person who I felt understood me. And my feelings for him never left me.

'I told him what felt like the truth at the time. I told him I had always loved him. I told him I waited for him when I was thirteen to rescue me and that I would wait again for him to come, that I was of age.' She takes another tissue. 'I probably wrote too much, said too much, but I felt so desperate. My parents had not been in contact for years, so I could not return to them. Being eighteen gave me the freedom I wanted, but I had no place to go and no skills to go with. I wanted to leave but to go where, do what? The only role that had ever been laid out for me was that of a wife.'

'Did Yanni write back?' Juliet asks.

'No,' Sophia says quietly and takes another tissue.

'Oh.' Juliet pulls her legs from the floor and tucks them under her.

'Maybe he never got it. I asked a woman who used to come up often from the village for a stamp, but when I asked her to post it, she said I must ask the abbess, which I did and she agreed to it. At the time, it felt like my one hope and as the days passed and no reply came, I realised Yanni didn't want to know.' Sophia sniffs in defiance. 'I considered leaving the convent by myself, but where would I go?' She looks directly at Juliet, who shrugs. 'On the island, everything is done through who you know. The jobs in the shops and tavernas, the renting of houses, everything is word of mouth, and away from the island, I knew no one. So I gave in and I tried to progress from being a novice to becoming a nun. But the abbess, thankfully, never thought me fit to become a tonsure. It has only been through getting to know Stella, who knew about the job in the sandwich shop, that I saw a way out now. That and my mama passing.' She crosses herself. The tears dry up.

'Mothers have a lot to answer for,' Juliet says flatly.

Chapter 24

'There's a power cut,' Sophia announces as she trots back into the drive less than an hour since she left Juliet's. The days since she first moved in with Juliet have spun by, and it feels like she has known Juliet forever. They have talked into the early hours of the morning nearly every night. Talked about her, talked about Juliet's brave and slightly crazy move to Greece. They have talked about cultures and education, English and Greek. Every new dawn, her eyes have been tired and have not wanted to open but her spirit has leapt from her bed ready for a new day. The days, with no hours of prayer and no strict adherence to routine, feel long and full of things to learn. Just being in the world, watching, feels fulfilling enough. 'All day. It's official,' she adds. 'The kafeneios are empty but Stella is busy. She only needs her grill, and Mitsos has brought his generator down from his house. It's like the whole village is in there. As for the sandwich shop, the fridges are off, there's been no delivery, so there's nothing to sell. The owner's wife came, told me that the pies have not even been baked so I should lock up and go. I have the day free.' Sophia kicks off her shoes, holds her arms in the air, fingers spread, and causes the cat to jump from the wickerwork chair in fear of her outburst of energy.

'Oh, sorry cat.' She lowers her arms.

'I know. No computer. I didn't leave it on to charge, so no work for me, either.' Juliet puts her book and glasses down. 'I don't think I'm going to finish that book.'

'You want a frappe? Oh no, well yes. I could make it by hand?' Sophia goes inside.

'No thanks. You know what, let's go into Saros, wander around like tourists. We can go for a coffee there. Sit and watch the world go by?'

Sophia stands in the doorway.

'Don't look so scared. It's only coffee in Saros.' Juliet laughs.

Saros is busy. The roads through the centre are closed off, men beyond the barriers are on hands and knees laying a pattern in bricks; it is all being pedestrianised. Juliet is not ruffled by it. She takes a left into a maze of roads and they come out by the water's edge, where they park the car.

The long harbour front is lined with gleaming white yachts. The clicking of the halyards against the masts takes Sophia back to her childhood, to the port on Orino, filled with the yachts of the rich. Yanni there with his baba and their one donkey, Suzi. She will be old now. He will be older, too. The yearning in her chest catches her unawares and her vision blurs. She keeps strolling, Juliet by her side, but she looks away from her, towards the town. Parallel to the quayside is the main road to the old town, and on the other side of that is a strip of grass dotted with bushes and flowers that edge the endless line of street cafés on the other side. From here a hum emanates, a burst of laughter every few seconds. The world is alive and people are happy. Sophia blinks away the tears and smiles. She is part of this now; she will find her place.

'I like these cafés by the harbour, but once you are sitting down, you are too low to see the sea. Are you all right if we go into the town and sit in the main square?'

Sophia shrugs. It is all new to her. Everything is all right as far as she is concerned. Where the yearning was a moment before, her stomach flips with excitement. They cross the road and walk up a narrow alley that brings them out into an open square that is heaving with people. Around the square's perimeter are chairs and tables sprawling out of cafés; in the middle, preschool children run and shout and kick balls. A woman stands clutching a huge cluster of bright, metallic-coloured balloons in the shape of dolphins and zebras, and some that look like a square sponge with eyes. There's a floating dog, a goldfish with black and white stripes on its orange body, a yellow smiling face. High above them, one of these balloons floats in the still air. There will be a child crying somewhere for the loss. Sophia's eyes return to earth, looking for the bereft child, but all she sees is people smiling, children laughing, joy everywhere.

'Here, this is the place I prefer.' Juliet heads for a café whose tables and chairs are littered under the spreading arms of a huge plane tree. Some of the branches are so old and heavy, they have wooden supports keeping them from bending to the ground.

'Is it safe?' Sophia asks, but she is not serious; there is nowhere she would rather sit. 'Here?' She chooses a chair turned to face the square, from where she can see everything.

'Sure.' Juliet sits, lithe, like a cat, her hips sliding between the table and chair; first her upper body and then her legs following. She kicks her shoes off even though they are out in public. There's no denying the excitement Sophia feels and it is just from being here in the square, alive, free. Yes, definitely from being free.

'Do you think you would have stayed the rest of your life in the convent if you had not met Stella?' Juliet asks once they are seated. Sophia is watching a boy with a ball who is using the people walking through the square as obstacles to be dribbled around. No one seems to mind. She hears Juliet's question but she does not really want to think about it.

A child with matted hair and a dirty face stands by her shoulder with its hand held out.

'Oh!' Sophia exclaims at the sight of her. That was one thing that always amazed her about the nuns, and which seemed to contradict their Christian beliefs. They firmly believed other people were different, that the Albanians were not like them, that the Romanians didn't feel as they felt, that the Gypsies had no hearts. It was as though they felt that the Greeks, the followers of the Orthodox faith, were somehow elevated. After years of listening to these attitudes, Sophia catches her first reaction to this Gypsy child, and it is one she classifies as repulsion, but her strength of logic tells her, on second analysis, that it is fear. Fear of the unknown. The child looks so far removed from any experience she has ever had.

'Give me a euro,' the child recites in a whining voice, but its eyes flick left and right, fear betraying the pretence of need. Sophia fumbles in her skirt pocket and finds a two euro piece. She looks up to give it to the child.

'Go.' The waiter speaks firmly and marches at the child. It takes one look at him and runs.

'Now madams, what can I get you?' The waiter keeps one eye towards the square, checking the Gypsy does not return.

'Do you have electricity?' Juliet asks.

'We have a generator for such times, so what will be your choice? We have everything.' His attention is still on the Gypsy child who is edging near a customer sitting further along.

'Right, I will have a freddo,' Juliets states. 'Oh and a toast. No ham, just cheese please.'

'What's a freddo?' Sophia asks, also watching the Gypsy child. The people she was edging towards are waving her away. The child's face is rigid, as if their dismissal has no bearing on her. It does look like she has no heart, but how terrible that such young life has been so hardened. Surely she would respond to love and encouragement like any other child, so equally she must be affected by cold indifference and worse. The poor child wears no shoes, her t-shirt is torn, and her shorts are very dirty.

'It's kind of a coffee milkshake I suppose, creamy and cold,' Juliet clarifies. 'Can I have caramel syrup with mine please?' The waiter nods.

'I'll have the same,' Sophia says. Right now, she could take on the world. The waiter moves off and within seconds, the child is by her side again, its hand held out, its head turned to follow the waiter's course, legs twitching, ready to run. She cannot be more than five, maybe six years old.

'Here you are.' Sophia gives her the coin. 'Where are your mama and ...' But there is no point in finishing the sentence because the child runs off.

'You cannot save them all.' Juliet has sunk into her chair, looking comfortable as always. Sophia tries to do the same, but she feels she is sliding and sits up straight. 'So do you?' Juliet asks.

'Do I what?' The Gypsy girl has reached the other side of the square and is approaching a group of tourists. So tiny.

'Think you would have ever left the convent?' Juliet links fingers across her stomach.

Watching the Gypsy being waved away by the tourists in their new clothes, designer shoes on their feet, Sophia considers Juliet's question.

'It was a constant question in my mind. Once I had come to terms with that fact that Yanni was not going to write back, not going to come and rescue me, my constant question was how could I leave? I had no money, one dress and one skirt, and the nuns thought I was possessed by a demon.'

'Were you an official nun—you know, ordained?' Juliet asks, her head turned to watch a toddler on a tricycle being chased by his baba.

'No, I never became ordained. I tried to go down that route for a while. In my early twenties, when I realised it would not be so easy to leave. For a while, I even believed it was my calling, but the abbess was not to be conned. Thank goodness.' She laughs. Juliet smiles, a lazy smile that grows as their coffees are delivered.

'Your toast is coming,' the waiter tells them and turns to invite a couple standing arm in arm to take a quiet seat around the far side of the tree. They follow his lead.

'So they let you stay anyway?' Juliet asks.

'I worked like a horse in that garden. I knew the seasons; the things I planted flourished. The garden kept my spirit alive and the food I produced kept the nuns alive. They weren't stupid.'

'So do you think you would have, then?' Juliet asks.

'Would have what?' Sophia asks.

'Stayed.' Juliet laughs.

'Oh, right. Well, I think the fact that I have left proves that I would not have stayed, if you see what

I mean. If you look for something, I think you find it. I was looking for a way out, so I found it. A bit late perhaps but now, I am here!'

'And your parents dying? Has that helped? Sorry that sounds terrible, but you know what I mean.' Juliet has ditched her straw and sports a freddo moustache.

'Ah. Well I'm not sure, really. Vetta will keep her shop in the port, no matter what the will says. Sotiria, well, she is in America, so I don't suppose she is interested at all in the old house. Angeliki has no need for anything. The last letter I got from Vetta was to say that Angeliki was opening another taverna down the coast on the island. They have bought and done up an old ruin there apparently and have boats to run customers back and forth to the town. Vetta said the waters are very deep not far from shore there so the big yachts can anchor, and it has become the place for the rich to dine. So that leaves Sada and me.' Sophia sighs.

'Sada with the drunk husband,' Juliet says. The toasted sandwiches arrive and she sits up, pulling the crusts off and eating them first. Sophia makes a small prayer, just a thank you, but it no longer feels like she is praying to the God that lived in the convent. This new God is more generous, more at one with nature. Bigger.

'Yes, Sada. She has her own home, so she won't want to live in the old house, but I am hoping she will not want to sell it. I think Aleko would just drink a lump sum away until he is dead, which would

252

leave Sada with nothing. But if I live in it, what will I do for money? To those who know me, I am the woman who stabbed Hectoras. They will not employ me. Those who don't know me will not give me a job because they don't know me. So I am thinking maybe I can rent the house. This might give Sada money to pay her bills and me money to live on. What do you think?' Sophia cuts her sandwich halves into quarters. 'But of course that leaves me nowhere to live.' She takes a bite.

'Do you want to go back to live on the island?' Juliet chews and swallows.

'Well, in truth, there is no reason to. But then, where else do I know? Also, I need to know for sure.'

'Know what for sure?' Juliet asks, pausing before she takes another bite.

'About Yanni.'

Chapter 25

'Yes, tell me more about this Yanni.' Juliet uses her tongue to dip into her cup, curling around the side of the glass at the caramel syrup sticking there. 'Oh sorry.' She stops and licks her lips. 'That must have looked disgusting.'

'Were you a wild child, Juliet?' Sophia asks, smiling.

'What's with the "were"?' But she lowers her chin and looks up at Sophia as if she is a little ashamed.

'At least you didn't get sent to a convent.' Sophia laughs, encouraging Juliet to do the same. The huskiness is contagious, and Juliet joins her despite herself. The people at the next table give slightly disapproving stares, and one of them tuts, the leaves of the plane tree dappling all their faces.

'I think life always tries to find a way to chip the edges of the fiery characters.' Juliet finally stops laughing long enough to speak. 'I think if it fails, those are the people who have the energy and enthusiasm to make big impacts on the world, business creators, charity organizers, stars.' Sophia nods her agreement. 'The rest of us have been through the mill to such a degree, we are just happy to be alive and no longer wish to climb to great heights. We just appreciate what we have.' Juliet uses

254

her little finger to get the last bit of caramel sauce from inside her glass. She licks it off her nail, then uses a serviette to wipe her hands. 'I'm such a pig,' she says.

'An appreciative pig,' Sophia agrees.

'So. Yanni.' Juliet slides down into her chair again.

'Yanni. How do I tell you about Yanni? He was a man, well a boy then, I suppose, who appreciated what he had, and he didn't have much. When we started school, he shone. He was the fastest at learning. He knew the alphabet before anyone else, he could read before anyone else, and then he was gone.'

'What do you mean "gone"?' Juliet turns her head, the static in her hair making it stick to the seat, curling up behind her where she slouches.

'He was a shepherd. His baba had a huge flock of goats and sheep, and come lambing or kidding time, he would have to help out. So he would start school in September, be there a few weeks, and then he would be gone, turning up for a day here and there when he could take the time off work.'

'Yes, but at what age did you start school? Six, isn't it here in Greece? Are you telling me he was working as a shepherd from the age of six?'

'Sure, why not? What choice does he have? What choice did his family have? He was lucky; there are children in the mountain villages at the other end of the island who have never been to school. How would they get there? Who would take them when it takes three hours to walk in to town? Greece is still an agricultural country; the seasons dictate our lives. Oh look!' She points to a boy on a skateboard who jumps and flicks the board over before he lands.

'So Yanni was bright but never got to go to school? So how did you see him?' Juliet shows very little interest in the boy with the skateboard. It's all new to Sophia, though, and she is fascinated.

'Do you think he would let me have a go?' she asks, and Juliet throws her a dark look. Sophia watches the boy on the board a little longer before she continues. 'I would go up through the trees after school. It was about an hour's walk all the way up, but often he was on his way to meet me. We would climb trees, or take the goats to the far pasture if they needed it. Wherever we were, we were alone. It would have been considered an engagement if we were older, and had we been caught. But we were kids, and no one knew.' She pauses, watching another balloon that has escaped a tiny grip, this time leaving a child crying. The metallic colours flash as the sun catches its surface, floating higher and higher.

'He had a quality like no one else.' Sophia speaks slowly, dreamily. 'This peaceful, sure quality that made me feel safe. It's funny because against the likes of Hectoras, he was the one in the corner or on the floor. But you know, it was as though he let himself be bullied and chose not to fight back. Rather than a lack of physical ability. I mean, he was built with lean muscle on lean muscle, even though he was only a child. But it was as if he had made a

256

choice not to use his strength, or as if it hadn't occurred to him to use his strength in that way.'

'He sounds very noble.' Juliet says.

'Noble doesn't quite fit; it was not for effect. It was something very personal to him. But I also sensed this fear. Not like the world scared him, more as if he was scared what he could do to the world if he responded, if he just let go. He was a non-conformist in every way. He never took what anyone said for the truth without questioning it, even if it was the teacher. The teacher in the first year loved his attitude and did everything she could to explain all he asked. We had her the next year as well, but he was not there for much of that year. In the third year, we had Kirio Polikouto, and he taught by rules and verses and he had no time for Yanni, who came less and less anyway. I would take my books when we met up. We would learn together.' Sophia's head tips right back, looking at the speck of the balloon which drifts higher and higher. Down in the square, the mother of the crying child is trying to buy her another, but it seems there are no more of that colour and the child will not be consoled.

'Fear's a funny thing.' Juliet says. 'It can take so many forms and so often, we don't even notice it. It has taken me a lifetime to work out that my mum was scared of being close to me, scared of her own feelings. It wasn't just me either, she pushed away my dad too. I didn't always go to school as a result. I would skive off, couldn't see the point. I wasn't a swot like you!' She laughs. 'The long-term effect was

257

that I chose my husband, Mick,' she looks to Sophia who is nodding, 'who also was afraid of being close. Sure, he was super attentive in the beginning, but I think we recognise tiny signs that our subconscious deciphers to let us know what a person is all about. I think I saw all the signs of his being a person who was afraid of being close and instead of it being a warning, it felt familiar.'

'You think Yanni was afraid to be close?' Sophia asks.

'Oh, I don't know. Just something you said made me think of my own experiences. Maybe, who knows? Have you heard anything from him recently? Is he married?'

Sophia partially stands up, straightens out her skirts under her, and sits back down. She folds her arms and one hand raises to her mouth to push against her bottom lip, which she chews.

'Sophia? Tell me,' Juliet invites.

'It's stupid, and now I suppose it doesn't matter,' Sophia says. 'A few days after I started working at the sandwich shop, I thought I saw him.'

'No!' Juliet gasps.

'Well I haven't seen him since he was thirteen and people change a lot, but there was something about this man that just made me think of Yanni. I was almost sure. I thought if it was him, he would come over and talk to me, but then I suppose I have changed, too.'

'So did you not go to talk to him?'

'When I saw him, he was with Babis. You know Babis the lawyer, right? Well, he was with him at Stella's, so I guessed they were talking business and I didn't want to interrupt. And then, after he was gone from Stella's, I doubted myself. How could it be that the boy from my childhood would be over here the same time I find a way out of the convent? It's all too perfect. So I told myself I was making it up, that I was imaging the things that made me feel safe.'

'Did you ever find out if it was him?' Juliet's eyes are fixed on Sophia.

'The next time, and the last time I saw this man, was up at the convent. I was still living there, even though I was working down here and it was the *panigyri*, so the whole village was up there. I had sat down to eat with Stella and a crowd from the village when he came in. He was looking around the room like he had lost someone, or something, and I can remember thinking "I am here. I'm here. Can't you see me?" I was so excited. But he just kept looking around and his eyes fell on a young nun at the back of the hall and he could not take his eyes from her. Then someone said his name. "Yanni, he's in the church." Or something like that, and that was the moment I knew it was him and my heart reached out.'

'Oh my goodness! What did you do?'

'Well I was going to stand and rush to him, but one of the older nuns said something to him and even as he was talking to her, he could not tear his gaze from the young nun. He just stared at her. He

259

didn't go up to her or say anything, he just stared. Then he glanced back at our table, I think Stella said hello, and he looked right through me. I had to look away quickly. I could not control myself. Tears were in my eyes.'

'Oh you poor thing.' Juliet's hand slides across the table and takes Sophia's.

'So I never spoke to him. All I know is that he saw me and he ignored me.'

'But how was he to know who you are? He has not seen you for twenty years, and in that time, you have been through things that will show on your face. Did you see a wedding band?'

'I didn't look. It was over in a second.'

'So you know nothing, just that he is alive and he is, or was, here.'

'I know he saw me. I know he walked away.'

'And that's it then?'

'Just because I stood still in my convent glass bubble doesn't mean the world also stood still. It goes on, Juliet. I accepted that years ago. To dream that I would walk out of there and find everything as I left it would be a ridiculous notion. Half the girls at school would have married him in a heartbeat if he had noticed any of them, and they have had twenty years to get his attention. He will be married with children, and, as events have shown, he doesn't even remember me.'

'And the young nun he was looking at?'

Sophia shrugs, looks away. 'It's none of my business.'

Chapter 26

With a shrug, something dark flickers through Sophia. One arm contracts across her chest. She bites her bottom lip so hard, she can taste iron. A stream of unleashed thoughts rages through her, unwholesome, black, and more damning than any thoughts she has had at any other time. She is half-inclined to cross herself, but all that symbolism seems like make believe and superstition in the moment. All she can think are that her thoughts are justified. Thoughts against Hectoras, her mama, the abbess, and all the nuns who had nothing better to do than to seek out the evil in her. Thoughts even against Yanni, who should have been more than he is, but mostly thoughts against herself for living in fear: the fear of walking out of those convent doors. It is just a shadow and it passes, but it leaves a trail behind it.

If she had just walked out, of course it was possible that many, many bad things could have happened to her, but there was also a chance that good things could have come her way, too. Yanni might have not forgotten her if she had acted years earlier. What does it say about her own state of mind if her belief was so strong that only bad things could happen outside of the convent, that she would be better off staying where she was? Surely that is to think evil of people—just like the nuns had of her. Perhaps she is no better than any of them. Maybe that's why Yanni ignored her, if that was what he could see in her face.

'Hey, Sophia, I asked if you are alright.' Juliet's hand on her forearm shakes her gently.

'Oh, what? Yes. No. Well, yes and no,' Sophia says. 'I just realised something, that's all.'

'What?'

'I just realised that all these years of listening to the nuns, or praying and trying to fit in, all this time, a part of me has considered myself better than them. A part that believed that I was not the judgemental one, not as condemning as they were. The same arrogance I had when I was a teenager is still with me, I guess.' The laugh is not warm and husky. 'But I just realised that in that very arrogance of believing I was better than them, I am just the same, just as condemning, just as closed-minded.'

'Best freedom in the world, realising you are human,' Juliet says, and her laughter is real. 'It allows you to kick your shoes off in public and lick the caramel off the inside of your cup and not to be embarrassed about it.' Her laughter settles to a content smile. Sophia is pleased for her, but cannot help but feel a little envious at her ease.

'You have absolute confidence in your survival, don't you, Juliet?'

'So far so good. But it's like most things in life. You get most of your confidence by doing it. It's the fear of failing that holds us back, well, held me back. I think ...' She is about to say more but they are interrupted.

'*Yeia sas* ladies. I am glad to bump into you, Sophia. All the papers have come through now, so if you would like to come to the office, we can go through them. Or call me and we can meet at my house if that is easier.' It's Babis, and he pulls a card from the breast pocket of his short-sleeved shirt and puts it on the table. 'Can't stop, I have an appointment. Bye.' With this, he hurries away, his shiny shoes clicking across the marble paving stones, a file under his arm.

'The abbess suggested I get a lawyer to help with the paperwork of the will and so on.' Sophia's words come out in monotone. It is hard to pull away from the thoughts she was having. Juliet doesn't seem to realize how big it all feels. Or maybe it isn't so big. Maybe most people have this sort of realisation and she has just taken her time to get there. Perhaps that is reasonable, seeing as she has been locked in a convent so long.

The sun is following its path and has found gaps between the leaves. Sophia puts a hand up to shade her eyes. Being part of the world seems to be triggering hosts of chaotic emotions. Do people get used to it, or are they all more stable than her? Maybe some people need more alone time than others, or maybe being with the nuns all these years, all the contemplation and meditation alone in her cell has made that her norm. Maybe she will never fit into daily life amongst people.

'Come on, let's go down the main street with the touristy shops.' Juliet stands and pulls a couple of crumpled notes out of her pocket.

'May I?' Sophia picks up the bill that sits in a shot glass by the ashtray. She cannot get the waiter's attention.

'Do you need change?' Juliet asks.

'No, it's right.' Sophia counts the coins in her hand.

'Oh just leave it on the table then and let's go,' Juliet suggests, pushing the shot glass towards her. Sophia drops the coins in it and leaves it by the ashtray. She takes a last look for the waiter as Juliet starts to walk away, worried that he will think they haven't paid. He sees her but doesn't focus. It seems the place works on trust.

The tourist street is bubbling over with things Sophia cannot imagine the use of. The jewellery she understands, but what is a fridge magnet for, and why would you want a t-shirt with rude words printed on it? The miniature donkeys carrying ceramic pots on either side of their saddles are sweet, but pointless, and you would need a home to put them in. Her breathing becomes shallow for a moment with this thought, but Juliet, the woman who moved from England, is by her side. Sophia just needs to trust herself and everything will come out all right. Her breathing returns to normal; her heartbeat slows.

'I think you need these.' Juliet hands her a pair of orange sunglasses with mirrored glass. Sophia smiles and tries them on, looking in a plastic mirror. The reflection is distorted, which fits. She has no idea who she is anyway, and how she looks is all vanity. She takes them off and hands them back. Juliet tries a pair of glasses that wrap around the sides of her face and sniggers as she puts them back.

The next shop sells things made from olive wood. Smooth bowls, plain chopping boards. At Juliet's house, she has noticed that all the wooden spoons are split and worn as if they are very old. She buys a new one whilst Juliet is playing with some bamboo wind chimes.

'Here you go.' Sophia gives her the wrapped spoon.

'What? Ah, Sophia, you needn't have. Is it a spoon? It feels spoon-shaped, and goodness knows I need a spoon. Do you know everything was just left in that house when I bought it, spoons and all? I boiled them, so don't worry, but you are right, I needed a new one.'

They have reached the end of the touristy part. If they turn left, they will come out at the harbour front where the car is. They make this turn of one accord.

Juliet unlocks the car and they open the doors. The heat rushes out at them and they stand there, not daring to get in. After a minute, Juliet reaches in and puts the key in the ignition and gives it a half turn so she can open all the windows. They gingerly get in. Once moving, the breeze cools them down.

'I really need to get the air conditioning fixed. The first year I was here, the air-con worked in the car but I had none in the house and I would go out for a drive just to cool down.

'By the way, this is the street Babis has his new office on. Do you want to stop now? I can stay in the car if it's private. Just that it will save you a journey.'

Sophia had been letting her mind go blank as the wind blew in her face. It takes her a second to answer.

'Okay, yes, if you don't mind. That's a good idea.'

Juliet pulls up in front of a block of flats. Several plaques by the door announce the businesses that are run from inside.

'I'll wait for you here,' Juliet offers.

'Oh no, come in. I would prefer it, actually,' Sophia says.

Chapter 27

Babis is on the phone. 'Yes that's right, your house is safe... No, there is no need to sell it ... No, there is no need to strengthen it ... Yes, all the houses, the whole village. There was never any fault, it was a mistake. No, I assure you ... Yes, that does include your mama's house ... Yes and your uncle's. Yes, please not to worry. Okay, goodbye.' He puts the phone down with a sigh and looks up as Juliet and Sophia enter the room.

'I hear congratulations are in order,' Juliet opens. 'Well done. What a low trick.' Babis straightens some papers on his desk. 'Who was behind it? Gerasimos or the mayor? I still haven't really understood ...'

Sophia looks around the office, which is new and crisp-edged. She cannot help but compare it to the offices in the convent: full of heavy, dark, old wooden furniture. This modern look is so much brighter and fresher.

'Anyway, it's great,' Juliet continues. 'So thank you, Babis, for saving the village. Maybe that sounds dramatic, but it's true, as far as I am told.'

'Ah well, you know, you do what you can, ladies. I am the lawyer for the people, I must act with their interests at heart.'

Instinctively, Sophia goes no further into the room. She does not trust him.

'Please, come, sit.' Babis flattens his tie down the front of his shirt and sits back in his big black swivelling leather office chair. It makes him look very small and he does not seem to have complete control over its dipping and swivelling. He comes to a standstill by placing his forearms on his desk.

'Oh, yes, right,' he says abruptly and pushes his chair back. He swivels round to take a file down from the floor-to-ceiling shelves of paperwork behind him, most of which are empty. An intricately carved wooden horse with plastic tack adorns one shelf, an orange and transparent glass cockerel on another. Pushing himself back, he grips the desk's edge to regain control. Juliet glances at Sophia, her eyes sparkling.

'Please sit,' he repeats to Sophia, who is still hovering. 'Right, it was your baba who made out the will, signed by them both. Let's see.' He turns over one of the loose sheets of paper that is covered with official looking stamps. 'Okay, so basically, he has left everything to you in the belief that you will do what is best for Vetta, Sotiria, Angeliki, Sada, and Sophia.' He looks at the list of names again. 'Oh, that last one is you. Five girls, eh, that cannot have been easy.' He looks up and smiles. Sophia shifts in her seat. The air conditioning is on full blast and it is blowing on the back of her neck. It is too cold to be pleasant.

'So that means the house then?'

'Well, no, there is more than the house. There is what is described as a net storage down in the port. That is prime property; you could sell that for a fortune.' His eyes glisten. Sophia's face is expressionless. 'If you wanted to,' Babis adds.

'That's Vetta's,' Sophia says.

'No, that is officially yours now.' Babis looks up from the papers.

'That's Vetta's.' Sophia repeats with a firm tone, and it is clear the subject is closed.

'I see. Do you want me to make that officially Vetta's? Technically she will have to …'

'She lives and works there. Nothing needs to change,' Sophia says.

'Yes, but in order for it to be officially Vetta's …' Babis begins, but the look Sophia gives him silences his words and he returns to shifting through the papers.

'Ah, here it is, I knew I had seen something more. Not that it is much use.' He reads. Sophia waits. He seems to read for a long time. Juliet and Sophia exchange looks.

'Right, so there's the house and the net storage, and it seems your family has had land for generations up on the ridge. As far as I can make out, somewhere south-east of the town. It covers over a hundred and fifty *stremas*, which is a big-sized plot.' He looks up at Sophia, his eyes wide. 'But I believe,' he looks back down at the papers, 'yes, here is a note. There is no water. So it is worthless land, really. You cannot graze livestock without water and you would

269

be hard pushed to get planning permission to build up there, and even if you did, what with no water and only donkeys to carry things up there, who would want it?' He looks at her again, his eyes no longer so wide.

'Why would my family have land up there?' Sophia asks.

Babis pulls down the corners of his mouth and sticks his chin out and back. 'Well, presumably they used to farm it when Orino still had water.'

'What, travelling up there every day and back?' Sophia asks.

Babis turns back to the file, turning over one page after the next. 'Ah no, here it is, or should I say was.' He laughs at his joke, but as it makes no sense to either Juliet or Sophia, he laughs alone. 'There was a house,' he clarifies. 'Two rooms, and a well and … and that's it. It says here that the roof has gone.' He looks up at Sophia. 'I imagine a lot more has gone as well now. It will probably just be a pile of stones.'

Juliet leans over to her and whispers, 'Are you okay?'

Sophia glances at her quickly and nods. The surprise is that her baba left it all in her hands. She who was meant to be evil, crazy even. Why not leave it for Sotiria? Well okay, she moved to America, but what about leaving it to Angeliki to sort out? He condemned himself by leaving it for her, Sophia, to sort it, condemned himself because it proved he thought her the most capable and still, he let her be

270

sent to the convent as if she was an evil monster to be controlled. Her chin lifts in defiance.

'I would like you to arrange to rent out the town house,' Sophia clips. This catches Babis by surprise; he had started to clear the papers away.

'Long-term rent, you mean?' he asks.

'Yes, to create an income for Sada and me,' Sophia replies.

'If it is money you are looking to make on an island like Orino, you would make more by holiday letting it.' Babis has stopped stacking the papers and is rubbing the fingers of one hand with the fingers of his other, one hand rolling around the other, a small movement.

'How does that work?' Sophia asks and Babis begins his explanations about licencing and arranging a housekeeper to clean and to show the guests in and out. He offers to advertise on the Internet, '… for a small commission, of course.' He jigs in his seat as he talks, becoming more and more animated until he finally cuts to the bottom line of how much she can expect to make. He freezes at this point to await her response.

'Fine, do it,' Sophia says, still with no emotion.

'Okay. I will need a setup fee. That will be separate from the fee for sorting out the will. I will need money upfront to pay the housekeeper and there will be expenses for me to go and find someone willing to do this job. The house may need some updating and repairs, so there may be costs for that, too.'

'I have no money,' Sophia says quietly. The words filter through Babis' monologue and he stops talking abruptly. 'I take it no money has been left?' The look on his face answers this question.

'And my fee for sorting out the will?' he asks. There is a slight edge to his voice. Juliet looks out the window.

'I will pay you when the first rent comes in,' Sophia says.

Babis pushes all the papers together and stuffs them back into the file. Some crease and get stuck, but he just pushes the harder and forces the file to close, pulling the elastic binder over it. He gives Sophia a long, hard stare before his eyes glaze over and he looks at his watch, muttering something about another appointment.

Sophia begins to stand.

'Just a minute, Babis. What happened to you being a lawyer for the people? That was short-lived, wasn't it?' Juliet asks, remaining seated.

'I have an office to run,' Babis replies and stands. Sophia stands. Juliet remains seated.

'If you had any sense, your reputation would be more important than your office.' Juliet still doesn't stand. Sophia slowly sits back down, obliging Babis to do the same.

Sophia looks at him long and hard. For a moment, she can only see the boy he must once have been, the boy before he lost his baba. He twitches under her gaze and is a man again, but a young man whose mama has gone to Athens to stay with her sister and not come back. There are so many people alone in the world, each trying to survive. Some with dignity like Juliet, others choosing to grab like Babis, but it is all a choice. It seems Juliet's grace leaves room for her to enjoy her life a great deal more than Babis' grabbing gives him. It is all down to fear. Juliet is not afraid; Babis is filled with fear.

'Babis,' Sophia says. 'I am terrified I am not going to be able to survive in the world. Living with nuns prepares you for nothing. I am like a child.' Although she says it for effect, the words ring true. She waits for the next words to come to her. 'But if I let this fear take hold of me, I will cower and lash out at everything around me. It is not the way.' Sophia looks into her lap and shakes her head as if consolidating her thoughts. 'I think the only way is to not give the fear we feel any power, to trust and give room to people so they can show that they are good, don't you?' She looks directly at Babis. 'All you have said about renting out my family home as a holiday let sounds expensive and complicated and my instinct is to be afraid and choose the route that I can understand more easily; just rent it out to some family, my instincts say. But if I choose that, I would not be trusting you, I would be giving in to the fear. I choose to trust you, Babis. I choose to believe that you will make the right choices, make the right purchases, and do all the right things to let the house out to its best advantage. That is a big trust, don't you think?' She still holds Babis with her eye contact.

273

He nods, sideways and down. 'How much would your fee be?'

He breaks her stare abruptly and looks instead to the ceiling, his lips moving. He takes his pen, scribbles some numbers, and then turns the paper to Sophia.

'And how much rent could you get each month if you let it to tourists?' Sophia asks. Juliet is no longer looking out of the window; she is staring at Sophia. Babis scribbles some more and turns another piece of paper towards her. She tries to show no reaction, but the amount is several times what she expected.

'You believe you could get that?' she asks. Babis nods. 'Then I believe you, too. I offer you the first two calendar months' rent to cover your fees and your costs and your own fear.'

His jaw drops open just a fraction and then he springs to life. 'My dear Sophia, I would not dream of asking for such a sum. If you are fearful, I can understand that. Let me take that fear from you. I will do all that is necessary to have your place fully booked. I have no fear. Let us settle for just eight weeks' rent to cover the setup charges and work forward from there …' He smiles, his hand smoothing the cover of the file, his fingers finding the folded corners and straightening them out in that glorious moment when his mind must be swimming in the knowledge that she has just agreed to double his fees.

'I can leave it in your hands then?' Sophia stands, followed by Babis, Juliet showing no hurry.

They say their formal goodbyes. Babis reassures her not to be afraid, and they leave.

The air outside is still and hot. Initially, it is delicious after the air conditioning, but before they even reach the car, the sun is burning them.

They have not spoken since they left the office as Juliet starts the car and begins the drive home.

'You know what, Sophia? I think you should train to be a lawyer.' Juliet takes a second to think. 'Or maybe even a boxer.'

Chapter 28

Sister Katerina hands Sophia the secateurs.

'I deadhead them every day.'

'I think perhaps they need to be pruned from lower down. Not now, but in the autumn, or at the latest, the spring.'

'I usually do it in the spring. Look!' Sister Katerina slowly straightens to point out a blue dragonfly.

'Beautiful,' Sophia replies.

'So are the builders there today?' Sister Katerina asks.

'Yes. They already had the roof on before I left the village. Babis, that's my lawyer, has been most helpful. Although I'm sure he will charge me for every step. You know, I think he thought I was quite mad, wanting to renovate the old house.'

'It will be lovely to have you up here, Sophia. Permanently, I mean.'

'Well, I'm not sure how it will work out. There's no water, you know. Well, I say no water; apparently the well dries up by about July and you have to wait for the autumn rains.'

'Trust in God,' Sister Katerina says. 'I'm sure you'll find a way to live up here.' She puts her basket of deadheads down and rubs her back.

'Sit a while, Sister,' Sophia says.

'You are kind, my dear. The convent outside Saros must have been very sorry to lose you.'

'I'm sure the abbess filled you in,' Sophia says with a sly look.

'It's what the abbess said about you that made me sure we would get on. She said that she had had to have a word with you on several occasions for laughing and encouraging others to laugh at most irreverent moments.' Sister Katerina sits on the bench by the church with a small sigh. 'And besides, we have a mutual friend.'

'Do we?' Sophia stops her weeding and looks up, interested. But Sister Katerina's eyes are closed and she seems to have nodded off. Sophia leaves the weeds and goes around the back of the church to the vegetable plot, which has been neglected in favour of the flowers. The sight of all there is to do thrills her, and she re-canes the peas and digs around the lettuces before Sister Katerina awakes and wanders round to find her.

'Ah, there you are.'

'I was just about to dig up some potatoes and some beetroots. I can make some *scordalia* to go with the beetroots for dinner tonight. Does that appeal?'

'You know, you are showing me how much I was neglecting myself. Too often, I would boil up a potato and make that do. Sometimes not even that: a lettuce and grated carrot. They are easier to get out of the ground.' Sister Katerina still has her gardening gloves on, which are far too big for her hands.

'It can't be easy living up here alone,' Sophia soothes.

'But now you are here! Has this Babis of yours given you any idea when the house will be ready?'

Sophia straightens up and pushes loose hairs from her face that have escaped from her ponytail, whilst watching a tortoise who clicks up the path. 'He'd better not be heading for the lettuces,' Sophia exclaims.

'He is always heading for the lettuces,' Sister Katerina laughs. Sophia gently lifts the big old tortoise and turns him around. His head darts in leaving just a shell, and the shell sits there unmoving. First his head reappears and then his legs. Without hesitation, he turns himself around and continues his route to the lettuce patch.

'I will have to fence them in,' Sophia says.

'It won't stop him.' Sister Katerina steps past Sophia, pulls up a lettuce that's about to flower, and puts it down in front of the tortoise. His beak opens and he begins to tear it to pieces, slowly chewing and swallowing, his neck stretching, his head pointing to the sky as he does so.

'In truth, Babis has been amazing. Last year, when I first left the convent and he started sorting out the will, I had no idea how my life was going to work out. But he was good to his word. He has transformed the house in town and it's fully booked for this summer. Without that, I could never have even thought to do up the house up here.'

'And in the same mysterious way, God will find a way for you to have enough water to live up here.'

'Well, I don't know how mysterious it all is.' Sophia chuckles. The night she went across the road to Stella's for supper with Juliet is a night she will never forget. Juliet was drinking beer. Stella left Mitsos to deal with the customers so she could join them, and she drank beer too. Was it Sophia's evil streak or just curiosity that made her decide to try some beer herself?

'Oh, I'm not sure what all the fuss is about. It has a bitter aftertaste.' But she took a second sip from Juliet's glass to make sure. There was something strangely nice about it and so Stella poured her a glass of her own. She sipped it very slowly but as the evening grew into night, the beer made her giggle, which infected first Juliet and quickly Stella.

'I think it's sending me crazy.' Sophia giggled.

'Everyone is a little crazy,' Stella replied.

'Each in their own way,' Juliet said.

'No, they are all the same.' Stella opened herself another bottle. 'The government accuses us of stealing from them before we have even made a penny and they tax us in advance to assure themselves that they get their share. So what do we do? We do what anybody who wants to live would do. We find ways to hide what we earn and get more and more sneaky and more and more paranoid and it makes us crazy. We are crazy with paranoia and we sneak about and tell lies, to even our closest friends and family, about our incomes. Everyone I know lies and lies again about how they have not been paid and what they owe and how they do not have money until you wonder how they can eat. Yet they smoke two packets of cigarettes a day and drive a four-by-four and come out to eat chicken and chips and drink enough ouzo to sink a fishing boat.'

She took a breath at this point and swallowed more beer. 'Listen to this, the latest gossip of the village. You know the photovoltaic field over there?' She waves her hand around in the vague direction of the hill opposite Juliet's, with the olive trees. 'Well, there were only so many grants being offered and so there was a scramble by the farmers to get one. It all became the usual matter of who you know. Well, the man who has his field now filled with photovoltaic panels got the grant because his cousin worked in the government office that dealt with the applications. The cousin agreed to put his application to the top for a share of the income.'

Sophia took another tiny sip of beer, listening intently.

'First the farmer had to pay for half of the installation. Then when the panels were working, he had to wait until the electricity they had generated paid off the European Union their half of the installation cost—in other words, pay back the grant. Then the cousin, who had also set up the bank accounts so they could be paid, took out all that was coming in to pay off the bribes he had had to give out to get the grant in the first place. And do you know what happened meanwhile?' Stella paused for effect.

'Two things happened. First, the electricity company took the signed agreements from all the fields they had made this deal with to the European court and reduced the amount they would pay the farmers for the energy, claiming they were in a state of national emergency. The people who signed the original deal had no say, and it cut their income by half.' Stella paused before adding, 'And secondly, because the farmer had spent all his money on the installation and the chopping down of his orange trees, he had no money and no income. His land was generating thousands of euros' worth of electricity every month but between the company and his cousin, he saw nothing. Well, his electricity bill came to his house. One hundred euros. And this man who created the electricity in the first place could not afford to pay the bill and they cut the electricity off in his house.' Stella knocked back the rest of her beer and slammed the glass on the table. The table shook and, as it was up against the tree with the fairy lights, they too shook, shadows bouncing for a moment.

Juliet shook her head, but it did not seem to be a surprise to her. Sophia was horrified and her mouth dropped partially open until Mitsos came out and asked if they wanted more beer. He had two bottles in his hand; he opened one and put it on the table. The other, he left with the cap on and put the opener next to it. His hand trailed across Stella's shoulders as he returned inside. A little gesture designed to help her relax, perhaps. She lifted her shoulders and dropped them and smiled the smile of the defeated.

'So we are all a little crazy, but in the same way,' she concluded.

'I see a different craziness,' Juliet raised her head, 'amongst the ex-pats.' Stella topped up her glass. Sophia put her hand over her own glass; one drink felt like more than enough. 'When they first move over here, they are so full of themselves. After years of grey sky and rain, just the sun makes you feel like a king, makes you feel blessed. They arrive with their handfuls of savings and dreams for the future and they begin to live as if they are on holiday. Beer at lunchtime, afternoons on the beach, eating out every night.'

Stella raised her glass to this thought and Juliet admitted the irony of her words by raising hers in return.

'But as the appreciative greetings fit for royalty made by the bartenders serving the lunchtime beer become normal, it loses its impact and as their savings begin to diminish, these ex-pat kings and queens start to buy their beer from the kiosk and drink at home. They no longer get their daily greeting as revered big spenders and their life becomes normal again. And here is the strange thing that I have seen happen over and over again: They begin to complain. They find things to complain about. They complain about the Greeks. After all, it must be their fault. Wasn't it them and their country who made them feel so fantastic in the first place? So why are they not making them feel fantastic now? That is the first thing that happens. Then the second thing. They begin to grandiose what they have left behind. The house they left in the UK or France or wherever was so big, so new. Everything worked properly. Their families are grandiosed: they were so loving, so well-known. I have met a half-Austrian woman claiming pictures of Austrian castles she had postcards of were old family seats. I have met English people claiming their fathers and grandfathers were these great people who made huge impacts on the government and you think, "If all this is true, why did they leave? It doesn't fit".' Juliet took a drink of her beer. 'They spend their days talking about these things until they can talk about nothing else. It's their own form of crazy.'

'I have seen that,' Stella agreed.

'I was crazy,' Sophia said, surprising herself. 'When they said I had this demon in me. At first, I knew it was nonsense but then as time passed and more and more accusations were made and evidence was presented to me, I began to think I was crazy and I think I became a little mad. I watched myself from the outside in everything I did, watched to see any sign of the demon. But as I saw nothing abnormal, I began to interpret the normal as abnormal. Everything had a different meaning. Everything I said and did. I tried to hide myself from the other sisters. I found the vegetable garden a great place to be, away from everybody. So I stayed amongst the plants and the insects and the chickens until slowly, and I mean slowly—it must have been years—I saw I was not crazy and I began to quite like who I was.'

'I'll drink to that.' Stella clicked glasses with them both.

'I think, and I am speaking from my own experience.' Juliet put on a pompous voice as she said this last sentence, but something about the way she did it implied that she was also serious. 'You have to find out where you need to be, what situation suits you best. In England, I felt I was struggling after my divorce from Mick. I was struggling to find a job and struggling to find a home. I don't mean I couldn't find these things, but it was my life and after years of Mick, it felt precious, so I was not about to short-change myself on a job I didn't like or a home that felt like make-do.' She turned her glass between her hands and looked up to the smudge of the Milky Way that hung over the village. 'So I thought of all the places I had been and all the times that seemed the most precious and that was it. I knew I had to be in Greece.'

'I did the same after my divorce,' Stella said. Sophia looked at her quickly. She had assumed Stella had been with Mitsos forever. 'I asked myself what I wanted most in the world, and the answer was I wanted to do business, big business.' Sophia turned her head to look at the facade of the taverna.

'Oh not this,' Stella laughed, light and childlike. She seemed too small to run even the taverna. 'No, this is just for fun now. I have a factory that makes candles just outside of Saros. I run it with an English friend. We make and distribute beeswax candles to the Orthodox churches all over the world and we make, you might have heard of them, "AromaLite" scented candles that people use as therapy. That is a growing industry.' Stella didn't seem so small as she talked. She had an air of authority that made Sophia reassess her.

'So you need to know where you want to be, either geographically or …' Stella did not finish her sentence. 'Although if I was living at Juliet's, I would not be sure if I would want to move. Did you put that swinging chair up on your front porch?'

'Um-hm.' Juliet grunted her answer. 'It's a thought, Sophia. Have you any idea where you want to be? That might be the place to start, rather than what you want to do. Not that you are not welcome to stay.'

There was no thought behind the image. The top of Orino Island came along with the feeling of peace and in that moment, with Juliet, who had rebuilt her old farmhouse, and Stella, who had built an international enterprise, she decided to rebuild the family house in its hundred and fifty *stremas* of land and live in semi-seclusion. She could think of nothing nicer. Occasional trips to the town and across to the village, Juliet and Stella and Mitsos to come to stay. The whole thing just slotted into place.

She shared her vision and Stella became very excited. She explained how she had started her candle factory in her baba's old barn on top of her own hill. Juliet said she would visit for sure and the

285

rest of the night, the three of them laid plans. No mysterious God, but there were one or two bottles of beer.

Chapter 29

'To answer your question, we've had several completion dates, and it keeps getting pushed back ... But when he asked me to come and look, I knew the day to move in could not be far way.'

'Well, I think it was very sensible of you to come and stay with me so you can keep an eye on things.'

'It was very kind of you to invite me.' Sophia realises she is not going to get any more digging done for the moment and so leads Sister Katerina into the shade, back to her bench by the church door; the most perfect spot to look over the garden.

Staying with Sister Katerina was the abbess' idea. After Sophia left the convent, it was agreed that she would visit the abbess once a month, and it was at one of these meetings she voiced her plans to move back to her island. The old nun turned very thoughtful for a moment before taking a large key from inside her robe and unlocking the bottom door of an oversized dark wood desk from where she withdrew a piece of paper folded many times and bound in string. Carefully undoing the knots and unfolding the sheet, she slowly read through the contents.

'This is a note from a fellow nun. I will divulge its contents, but you must keep complete confidence,' she rasped.

'Of course, Sister.' Sophia was curious.

'It is from Sister Katerina in the convent on Orino.' She looked at the note. 'She says that despite her prayers and God's strong arm of support, she grows physically weak. Her vegetable garden is not producing enough to live on because she does not have the strength to do all the work that is necessary. In this note, she asks if I could send a younger nun to support her. Preferably someone quiet who will not get in the way.' She paused before adding, 'Those are my words, not hers, but I can read between the lines.' She cleared her throat, re-folded the note, re-tied the string around it, and replaced it in the bottom drawer. 'It strikes me that you are the answer to her prayers. You can stay with her to begin with, sort out all the major jobs she lists as being beyond her, and use your God-given talent on her vegetable plot.' She crossed herself. 'Then when your house is done, it will give her the space she needs if you were to attend her garden a few times a week. I think this is God's purpose for you. This is what he would like you to do to recompense the church for all the years you lived here.'

The anger boiled in Sophia, rendering her speechless. But after a moment's reflection, reason filtered through her wrath and she slowly realised that this presumption by the abbess could in fact be the answer to her living up on the top of Orino Island long-term without water to grow her food.

'I will write to her, telling her to expect you.' Sophia was dismissed and she walked once more from the convent wishing, hoping, that would be the last time she would ever see the abbess.

In the shade of the small church, Sophia sits by Sister Katerina's side and they gaze over the garden.

'Look what a difference you've made in just two days.' Sister Katerina surveys her blossoms and blooms. 'It is wondrous.'

Sophia checks over the lupins and the geraniums and notes several things in that area that she must attend to. There are weeds poking through here and there and behind them, the climbing rose by the front gate needs to be cut back to one or two stems to give it strength. It thrills her. The whole garden thrills her. There were so few flowers at the convent near Saros, but here, there is so much that is new, so much she can learn, and Sister Katerina has so much she can teach her, which she seems to enjoy doing in her own meditative way.

Her happiness is all but complete. She can ask for no more. If there is a God, a bigger, more real, more live, all-encompassing force of nature that governs the universe than the icon gods of the convent, then maybe that force has turned the wheels of her life, that force has moulded her steps to bring her out into her own garden of Eden and for this, she gives thanks, as she could not be happier.

289

Presently there is a tapping noise that breaks Sophia's reflection.

'Oh.' Sister Katerina stands and her old legs seem to take on new life. 'I have just thought of something I really must do inside.'

Sophia has stood automatically, ready to support Sister Katerina. The tapping is repeated. Sister Katerina has moved with alarming speed and is almost inside when she turns to say, 'Open the door, will you? That will be my weekly delivery from town.' With this, the old nun goes inside and closes the door behind her, leaving Sophia alone in the garden.

The tapping repeats itself. A butterfly on the roses nearby takes to the air.

A donkey brays just outside. Sophia opens the door.

Good reviews are important to a novel's success and will help others find The Illegal Gardener. If you enjoyed it, please be kind and leave a review wherever you purchased the book.

I'm always delighted to receive email from readers, and I welcome new friends on Facebook.

https://www.facebook.com/authorsaraalexi
saraalexi@me.com

Happy reading,

Sara Alexi

Also by Sara Alexi

The Illegal Gardener
Black Butterflies
The Explosive Nature of Friendship
The Gypsy's Dream
The Art of Becoming Homeless
In the Shade of the Monkey Puzzle Tree
A Handful of Pebbles

KI

C.1

Made in the USA
Middletown, DE
30 September 2015